Vulture House

Vulture House

D. L. Wilburn Jr.

ISBN: 979-8-9912868-0-0 (eBook)

ISBN: 979-8-9912868-2-4 (Paperback)

ISBN: 979-8-9912868-1-7 (Hardcover)

Library of Congress Control Number: 2024921565

Any references to historical events, real people, or places are fictitious. Names, characters, and places are products of the author's imagination.

Printed in the United States of America.

Cover by Suvajit Das, Architect of Design

Interior Art by Adena Sheridan

Edited by Elaine Wilburn.

Beta Readers: George Engel and Adena Sheridan

First printing edition 2024.

W-III Publishing

Permissions@W-III.org

To my cousin Rudell "Dale" Wilburn Jr.,

for his love of horror stories.

by D. L. Wilburn Jr.

The God Protocol: Dragon

The God Protocol: Worshippers

The God Protocol: Judgment

Co-Author as Leilana Rae

The Meaning Between Us

The vultures do not circle in the sky for death alone,
but for the secrets the living cannot keep.

# Chapter 1

Saturday

The back door of Mountains and Molehills squealed before slamming shut, the thick metal grinding on the frame.

Ka-lack, Ka-lack, Ka-lack, Ka-lack.

Jenny hurried toward her car, despite being exhausted. It had been a busy night. Enough customers were vying for the girls' attention that she felt like she was being pulled between the stage and private dances all night. Jenny fished through her small clutch for her keys.

The parking lot exuded an eerie darkness, with only one of the six lights in operation, and even that solitary light flickered, signaling its imminent extinction. She made a face as the stench of decaying meat wafted through the warm summer air. That Korean BBQ place was most likely the one. It would sit for days in the heat if they were late getting their trash out on time. Her car wasn't right under the light. The lot had been full when she arrived. An oversized truck parked next to her small Mazda. She adjusted her path to stay in the light.

Ka-lack, Ka-lack, Ka-lack, Ka-lack.

A can bounced under another car in the lot, causing her to jump. A shape stumbled from around a car, illuminated faintly by the light. She recognized the man. He had been drinking scotch and water all night. He tipped her before being ejected for getting too handsy with her.

"Jesus! You scared me."

"I've been waitin' Candy. You didn't finish my lap dance." He was near enough that she could detect the liquor on his breath.

She laughed, fidgeting as she continued on her way to her car.

"Sorry, I'm off the clock. I've got class in the morning." She watched him while stealing a glance around the dark lot. She was closer to her car now. All feelings of exhaustion were gone as her adrenaline kicked in.

"Wait! Where are you going? I paid, and I want my money's worth." He slurred his words, picking up the pace to match hers.

Her heart raced. Her car was close by, parked a few spots away from the parking light. Mountains and Molehills had a camera above its back door. Maybe the bouncer was paying attention. She hooked her pinky through her car keys and grabbed the small bottle of mace, feeling the little nub with her thumb telling her which way to point it.

Her smile lacked conviction. "I get it. Come back Thursday, I'll give you another dance."

He grabbed her arm. She winced as his fingers dug into her arm. "I don't wanna wait!" He pushed her into the front of her car, pain erupted from her thigh.

"Help!" She raised her hand and sprayed, her voice piercing the night.

The man brought his arm to his face, shielding his eyes from the spray. He coughed, swinging his other arm out and down on her forearm, causing her hand to drop the spray and her keys.

"You're gonna pay for that, bitch! I'm a cop," he huffed. He continued coughing.

He followed the strike on her arm with a backhand across her face. She dropped to her knees.

"Now, that's more like it." Snot was running from his nose as he tried to clear his throat. The nearby light flickered.

Jenny looked around for anything she could use to keep him away. "Help!" she yelled, waiting for the next blow. When it didn't come, she glanced at the stocky man. His eyes focused past her, wide with fear. She felt a scratch along the base of her neck.

A tingling sensation coursed through her body as she lost sensation. Her muscles gave out, unable to answer her desire to flee, and she slumped to the ground, falling to her side. She tried to close her eyes but couldn't. The parking light continued to flicker. Her chest tightened. Breathing was a struggle. It felt like something was wrapped tightly around her chest, constricting her. She tried to scream, but no sound came out.

A dark form moved across her line of sight.

"Aaar—"

She heard a gurgling. The dark shape shifted. She saw the man who attacked her lying on the rough asphalt. Looking directly at her, his face locked in terror, caught in a silent scream. She wanted to yell, to get up and run away as fast as she could, but she couldn't. The dark shape moved between her and the man. She heard the wet gurgling sound and watched as a pool of blood crept toward her. The sensation of the warm asphalt pressing against her cheek was unmistakable as the liquid spread. A pungent scent resembling burned meat on a grill permeated her nasal passages.

The light flickered once more, then went out.

She watched the silhouette of the person kneeling over her assailant. Her breathing became more difficult. She tried to scream again but couldn't. The dark crimson puddle reached her, and she felt the warm liquid on her cheek. She heard a dry ripping sound like cardboard being pulled apart as the night faded to black.

Chapter 2

Sunday

Tanya sat at the small white desk in her room, pencil in hand, looking at her laptop screen, listening to a young, almost cute professor on YouTube explain the basics of derivatives.

"Tanya! Hello? Can you hear me?"

The voice got her attention. She had turned up the volume to cover the raised voices coming through the floor from the kitchen. "Yes, Sheri, sorry."

"I said, you don't need to look it up. Just tell your mom you need to come over to study. I'll show you how to finish our assignment, and then we can hang out for a while."

Tanya smiled at the small box on the upper right of her screen. Sheri's discerning hazel eyes peered at her with anticipation. Sheri was wearing a University of Texas Sweatshirt, her curly light brown hair framing her face. Her mother's pendant hung around her neck; tiny sparkling diamonds surrounding a sapphire.

Tanya looked away, her brown hair slipping forward. "I don't know. It's late already." She undid the large hair clip, gathered the stray locks, and clipped it again.

"Tell your parents we have a project we need to work on. You could stay over here if you need to."

"I'll be ok. Let me get this done. I'll meet up with you in the morning. Thanks, Sher."

"Ok, I'm only three houses down. Call me back if you need anything."

The small box disappeared, and she refocused on the video and homework.

After thirty minutes, in the absence of noise, she crept downstairs to get a snack. Her dad was sitting at the round kitchen table, eating chips. He was still in work clothes, a button-down light-yellow shirt, and blue slacks. His rolled-up sleeves revealed the anchor tattoo on his forearm, which peeked out.

She heard the sizzle and smelled chicken. Her mom was shifting the meat around the cast iron skillet. Her hair was down, long brown, and hanging over her shoulders. She wore a *Rice* T-shirt and jeans. She concentrated on the skillet, avoiding eye contact. Tanya glanced at her dad and kissed her mom on the cheek before going to the refrigerator.

Her mom smiled discreetly. "Thank you."

"What, no hug for your dad?"

She forced a smile and went to the table and hugged him. She smelled the acrid odor of the sanitary soap he used at work. "Hi, Daddy. How was work?" Tanya asked as she went back to looking for a snack.

"It could have been better. Your mom forgot to pack my lunch again, so I had to stand in line at the food truck with everyone else. Obviously, I got home late, and dinner was cold."

Tanya tried to smile at him, glancing at her mom to check if she was ok. "The chicken is good. It's a new recipe."

"I don't know what was wrong with our normal chicken."

"Chris, you need to expand your palate. We can't eat the same thing week after week."

Her father looked at her mother. "At least the potatoes smell normal." He took a drink of his beer, shaking it afterward. "Tanya, get me another one."

"Yes, Daddy." She went to the refrigerator and grabbed another beer. She set the cold Coors Light by his plate, picking up the empty can and tossing it in the recycling bin. She opened a drawer and got a spoon. "I'll be in my room, working on my homework."

"Tanya, you better bring that back down. I don't want ants in the house," her dad called after her.

"I will," she yelled back. She stood at the top of the stairs, listening to her parents, hoping it would be a good night.

He grunted in response. "Kaitlyn, is that damned chicken ready yet? Are you trying to starve me?"

"I said just a minute, Chris. It's almost done."

"I don't need the attitude. This is your fault. If you had made it right the first time, we'd be relaxing, watching our shows." Their shows comprised of whatever he wanted to watch. He usually settled on sports, which her mom couldn't care less about.

Tanya closed the door and inserted her earbuds, expecting an argument soon. She unplugged her laptop and jumped into bed, sinking into her puffy lavender comforter and pillows, and peeling back the top of the yogurt. In over a dozen forms, Smurfette stared at her from the shelf above her desk. Her mom passed down the collection to her when she was little. Supposedly, the cartoon show was the only thing that would stop her crying when she was a baby. They still gave her a sense of security, but Smurfette's smile was sometimes judgmental. She appreciated how the character lived her own life in a male dominated world.

"What? I need to relax before I finish my homework. You know how it is."

She searched for a song to play.

Arr, Arr, Arr, Arr, Arr. She heard their Scottish terrier, Jackson, in the backyard. She slid out of bed to look out the window, taking her earbuds out and laying them on the desk. Their Scotty stood at the back fence, barking at something on the other side. Probably the Burkes's little bulldog, Coolio. The two dogs were friends and rivals, always competing to establish who the neighborhood alpha was. And according to her dad, who could be the most annoying.

She opened her window. *What was he into now?*

Rowf, Rowf, grrr, Rowf.

Yep, it was Coolio. Jackson was standing tall for his small size, staring at the fence in the backyard, illuminated by the backyard light. The two dogs traded barks through the fence before the other dogs in the neighborhood joined the conversation. She found it amusing when they all got excited. Her dad would get mad soon and put Jackson in the garage. After about fifteen minutes, Jackson would start barking to get out, and then her dad would discipline him by sending him to the backyard again with a smack on his butt that would quiet him for a few minutes. Then Jackson would smell the dog on the other side, and it would all start again.

She felt as much as heard the back door fly open beneath her. "Damnit Jackson! Shut the hell up. People are trying to relax, and they can't with all the damned noise you're making out there."

Arr, Arr, Arr, Arr, Arr.

"I'm gonna put you in the garage!"

She closed the window and put her earbuds back in, turning up the latest Taylor Swift song.

Ding.

She picked up her phone.

> Sheri: Don't forget you said you'd stay after school with me tomorrow.

> Tanya: I didn't forget. I told my mom that I'd be home late.

> Sheri: Ok. It's college color day.

> Tanya: I know. I remember. I'm not eight.

Sheri: You still forget. Did you finish the Calc?

Tanya: Most of it. I have a few more to do.

Sheri: OK, I'll see you in the morning.

She scooped the last yogurt out of the cup and set it on her nightstand. Closing her eyes and taking a deep breath, she let the music flow through her thoughts. As she drifted off to sleep, the sound of the back door slamming startled her.

Tanya turned the music down and heard her father yell at the dog, "Jackson, get over here!" A moment later, she heard a yelp, and the door closed again. She resisted the urge to go downstairs. Jackson would be fine. Her dad never hit the dog.

A few minutes later, there was a knock at the door.

"Yeah."

Her mom peeked her head in. "Tanya, I'm doing laundry tomorrow. Could you make sure you sort everything?"

"Yes, Mom. Don't forget, I'm staying after school with Sheri tomorrow. We'll grab something to eat. So, I won't be home until later."

"Um, ok. Your dad wants pork chops tomorrow, so I need to run to the store early. Let me know before you go to school if you need anything."

"I'm good, Mom. Do you need me to do anything?"

Her mom looked at her, smiling despite her sad eyes. "No, dear, I'm good. Don't stay up too late."

"I won't. Love you, Mom."

Her dad's voice came down the hall from their room. "Kaitlyn, what are you doing? I'm waiting in here to start our show."

"I'm coming." She smiled, closing the door behind her.

Tanya: I reminded my mom that I'd be staying after school. All good!

Sheri: Great!

Tanya got up to turn off her desk lamp. She stared for a moment at the corkboard filled with pictures. In the middle were her and Sheri at the Texas State Fair. They were smiling from the top of the Ferris wheel, arms up. The wind whipped her long, brown hair. They were happy. She smiled at the memory.

Chapter 3

Tuesday Morning

"Did you get everything done?" Sheri leaned over, bumping her shoulder as they walked down the sidewalk. She enjoyed the morning walks to school. She was out of the house, and the trees along both sides of the road made it a long, colorful tunnel in the fall.

"Of course. It just took a little longer than expected. I think I have it, though." Tanya adjusted her backpack.

The sun was peeking above the fences between the houses, not too warm yet. People anticipated the temperature to surpass a hundred degrees once more. *Six days in a row.* They both wore shorts and a T-shirt with a college logo on the front. Sheri wore a light gray tee with the orange longhorn for the University of Texas, and Tanya's was dark blue with the white calligraphy 'R' for Rice University.

"Have you started your applications yet?"

Tanya shook her head. "No. I've got them saved. Every time I bring up Rice, my dad goes off on earning a nomination to the Naval Academy and how he saved my grandparents' money for tuition."

"Eww. Why would you want that?"

"I don't. But he goes on and on about how he didn't have to get student loans."

"What does your mom say?"

"She says I should find a school with the major I want, go there, and enjoy the experience."

"So, you need to get the applications done."

"Are yours done, Sher?"

"Yes, I sent them in last week." She shrugged.

Tanya threw her head back. "Of course they are."

The black vulture's call echoed through the air, a sound reminiscent of coarse gravel scraping against aluminum siding, a harsh and raspy 'Krsssshhhk.'

They jumped at the cry of the vulture. Tanya almost dropped her flute case. "Oh my God!"

Sheri clenched her hand to her chest.

A group of birds perched on the roof. Some stretched their wings and others watched them pass. Their dark, unblinking eyes focused on the pair. The two-story home had been abandoned for a few years, and whoever handled maintenance had failed. Shingles were missing in several sloped roof areas, and the gray siding looked dingy. The front porch overhang created too many shadows, making the front door uninviting. The windows were dark and covered with white sheets. No one had taken the time to edge the lawn all summer. Another vulture swooped in as she looked at the house and landed on the angled roof.

"I don't know why animal control can't do something about those birds," said Tanya.

"I heard that the last agent that tried to sell it disappeared. No one wants to sell it. It's probably cursed or haunted."

"That's not true," Tanya replied and started walking again.

"It's just what I heard. Besides, it's well known that vultures like that are omens of death."

"Maybe in the desert, not here."

"You don't know. They like that house for some reason."

"Well, I'm sure someone's gonna buy it eventually. Luke's parents sold their house in two weeks, and they're just one street over. They

12

moved out before school started. Someone just needs to fix it up a bit, and a nice, happy family will move right in."

"Whatever. I'd drive us to school if gas weren't so expensive."

"At least your parents got you a car. Every time I bring it up, my dad tells me the story about how he didn't get his first car until he was in the Navy and paid for it himself. There's an important lesson in self-reliance."

"Yeah, ok." Sheri shook her head.

Tanya waved. "There's Amara."

Amara came down the steps, waving to the pair, with her black hair pulled back in a Dutch braid below her shoulder blades. Her dark brown, almost black eyes contrasted with her light brown complexion. She wore jeans and a thin long-sleeved navy blue top with the Rice logo.

"Hey! Just in time." Amara smiled, flashing her perfect white teeth.

"Hey Amara," Tanya said, making room to walk three across. She glanced again at her friend. She always looked put together and in charge.

"You took your flute home? Did you practice?"

"Of course," Tanya said.

Sheri chimed in, "She has to keep that first chair."

Tanya pushed Sheri. "I practiced. Last night's calculus just took a little longer to do."

"Really? I didn't think it was too bad." Amara shrugged.

"Yeah, neither did Sheri."

Amara looked around her to Sheri, who smiled. "We may have to tutor Tanya if we're all going to Rice."

Amara furrowed her brow. "You keep saying that, but you wear UT colors every college day."

They stopped behind a group of students waiting to cross the road. Tanya leaned over to Amara and said. "Ted Baxter wants to go to UT."

Sheri's cheeks flushed red and she slapped Tanya on the shoulder, glaring at her.

"You need to say something."

"Shhh. He only goes out with the girls on the swim team."

Amara leaned in and whispered, "So, join the swim team."

Tanya held a hand over her mouth, stifling a laugh. "Have you seen her swim? Don't you remember Sandra's birthday party?"

Sheri looked between the two. "That was three years ago."

"I think her swimming has gotten worse." She looked at Sheri, whose cheeks were red, and she was staring daggers at her. "What? It's true."

Sheri whispered, "You don't have to say it."

Amara shook her head. "He doesn't know what he's missing. You're cute and the smartest girl in our class."

"She's right. You should say something."

Sheri stood straight and brushed her hands down her Longhorns T-shirt. "I am saying something."

Amara squinted. "I don't think he's gonna get it."

"Me neither," said Tanya.

They waited at the crossing for the four-lane road in front of Cedar Ridge Central High School. The school was a two-story light orange brick building on the right and a swooping open glass area to the left, where the cafeteria was. The top of the building angled up in a smooth curve, reminiscent of something she had seen at an airport. Traffic split to either side of a large paved circular grass area surrounded by a white sidewalk. A flagpole extended from the center of the grass another twenty feet above the building, the American flag flying. Student drop-off was on the right, and senior and faculty parking was on the left. Past the parking area was the football stadium. Larger than some college fields, they were told.

"Look," Amara pointed to a lone figure sitting under one of the tall trees in front of the school.

14

"We should go say hi," Tanya suggested. The girl, Yasmin, was a transfer at the beginning of the school year. She kept to herself. Most people felt intimidated by her.

"Why?"

"She's new. It's been six weeks, and I haven't seen her hanging out with anyone. That would suck if it was any of us. Her family moved here from Iran."

Amara turned to her. "What's that supposed to mean? Are you friends with everyone born here in Texas?" She exaggerated a southern drawl.

Sheri giggled.

"No. I thought you might have something in common since your family is from Iran, too."

"Well, I think I have enough friends, and you two understand me." Amara put her arms around them and pulled them in. "I don't need anyone else."

Tanya smiled and her eyes were drawn toward Yasmin, who was sitting alone and watching everyone enter the school. Amara had disliked her since the beginning of the school year. She had thick, dark brown, gently curled hair, upturned brown eyes, and full lips. Surprisingly, none of the boys had taken an interest. Yasmin dressed in dark colors, predominantly blacks, grays, and browns. Today, despite the heat, she wore dark jeans and a tight, long-sleeved brown shirt.

Tanya felt drawn to the girl, not wanting anyone to feel left out. They were in their final year of high school. Everyone deserves to have a great senior year. She made a mental note to talk to Yasmin when she had a chance.

"Let's go." Amara pulled her arm. As the last kids crossed to the school, the crossing guards held the traffic at bay.

 # Chapter 4

Tuesday Afternoon

Tanya and Sheri crossed the road along the school grounds, just past the football stadium. They followed the sidewalk to the church off the side of the main building with the traditional steeples.

She paused at the door. "I don't know, Sher. Maybe this is a bad idea."

"Tanya, just try it. I looked at their website. The reviews are excellent and it's close to school."

She was unsure, looking at the glass door. She wanted to open the door and walk right in, full of courage for whatever would be inside, but fear stayed in her head. What if someone noticed her?

"It's ok, I'll be here with you."

Tanya looked at Sheri. "Let's go." She pulled the handle and walked through. Children's artwork adorned the walls on either side of the long hall.

They followed the meeting announcement signs to a set of double doors, one propped open and the other with a large paper sign that read, 'Meeting inside.'

As expected, inside the organizers had set up a large circle of chairs with a table against the wall, which was surrounded by women of all ages mingling. The girls made their way over to the table, finding coffee, ice water, blue punch, cookies, carrots, and celery.

Tanya took a cup of ice water and turned to scope out a seat in the circle. Over a dozen women were present.

A woman with gray hair and inviting but sad, icy blue eyes approached them. "Welcome, I'm Diane. We have name tags on the other table, if you don't mind. You don't have to, but it sometimes helps break the ice." She smiled, revealing coffee or tea stained teeth.

"Thank you," Tanya replied. "What time does the meeting start?"

"In just a few minutes. I try to get as close to six as we can. A few will come in after we start."

"Is there assigned seating?"

"No, you can sit wherever you are. Mingle. This is a safe place."

Tanya expected the woman to reach out to pat her on the arm or shoulder, but she didn't. "Thank you, Diane."

The older woman smiled and moved to another group of women gathered at the other end of the refreshments.

"You wanna sit down?" Sheri asked.

"Sure." Tanya looked around the room again, seeing most women making their way to a seat in the circle.

Diane took one of the empty seats in the circle. She glanced at the other participants, making eye contact and smiling at each woman. "I am glad you all are here with us tonight. This is a safe place. Those around you are victims of domestic abuse or violence, including myself. As always, you can share if you are comfortable. We don't judge anyone and love every one of you."

Nods circulated throughout the room. Tanya experienced a tightness in her chest, tears welling up in her eyes as her emotions surged. She looked down as Sheri took her hand, gently squeezing.

"We don't have a speaking stick or a specific order. If you have something to share, please raise your hand and talk to the group. Would anyone like to start tonight?"

A middle-aged woman to their left raised her hand. She wore light blue sweatpants and a yellow T-shirt. She had her hair trimmed to a short length above her shoulders. "I'd like to share."

Diane nodded to her. "Go ahead, Sharon."

The woman looked around, swallowing with apprehension. "Hello everyone, I'm Sharon. I want to let you know that I'm closer to taking charge of my life." A smattering of claps echoed throughout the room.

"I told my boyfriend that we should get our own places." She looked at Diane.

"That's good, Sharon. How did he take it?"

"Um, he wasn't happy. He said that I needed him to take care of me and that I would waste all my money if he didn't manage our budget."

"How did that make you feel?"

"Unsure. Um, I do like to buy things. Sometimes, I get things we don't need."

"Sharon, is that what he says or what you believe?"

"It's what he says, I buy things. Last week, I bought a laundry basket. But I guess I didn't really need it. I could just pick up the clothes from around the apartment and bring them to the laundry room."

"That's bullshit!"

"Arline, let her finish."

Arline looked to be in her late twenties. Long dark hair cascading down. She wore a red floral blouse, a black skirt, and black flats. "I'm just saying that if she wants a laundry basket or whatever, she's the one working. Unless he got a job since last week."

Sharon shook her head, glancing at Arline before looking down.

"Then honey, you spend your damned money on whatever you want."

A sparse applause emanated from various corners of the room.

Diane held a hand up. "Sharon, that's a wonderful step. When he got angry, what did you do?"

"Reflecting on our previous conversation, I remembered what you taught us about coercive and controlling behavior. I told him I would be ok in my own place. I had an apartment before and was fine."

"What was his response?"

"He got mad, then got a text and left. He said I'd realize I need him to take care of me since I'm useless alone."

Diane clapped and the group joined her.

Tanya heard the door behind her open. She turned to see who had come in, and her breath caught for a second. The new girl from school, Yasmin, closed the door and moved to an open seat across the circle. Yasmin didn't react to their presence. Maybe she didn't recognize them from school.

Diane led the group, allowing those who wanted to share to do so. Tanya squeezed Sheri's hand and leaned over to whisper. "Thank you for talking me into this."

Sheri smiled in return.

Several of the women discussed their situations and what efforts they took to confront their harasser, extract themselves from the situation, or cope with their feelings more effectively. Tanya caught Yasmin's eyes a few times, but still hadn't seen a reaction. *That girl is a stoic.*

"Thank you all for coming. Remember, you can call me anytime. Take a card from the refreshment table. Hang out. We have the room for another half hour. If anyone is looking for an advocate, let me know, and I'll set up a meeting for you to meet them to make sure there is a match."

The women in the group stood and milled about, working their way back to the groups they had been in before the meeting started.

"I want to say hi."

"Sure."

Tanya walked over to Yasmin, who was refilling a cup of coffee.

"Hi, Yasmin. I'm Tanya, and this is Sheri."

She sipped the coffee and looked up from the cup. "Cold, but not bad. You are in my AP World History class." Her voice was warm and rich, pleasant to listen to, inviting.

Tanya smiled. "I'm sorry I haven't said hi to you before."

Yasmin had a defiant demeanor. Her stance was defensive. In a fight-or-flight situation, she looked like she was all in. The coffee finished, she tossed the cup in the trash. She took a few packs of cookies, stuffing them into her pocket. She shrugged. "In case I get hungry on the way home."

"Do you live around here?"

"Not too close. I think we are just inside the school district." She looked distracted, watching the other women. "Thank you for coming over. Maybe I'll see you at school."

"Um, ok. It was good to finally talk to you. Maybe I'll see you at lunch."

"Or in class." She flashed a quick smile before her face returned to its normal solemn.

Yasmin walked to Diane, said something that got a hand pat from the woman, and then left.

Diane came over to the pair. "I hope your first time didn't scare you off."

Tanya shook her head. "No, I told Sheri I'm glad she talked me into this. I think I'll be coming back."

"That's good. I hope you can find the support you are looking for. I understand it's frightening to share in front of strangers. Do you mind if I ask you a question?"

"Sure," Tanya replied, feeling defensive.

"Is your situation sexual?"

Tanya blushed. "No, ma'am," she blurted.

"Ok, I'm sorry to be forward, but you're young, and if there is a chance to intervene, I don't want to wait."

Tanya looked down, feeling ashamed to discuss her home life. "It's not that." She felt the flush in her face.

"Ok, I look forward to seeing you next week if you can make it." She reached into her back pocket and pulled out a card. She handed one each to her and Sheri. "Those are my personal numbers. Call me anytime if you need anything."

Tanya looked up into the older woman's face. "Thank you, Diane." She looked at the card. The area code was 312, not local.

Diane nodded and moved to another group near the door.

The sun was still up when they left the church and it would be light for another half hour. Tanya didn't want to call her parents to come to get them.

"Are you gonna come back?" Sheri asked.

"Yeah, I think so. I don't know if I'm ready to share, but hearing their stories helped. I wish I could bring Mom down here, but my dad would lose it if he found out." She looked at the card Diane had given her, noting that it only had her name, phone number, email address, and the title 'Advocate' under her name. If her dad found it, he might ask who it was, but he wouldn't be able to get mad. For all he knew, it was a person from college admissions.

Tanya cheered up, tapping Sheri on the arm. "Do you want to swing by the Natatorium? Just to see if someone is practicing."

Sheri raised her chin in mock anger. "He has practice from five to seven thirty in the morning. The JV and dive teams are there now."

"Ok, I thought I'd offer since it's on the way home. Wait, how do you know the schedule?"

Sheri flashed her a quick grin before walking toward their street in silence.

Chapter 5

Tuesday Night

The sun had set by the time she got home. While she couldn't see the horizon in her suburban setting, the brilliant colors in the western sky made her smile. She looked around the front yard and up the street. It was a pleasant area with neighbors, pretty lawns, and happy little families. Her eyes drifted back to the metallic blue BMW in the driveway, bringing up thoughts of her dad. How many have dark little secrets hidden away behind the closed doors of happy little suburban homes? She reached into her pocket, feeling the card from Diane. She opened the front door and returned to her world.

"Where have you been?" her father questioned her without looking up from the TV. He was in his work slacks and his undershirt. He propped his feet up on the coffee table—something her mom hated.

"I was with Sheri at school. I told Mom."

"Figures, she didn't tell me. There weren't any boys, were there?"

"No, Daddy, all girls. It was good and I had fun. Do you want to hear about it?"

"No, I'm good. I don't need to hear about chick stuff. Your mom should be in the kitchen or out back with the dog. I never know what the hell she does. Certainly not keeping the house clean." He swiped a finger across the end table where his drink sat next to a coaster.

She moved towards the kitchen, then went back to kiss him on the head before he said something.

"Hey! Is this project or whatever gonna help you getting into college?"

"Yes, Daddy, I think it will help."

"Good."

She waited for a second, in case he was going to say something else, but he just sat staring at his show.

In the kitchen, her mother was running water in the sink, getting ready to wash the dishes. Tanya gave her a hug from behind.

"Hey baby, how was your day?"

"It was good, Momma. You relax, I'll do the dishes."

"I won't argue with that. Anyway, I have some things that need to go upstairs."

Arr, Arr, Arr, Arr, Arr.

"I don't know what has gotten into that dog." Her mom leaned against the sink to look out the window into the backyard.

Tanya looked out the window. Jackson was staring at the right side fence, growling. His hackles were up. "He's barking at the Phillip's yard. I thought they were on vacation for a few more weeks."

"They are. And they took Champ with them."

"Who knows with Jackson. He's the smallest dog of all the neighbors and thinks he runs everything."

Her mom smiled, something she didn't do too often. "Do you remember that movie we used to watch when you were little? The one with the talking pets."

Tanya smiled. "*The Secret Life of Pets?*"

"You loved that movie. Jackson's definitely the bunny. Our little guy with the big attitude."

Tanya laughed, "Yeah, he is. All attitudes."

Her mom's smile faded. "If he keeps it up, bring him in before your father gets annoyed."

"I will. Love you, Mom."

"Aww, I love you too." She turned and left.

Tanya felt the water and pulled her hand back, turning the knob to cool it just a bit. She swung the faucet to the other sink basin, grabbed the plates, and sunk them in the soapy water, splitting the tall pile of suds.

Arr, Arr, Arr, Arr, Arr.

Jackson had moved closer to the neighbor's fence. *Oh, please don't be a skunk.* She washed the plates while watching the dog out the window.

"Kaitlyn, shut that damned dog up!"

Tanya dried her hands and went out back, stepping down to their small deck. "Jackson, what are you doing?" She walked toward the dog. "Come!"

The gray and white Scotty continued barking. The backyard lights flickered off, leaving the right side of the yard in shadows. She stopped, looking in the direction Jackson was barking. The darkness was almost overwhelming. She walked into the grass, focusing on the back corner. She recoiled as an unpleasant odor overwhelmed her. "Oh my gosh." She pinched her nose. "It smells like roadkill that's been sitting in the sun all day." She turned and stopped. A shot of adrenaline hit her as she froze. Something moved in the shadows, a darker shape inside the darkness. Her heart jumped and she let out a brief scream. She returned to the house, grabbing Jackson on the way—the little dog squirming in her arms.

She burst into the kitchen, putting the dog down.

"Daddy, something's in the backyard. To the right side. The light's out."

"Damnit. Ok, ok, calm the hell down. I'll look."

She followed him into the kitchen and went back to the window to watch. Using a flashlight, he swept over the yard, illuminating all the dark areas with the beam of light. He moved to the fence, shining his light down and along the length of the side of the house.

He closed the door behind him. With a shake of his head, he conveyed his disapproval. "Something dug under the fence. Probably a possum. Something smells bad, but not like a skunk. I'll fill it in tomorrow or this weekend."

He patted her on the head. "Don't worry, darlin'. I'm here to protect you and your mom. You'll be ok." He chuckled as he put the light back in the drawer and returned to the living room.

She felt her anger rise. She finished the dishes, glancing out the window throughout. Nothing moved outside. Jackson lay down next to the back door. After cleaning up, she grabbed a snack bar and looked out the window again. The motion sensor lights were off. Her gaze was fixated on the darkness. She felt goosebumps prickle her arm as a feeling of unease overwhelmed her. Tanya had a sense of being watched despite not seeing anything.

With her eyes on the window, she stepped back. Fear gripped her. She ran through the living room and up the stairs to her bedroom, closing the curtains and turning on all her lights.

Chapter 6

Thursday Midday

Tanya carried her tray from the lunch line into the main room. The cafeteria smells filled the air. A constant hum of conversation drowned out all but the most determined speakers. She paused, looking around the expansive room.

"What are you looking for?" asked Sheri.

"Amara."

Sheri touched her elbow and pointed. "There she is."

Amara was waving from a table along the edge of the room, near the windows. When they got to the table, she saw their friend had her lunch laid out in front of her. Every part of her meal had its proper place. She was eating apple slices. It wasn't as loud as expected. At least one-third of the seats were empty. Tanya set her tray down, unwrapping her fork and mixing the small salad with the cup of Italian dressing.

"You two are going to look back on this time in your lives and wonder why you didn't enjoy your food," said Sheri, dipping her fries in ketchup. She placed her lettuce and tomato on her cheeseburger and pointed at it. "Salad." She then took a bite, making exaggerated sounds of enjoyment.

Amara rolled her eyes, taking another apple slice. "I like my food. I don't know how you can eat that."

Tanya was quietly eating her salad.

"You don't know what you're missing." Sheri took another bite of her cheeseburger.

Tanya looked around the room, not paying attention to the back and forth banter.

"Tanya, did you hear me?"

"I'm sorry, Amara, no. What did you say?"

"What's got you distracted?"

"You'll probably think it's silly."

Amara shook her head, "No, what's up?"

"Last night, Jackson was going crazy, barking at something on the other side of the fence."

"That seems normal." Sheri shrugged.

"True," added Amara.

"Not that. I went out, and I swear I saw something move in the dark. It was weird. I didn't see anything, but it felt strange. It's like there was a shadow inside the shadows."

"It's just your imagination. We are in the most boring neighborhood in Cedar Ridge."

Tanya noticed Yasmin enter after taking another bite of her salad. She waved enthusiastically, motioning her over.

Amara's eyes widened. "What are you doing?"

Tanya leaned across the table. "I'm inviting her over."

"I see that. Why?"

"She's in my AP World History class, and she's nice."

Yasmin made her way to the table.

Tanya scooched over, making room at the end of the bench. "Join us."

"Sure." She sat down, opening her thermos.

"Aren't you gonna get lunch?" asked Tanya.

"No. I usually skip lunch. I prefer to sit outside, but since you invited me, here I am."

"You like it outside."

Yasmin shrugged.

"What's up with your nails?"

"Amara!"

"What, she doesn't look the goth part. I'm just curious."

Yasmin held her hand up and turned it to look at her nails. "It's no big deal. My grandmother lets me work in the garden when I get home. Black hides the dirt better."

Amara held her hands out. "See, harmless question."

"I like your necklace. It's from the Yazd area, correct?" Yasmin nodded toward Amara's necklace.

Amara reached up and rubbed the intricate silver and gold pendant. "Yes, it is. Is that where you're from?"

"No, I'm from the Gilan province."

"I'm not familiar with it, or any region, actually. We moved here when I was two."

Yasmin dropped her eyes for a moment before straightening out. "I came here with my grandmother when I was thirteen." Her eyes darted to Tanya for a moment. "My mother died before we could go together."

"I'm sorry," said Amara, suddenly looking uncomfortable.

"Me too," added Tanya. "It must have been difficult."

"It's ok. I think about her often. I wish she could have seen America."

Yasmin abruptly looked uncomfortable and stood up. "Thanks for inviting me over. I need to do something before class." She turned and left the cafeteria.

"That wasn't too bad."

"I guess not. I'm surprised she recognized my necklace, though. It was my grandmother's."

"That was cool," said Tanya, before taking the last bite of her salad.

Amara leaned in. "Are you still good for Friday night?"

"I am," said Sheri.

Tanya nodded. "I think so. I'll check again later."

"Ok, it's for school, so bring your laptops and swimsuits."

"I will," said Tanya.

"Maybe we'll watch a scary movie, too," added Amara.

Tanya sat back. "I'm not afraid of scary movies. It was just creepy. Whatever." She threw her hands up and stood, picking up her tray. "I've gotta go to my locker. I'll see you in class."

Tanya walked down the hall to her locker, taking out her notebook and *The Catcher in the Rye*. She had fifteen minutes until class, so she headed to the bathroom. She caught sight of Yasmin looking out the window, facing the open grassy area behind the school.

Tanya walked up beside her. "What's going on?"

Yasmin didn't jump or react. She looked down at two boys pushing a smaller boy. They moved toward him, and he tripped, falling back into the grass. The larger boys laughed. "I hate bullies."

"Yeah."

Yasmin whirled and made her way down the stairs. Tanya heard the door open. She leaned in toward the window and pressed up to the glass. Yasmin walked toward the bullies, not looking around. She said something and the first boy turned around, holding his hands to his side, daring her to do something. She walked right up and kicked him between the legs. The second boy tried to grab her. She grabbed the second boy by the wrist, twisted his arm, and forced him down next to his friend. Yasmin kneeled, putting her knee in the second boy's ribs, and said something to the boys, who both nodded. Standing up, she let them go and pointed at them both while saying something else. Kneeling by the smaller boy, she said something, his head nodding rapidly. She left them on the ground and walked back inside.

Tanya hurried down the stairs, rounding the corner, narrowly missing a collision with Yasmin.

"Oh my God, that was amazing. What if someone saw you?"

"No one saw it and they won't say anything. Bullies are afraid of looking weak. I'll keep my mouth shut if they don't bully anyone else."

Yasmin looked at her. She noticed flecks of yellow or light brown in her brown eyes. "You'll keep my secret, right?"

"Of course."

"Thanks. I have to get to class. I'll see you."

"Bye." Tanya looked back out the window. The three boys had cleared out. *That was cool. Most people would've ignored them.* Tanya headed to her English class, smiling at the thought of keeping a secret.

Chapter 7

Thursday Afternoon

Tanya strolled, staying in the shade of the trees along the street toward her house. Sheri walked beside her.

"This is too hot. Will you please drive tomorrow?"

"Fine."

"I'll split the gas with you. I'm so drained when I get home. My plan is to shower and do nothing."

"At least you're not doing marching band."

"Mr. Bilby asked and I politely declined. I said I was happy to stick to jazz and performance."

"You know, if we drive, we'll miss our chance to look for ghosts in the Vulture House." Sheri pointed to the house ahead of them.

They stopped in front of the run-down home. "It gets gloomier every day."

"Maybe your shadow is hiding in there."

"I told you I'm not afraid. It was just creepy. I know it was my imagination." She teased Sheri with a push.

"Ok, I dare you to go look inside the windows."

"No, that's trespassing."

"It's not. That 'For Sale' sign means that it's fair game."

Tanya looked at her friend and back at the gloomy house. She raised her chin and approached the house with determination. The shadows on the front porch looked deeper, accented by the dark black door. More shingles had come loose and were hanging over the gutter, close to joining the broken few that had fallen into the bushes. The sheet covering one of the attic windows moved with the slight summer breeze. Someone left the window open. It didn't look too bad. She pulled her shoulders back and walked up the concrete path to the front steps. A sense of dread washed over her as she neared. Her imagination played tricks on her. What if she got up to the door and someone opened it? She swallowed and continued hesitantly.

"Let me know if you see a ghost. Victims like to haunt their resting place."

That did it. Her resolve broke and her imagination took off. Something moved in the front window. She turned around and ran back to the sidewalk. "That wasn't fair."

"What? I was trying to build suspense."

"It worked. Look." Tanya held up her arm, which was covered in goosebumps. She looked over her shoulder, squinting, trying to focus on the dirty second floor. It was dark and weathered. Adrenaline shot through her heart as she thought she glimpsed someone. "Someone's in there." She pulled Sheri's arm and pointed to the second-floor window. They turned, looking at the window for a moment.

Sheri looked at her, shaking her head. "It's the curtain up there. How does the agent not see that it's always open? That room has to be trashed by rain, leaves, and whatever."

She didn't think so, but she held her gaze on the shifting curtain. There wasn't anything there. If she stepped side to side, the dirt on the window could look like a person. "You're right, just the dirty curtain."

"You're just trying to get me back."

Tanya smiled weakly. "Maybe."

As they neared Tanya's house, her dad was out front mowing the lawn. His Scorpion shirt looked black, soaked in sweat. He wore long gray sweat-shorts that were just above his knees.

"Hi, Mr. Janessy."

He grunted in acknowledgment. "Tanya, go inside and help your mother clean up the mess in the kitchen."

Tanya glanced at Sheri, all traces of a smile disappearing. "Yes, Daddy."

She hurried up the path to the steps and into the house.

The kitchen door stood open. She saw broken glass on the white-speckled marble counter and the floor underneath it. Several glasses lay broken on the shelves.

She dropped her backpack and ran to the kitchen. "Momma?"

Her mom was sweeping broken glass from around the table. It looked like a glass had dropped on the floor.

She had a band-aid on her cheek that appeared to have fresh blood soaking the gauze. "Are you all right?" Tanya reached toward her mom's cheek.

"Yes. I'm ok. A piece of glass hit me. I'm lucky. It could have been worse."

Tanya looked back toward the glass on the counter and floor, the glass from the cabinet door panes. It looked like something had gone through it.

"What happened?"

"Your dad is under a lot of stress at work."

"That doesn't excuse this." She waved her hand over the glass.

"It was an accident. He didn't throw it at me."

"Momma, this isn't right."

"Tanya, it'll be ok. You know how he gets worked up sometimes."

"How did the cabinet get broken?"

"It's not important. I need to clean this up. Why don't you go up to your room? I'll call you down for dinner."

"Let me help."

"No, it's my mess. I'll get it. You go on."

Tanya shook her head. "Momma, he needs to get some help and talk to someone about his anger issues."

"Don't you let him hear you say that."

"It's the truth. We both know that."

"I've got this, dear. I need to get this cleaned up so I can get dinner on."

She looked at her mother. Serenely, she swept up the mess created by her father. She looked like any other suburban housewife: jeans, a V-neck green short-sleeve shirt, and plain white shoes. Her long brown hair, though tousled, framed her face. Only her eyes looked sad.

Tanya grabbed a juice from the refrigerator and stopped before leaving the kitchen. "I love you, Momma."

Her mom smiled. "I know you do, baby. I'll call you for dinner."

Tanya picked up her backpack and went upstairs to her room. She looked at the family pictures on the wall up the stairs. *So fake.* She didn't believe them anymore. The cheerful smiles of the three of them from when she was little, at the beach, camping, and a few professionals.

"What a lie."

She shut the door to her room and opened her clutch, pulling out the card again. Her mother looked broken, accepting. She looked out the window at nothing in particular.

She grabbed her phone.

Tanya: Not a good day.

Sheri: What's going on?

Tanya: The same.

Sheri: Sorry. Do you want to come over?

Tanya: Probably not.

Sheri: I could use the help with my homework.

Tanya understood that Sheri had picked up on the innuendo and was giving her an excuse her dad might miss. He was demanding of her and her schoolwork, and made exceptions for her to do what she needed. Sheri didn't need help. She was on her way to being class valedictorian.

Tanya: Maybe. I'll let you know.

Sheri: Text me if you need anything.

Tanya: You're the best, Sher.

Sheri: I know. =)

She tossed her phone on the bed and lay back on her pillows. Smurfette watched her from across the room, a wide, sweet smile on her face. *Are you going to do anything?* She looked around her room at the trinkets of her life. Band trophies, academic awards, pictures with her friends, and traces of lavender all around. The relaxing scent of Sea Breeze Vanilla filled the air as she lit a scented candle. She jumped onto her bed, closed her eyes, and sank into her pillows, letting the scent calm her.

Chapter 8

Thursday Night

Arr, Arr, Arr, Arr, Arr.

In search of her phone, she rolled over. The light from the backyard came through her window from the left, the right side was still out. She located and raised it, realizing it was past nine.

"Noooo." She struggled to get up, feeling lethargic, after sleeping almost four hours.

Arr, Arr, Arr, Arr, Arr.

She got up and went downstairs to let Jackson in. She noticed the light shining from under her parents' door. They were already in bed, which was a good sign, although they left Jackson in the backyard. If her dad were really mad, he'd sit downstairs watching something in the living room.

She went into the kitchen, which looked normal except for the missing cabinet door. She grabbed a glass and filled it with water. Jackson stood in his big dog stance, legs and back straight, barking defiantly toward the back fence and his buddy Coolio's yard. His shadow spread to the right into the darkness of that half of the yard. His little tail was rigid, his ears straight up. He was not a happy puppy.

She set the glass by the sink and turned on the back door light, getting Jackson's attention. He turned to her, his tail wagging quickly before looking back at the fence.

Arr, Arr, Arr, Arr, Arr.

"Jackson, shh. People are trying to sleep."

The little dog adjusted his stance. She almost cracked up.

"My little guardian. Leave Coolio alone."

Jackson sniffed the air and ambled toward the fence.

"Jackson, c'mon, let's go in."

The light on the left side of the yard flickered on and off a few times before going out. Her shadow from the back door light shot forward, falling over Jackson. She thought she heard digging from the back fence. Jackson whimpered and backed up.

"C'mon boy, let's go in."

She picked up the dog and went back inside, looking at the surrounding darkness.

The scraping and digging continued from the back fence. Hopefully, Coolio would give up once Jackson was inside.

She grabbed a yogurt cup from the refrigerator and went upstairs. Her phone rang as she reached the top. She fumbled, trying to answer, catching it without dropping the yogurt.

"Tanya, turn your ringer off after nine. I'll take that phone if you can't follow the rules," her father's voice came from behind the closed door.

"Sorry, Daddy."

She made her way to her room and closed the door.

"Hello. Hello? Are you there? Tanya."

"Amara, what?"

"Just making sure you are coming tomorrow night."

"I told you I am. You know my dad gets mad if I get calls after nine."

"It was close."

"I'm serious, Amara. If he gets pissed, I'll be stuck here all weekend."

"Fine, sorry. I'm gonna check with Sheri."

"Ok, I'll see you tomorrow."

Tanya opened her laptop and clicked the link to her student account and assignments.

The incoming call box popped up. She hit *Accept Call* and pushed back from the desk, fully reclining in her chair. Sheri's nose filled the screen.

"Aaagh, what are you doing?" She slipped her earbuds in.

"Sorry, I was getting a pen from the back of my desk." She sat back, and her friend appeared in the box. A light blue headband held up her curly hair, moisturizer covered her face.

"What's up?"

"You're late. I saw you go green. Are you just starting your assignments?"

"Yeah, I fell asleep."

"Need help?"

"No, I'll look at the questions and then read the assignment. I'm gonna get up early and do it."

"What are you doing?"

"Watching Netflix."

"Ugh, don't tempt me."

"Hopefully, not too long. My dad's at work."

"Still?"

"Yeah, a detective is missing."

"How long? Maybe they went on vacation and forgot to tell your dad."

Sheri laughed. "Right, you know my dad. Who knows? How are you doing? You, ok?"

Tanya lowered her voice, "I'm ok. I wish I could get my mom to go with me to the meeting next week, though."

"Just ask her, say you need to go shopping for an outfit for the dance or whatever."

"Yeah, right? It'll be a big no from my dad if he thinks I'm doing anything that might hurt my chance to get into college."

Sheri deepened her voice, "You can chase boys after you graduate from college. Worry about that, MRS degree, when you're on your own."

Tanya laughed, covering her mouth. "Oh my god, if he heard you, he would ground me for the rest of the year."

"I like it when you laugh."

"Thanks, Sher. I needed that."

"Ok, get back to reading, or Amara's going to catch up to you."

"I will. I'll catch up with you in the morning."

Tanya closed the window and read through the questions. They weren't too bad. She heard a scraping noise outside her window.

She got up, turned off the desk light, and looked out the window. The neighborhood was quiet at this time of the night. Most people were winding down. It was dark out as her house was between streetlights and got little residual light from the front. She looked into the surrounding yards. None of their backyard lights were on. She opened her window and slid the screen up. A gentle breeze added to the pleasantness of the night. Moving her desk lamp to the windowsill, she picked up her book and stepped out onto the back deck cover. She sat, leaning against the house, next to her window. She looked up at the stars, only the brightest making it through. The scent of whatever had died in the Phillips yard caught her attention. It wasn't as strong, but it was still noxious. She reached over her shoulder and adjusted the light. The light illuminated the backyard, creating a stark contrast with the darkness. Her shadow stretched almost to the back fence. She could have gotten the book light from her nightstand, but she was already here. Settling in, she adjusted to read.

 Chapter 9

Friday Evening

Amara pulled into the parking lot of Friendly's. "I've been waiting for this all week."

"Me too," added Sheri.

"I'm going to get a banana split," said Tanya.

"Ok, Mom," teased Sheri. "You need to live a little."

"I'm getting the Vegan Coffee Caramel twist. One is almond milk, and the other is oat. You should try it. It's good for you," Amara added.

As they got out of the car, they looked at each other. Sheri and Tanya shook their heads at each other before nodding to Amara. "No, you can let us know how it is."

Amara rolled her eyes.

They picked up their orders and went into the main seating area. "There's a table right there." She led them over. Sheri bumped into a table while licking the chocolate syrup from her medium chocolate cookie dough cup, getting a bit of chocolate on her nose. Tanya saw Ted Crawford and a few of his friends in the booth behind them. Tanya looked from Ted to Sheri. Her cheeks had flushed red, and she hadn't noticed the chocolate on her nose. Tanya stepped in front of her friend and swiftly passed her a napkin. "Your nose."

Sheri's eyes widened, and she quickly wiped the syrup away, returning to her booth. Ted smiled at her before rejoining the conversation.

Amara sat across from them, smiling, eating her ice cream from the cone with a spoon.

Sheri glared at Amara.

"What?" Amara ate another spoonful of ice cream, a twinkle in her eye.

"What are we going to do tonight?" Tanya interjected.

"I think we should drive out to the lake, where we meet a few hot guys, sneak off, and then get taken out by a random monster."

Sheri tilted her head. "Well, that's cliché. Shouldn't we wait for spring break when we all go out to celebrate getting into college, and we're in relationships that will last past graduation?"

"Now that sounds like a plan." Tanya nodded.

Amara looked out the window. A police car drove by with its lights on. "So, Cabin in the Woods?"

"Yes, if Sheri's ok with it. You know she doesn't like to violate the seasons."

Sheri sat back, looking past Amara to the other table.

Tanya leaned in and whispered, "Say something or smile at him."

"It's not really horror. More of a behind-the-scenes documentary on all the shows our parents grew up on."

Sheri started to say something, but the sound of more sirens caught her attention. They looked out the front window, and three more Cedar Ridge Police cars sped by.

Sheri's phone buzzed. Tanya scooched forward to see where the cars were going.

"Something's going on. My dad got called in."

"Ask him if it's near here."

Sheri typed the message and waited for the response. Her phone buzzed. "Yes, a few blocks down by the strip mall."

Amara leaned in. "Let's go see. It's better than a movie."

Tanya slid out from the booth and caught her foot on the bench, tripping. She dropped her ice cream cup. Two of the guys at the other table were getting up and caught her.

"Thank you."

She looked from one to the other. "No problem. Tanya, right?"

"Yes."

"I'm Terry. Those benches will get you."

Ted stepped in, "We're gonna go down and see what's going on. You wanna go?" He looked around.

Amara slid out. "Yes, we would."

Sheri spoke up, "It's a few blocks down."

They left Friendly's and headed toward the strip mall. More police cars passed, pulling into the parking lot and around the buildings. They followed the lights around the building. The police already had the area cordoned off. Their searchlight lit the back of the building. A pair of EMTs were moving a woman's body to a gurney. She didn't appear to be moving.

Amara held her hand to her mouth. "Look at the ground. Is that blood?"

A large, dark, wet area stained the asphalt.

Tanya felt a tug on her sleeve. She looked over at Sheri. "That's Sharon." She looked toward the ambulance. "From the meeting."

Tanya looked at the ambulance. "Let's move closer."

As they moved along the police line, Sheri ducked down behind her shoulder. "It's my dad."

Tanya saw him and turned her face away, continuing forward. "You're right, it is her. They're treating her. This can't be her blood. The average human holds one and a half gallons. I've spilled a gallon of milk in the kitchen. If she lost that much, she'd be dead," she whispered.

"Whose is it then? I don't see anyone else."

"What are you two doing here?"

Tanya looked up at the Sheriff, Sheri's dad. "Hi, Mr. Downes."

Sheri stepped around Tanya. "Hey, Dad."

"You two," he paused, "three." Amara joined them. "Need to go home. Now."

Amara nodded, "Yes, sir."

Sheri stepped in, "Dad, what happened? Is she all right?"

"I don't know, but you girls shouldn't be here. Go home. I'm gonna be late. Don't wait up."

Sheri reached around her father, hugging him.

"Whose blood is that?" Tanya asked, regretting it immediately.

The sheriff scowled at her, and then back at the puddle. "You girls go home now."

"Yes, sir," they said in unison.

"Amara, are you ok? You look pale," said Tanya from the passenger's seat.

"It's the blood. Remember when I cut my leg at the playground in third grade? She passed out."

Tanya laughed. "Oh, yeah, Mrs. Kascinsky froze, trying to decide which of you needed help more."

"Where was the body?" asked Amara, her voice shaking.

"Maybe they already put it in the ambulance."

"I don't know. We saw the cars going by. They would try to figure out what happened," Sheri said from the back seat. "The woman in the ambulance was completely out of it. Her eyes were open, but she wasn't moving."

Tanya turned in her seat. "Do you think she killed someone, maybe her boyfriend or something?"

Sheri looked up at the rearview mirror before shaking her head. "She looked like she was in shock. She was out of it."

"Can we talk about something else?"

"Sorry, Amara, yeah." Tanya looked at her friend; her knuckles were white, and she was gripping the steering wheel. Her eyes focused on the road.

Amara slammed on the brakes and let out a piercing scream. Tanya just had time to put her arms up before the seatbelt dug into her shoulder, locking her in place. A dark shape jumped into the air, rising over the hood and above the windshield.

She could feel her heart pounding. With her arms locked forward, Amara clenched the wheel.

"Amara."

"Amara!" She yelled, her friend finally turning to acknowledge her.

"I'm ok, I'm ok." She relaxed her arms, leaning forward to see what was on the road. Something was being eaten.

Tanya leaned forward, not seeing anything. She unbuckled and opened her door.

"What are you doing?" Amara glared at her. "I want to go home."

"Just a sec." Tanya got out of the car and walked to the front. "Aww, it's a chihuahua. Yeah, don't get out."

She got back in the car. "Someone's dog got hit."

"What flew over the car?"

"What do you think it was?" Tanya asked calmly.

"I don't know. It could be anything. We don't know where all that blood came from at the crime scene."

"Or that could have been a domestic dispute, which is bad luck for the poor puppy. It was a vulture."

"How do you know?" Amara's eyes were wide and she looked pale as she sat there shaking.

"You're ok." She turned and pointed at the next house they were approaching. "I'm guessing it came from there."

Amara looked past her.

Tanya turned and looked at the dark house. The shadows appeared more profound in the moonlight. The lack of lights from any of the windows set it apart from all the other houses on the street. It sat in place like death or a disease, draining life from everything around it.

Amara put the car in gear and sped down the road to her house, pulling into the driveway too fast and running over the flowers along the side. "I don't want to watch the movie anymore," declared Amara. "We're watching a comedy."

Sheri looked at Tanya as they exited the car and followed Amara up the front steps. "Yeah, that sounds good."

Chapter 10

Tuesday Afternoon

Maintaining focus was a struggle. Tanya had just read the same paragraph for a third time. She checked her phone. The clock showed five-forty. Sheri was supposed to meet her here ten minutes ago. Tanya wanted to get to the meeting in time to talk to Diane.

"Hey."

She looked up from her book. Yasmin sat across from her. She had added a slight point on the outer corner of her eyes with a liner, which made them pop more. She smiled up at her. "Hi. Are you going tonight?"

"Yes. Are you?"

"Yeah. I was waiting for Sheri." She checked her phone, not seeing a text. "But she's late. Do you want to walk over?"

Yasmin looked around the library, seeing another person a few tables away. "Sure. You know that he's been watching you, right?" She pointed at the only other person sitting in the library, a younger-looking boy with a small stack of books.

Tanya turned, looking over her shoulder at the boy. He seemed young, possibly a freshman. "No. Let me get my things." She put the history book in her backpack and scooped up her things, adding them to her pack.

They walked by the boy and Tanya leaned over, tapping the table as he tried not to look up. "Good luck with your studies." She flashed him a smile as they walked away.

"Do you know him?"

"No."

"Are you attracted to him?"

She reached up to push Yasmin like she would Sheri, but stopped short. She caught herself and looked into Yasmin's eyes, feeling drawn in. The tiny yellow flecks stood out against the brown of her eyes. "You have pretty eyes."

Yasmin didn't flinch or react. "Do you prefer girls?"

Tanya realized what she said. "I'm sorry, I didn't mean, um, yes, I like boys. People like who they like, either option is fine, I guess. I uh." She just stopped talking, looking down, and walking toward the exit.

"Relax. I wasn't asking in that way."

Tanya looked up, her face still flushed. She liked boys but hadn't had a boyfriend since eighth grade when she introduced Henry Thompson to her dad. The next day, he told her they couldn't hang out anymore. He kept silent about her dad's words to him, but she envisioned it was horrendous. He wouldn't even talk to her after that. Since then, she only hung out with Sheri until Amara joined them at the freshman high school.

"Of course. Is there anyone you're interested in?"

"Not yet, but I'm open to either. Does that bother you?"

"No."

They walked in silence outside of the football field. She looked at the team practicing, then back toward the church in the distance.

"Hey, did you hear about what happened on Friday night?"

"No. The sun has been brutal on the vegetables, so I was in the garden all weekend and my grandmother only watches the news from Iran."

"Something happened behind the Italian-French restaurant on Cedar Ridge Hicks Road. You remember Sharon from last week?"

"No. What class is she in?"

"Oh, she's not in school. From the meeting, she was finishing up when you came into *the meeting* last week. She had a boyfriend that was controlling her, treating her like crap, and spending all of her money."

Yasmin listened, looking over for her to continue.

"I don't know what happened, but there was a large area of blood, and Sharon was in an ambulance, but she looked completely out of it. She didn't move or say anything, as far as I could see. I think she was in shock."

"What happened?"

"We don't know. Sheri, Amara, and I were close by and walked over to see what was happening. Sheri's dad wouldn't tell us what it was. When Sheri asked him, he refused to disclose anything except that someone was missing."

"What does Sheri's dad do?"

"He's the Sheriff."

"Ah, ok. Has anything like this happened before? My grandmother sometimes goes out to the store at night. I may need to convince her to stay in."

"Oh god, no. Cedar Ridge is quiet. I'm sure there are bad things, but I never see anything on the news."

"You watch the news?"

"Not like sitting down and watching it. I read the headlines online. You never know when some historical event is going to happen. I don't want to answer my grandkids questions about some event with, 'I'm not sure, I was watching funny videos.'" She smiled.

They waited at the crosswalk for the light to change before going to the church building. She hoped Sheri would show up, but at least she was here with Yasmin.

Tanya and Yasmin went into the room. The circle of chairs occupied the center of the room. A dozen women had assembled in their cliques. The mood was more somber than the previous week. It wasn't fun. There were forced smiles and a few genuine ones as the women received support from friends. She took a cup of coffee, added creamer and sugar, and stirred it, glancing back to the door for Sheri.

"Good evening. Thank you for coming. If you would take a chair, we'll get started," Diane greeted them.

A young brunette woman with a short bob cut, wearing a green button-down blouse and black knee-length skirt, raised her hand. She looked professional. "Uh, Diane, a few of us heard rumors that Sharon was under arrest. What's going on?"

"You know I can't share personal details. That is against our creed as an advocate." She looked around the group. "Sharon is not under arrest. She is in the hospital. Sharon hasn't been able to share anything about what happened, and apparently, there were no other witnesses."

Tanya raised her hand. "There was a lot of blood. Have they found her boyfriend? The one she talked about last week?"

"I hadn't heard that. If there was blood, I'm sure the police are on it. The important thing is not solving a mystery; Sharon is ok or stable right now, and we should all pray for her recovery."

The room buzzed with murmurs of support.

"Ok, tonight I want to discuss the next section of the power and control wheel." She walked over to the large easel with a circle broken into eight areas, each filled with a type of abuse. "Using Isolation. Can anyone tell me what this means or how you can identify it?" She waited for a moment before continuing. "That's alright. Chances are, it would be difficult to be here tonight if you were experiencing this type of control. Has anyone here had someone demand access to your cell phone, email, or social media?"

A few hands went up.

"How about someone wanting to know where you were all the time and encouraging you to stay home, even under positive influence?"

More hands, some of the same.

"In those instances, the person exerts control over you, trying to keep you isolated. Their insecurities and need to control you make them want to keep you near and subservient to them by allowing them to have control over what you say."

Tanya turned to Yasmin. "Do you mind if I ask what brought you here? You seemed pretty sure of yourself with the bullies at school."

Yasmin looked to the side, then coyly glanced back at her. "I'm not in a place where I can talk about it right now."

"I'm sorry. It wasn't my intention to be nosy. I read through all this last week. I wonder if it's like searching for symptoms on WebMD. You end up focusing on a rare condition with the worst consequences, when it's actually something you ate."

Yasmin gave her a stern glare.

"No, no, I don't mean it that way. It's just." She was wringing her hands in her lap. "In every section of the wheel, I see my father. I don't know why he is the way he is. Despite the pictures around the house and our apparent happiness, it's all a facade. I didn't realize it until this week, but I think my mom puts up with it because of me, and that sucks."

"You feel guilty?"

"Yeah, I guess."

"Don't."

"What?"

"Don't feel guilty. It's not your fault. Some of the blame is hers, but most is with your father."

Tanya slid away. "I don't know about that."

"Tanya, you do. You are enabling the behavior. Has he ever touched you?"

"Eww, no."

"Not like that. I mean, has he hit you or anything?"

"Not in a while. I've learned how to avoid making him mad."

"That's what I'm talking about. You say you have learned. He has trained you, like a pet, to act how he wants when he wants."

Tanya raised her voice, "That's not fair!"

Yasmin looked at her, holding her gaze. "Fair has nothing to do with it. It is not your fault. It is his."

Tanya sat back, crossing her arms. She clenched her jaw, staring across the room. She was right. A crack formed in her world and her emotions broke through. Tears welled up in her eyes and cascaded down her cheek.

She felt a hand take hers. The weather was chilly and arid. She looked down at her fingers intertwined with Yasmin's, the black polish standing out against her fair skin.

"Thank you."

"You're welcome."

Chapter 11

Tuesday Night

Tanya sat at the kitchen table, eating dinner. Her mom made baked chicken, mashed potatoes, and corn. She had the light over the table, but the rest of the kitchen was off. Her thoughts drifted back to the meeting. How had Yasmin broken her down in such a short time? Her life was a lie covered by a blanket of faux love and caring. She thought of what it would be like when she left for college. She was worried about her mom. Maybe her mom would leave him after Tanya was out of the house with muted encouragement.

She took another bite of the mashed potatoes. They were cold in the middle. The fork slipped from her hand and clattered onto the plate. She didn't feel like heating them again. Tanya got up and looked around. Jackson wasn't underfoot, which wasn't like him. She set her plate by the sink and looked outside. As night fell, the backyard was bathed in the sole glow of the back porch light. Her dad said he would fix the motion sensor lights this weekend if he had time. Shadows concealed the edge of the yard. A chill ran up her spine as she spotted Jackson sitting motionless and staring at the back fence.

She opened the door. "Jackson."

He didn't move.

She looked around. "Be brave, Tanya."

She walked out into the yard. "Jackson, what are you doing?"

Her mind flashed to Sharon, lying in the ambulance, alive but not moving. She took the last few steps and gently reached down and touched his head behind the ears.

He let out a yelp and jumped, spinning around. His tail started wagging when he caught sight of her.

She let out a high-pitched scream, and her heart jumped to her throat. As she fell backward, Jackson circled closely around her.

The voice of her father came to her from the back door. "Tanya, what the hell is going on out here? Why are you playing with the dog in the dark? Bring him inside and quit making all that racket!"

"Yes, sir." She got up and picked up Jackson, his little tail wagging.

While nuzzling his neck with her nose, she turned to go into the house, oblivious to the small red points resembling burning coals that were observing her from the rooftop of her neighbor's house.

She went to her room, opened the window, and stepped out on the back overhang. The sky was full of stars.

Tanya: Where were you tonight?

She set her phone down and opened her laptop, searching for any news on Sharon and whatever had happened.

Ding!

Sheri: I had to tell my dad where I was going and he said I couldn't go.

Tanya: We talked about Sharon. She's in the hospital.

Sheri: I know. They haven't identified whose blood it was, but it isn't hers. He wants me to stay away from the group.

Tanya: That's good, I suppose. Hopefully, she'll wake up soon and can tell them. It sucks you can't go with me.

Sheri: They discovered a woman in the parking lot of a strip club who bore a striking resemblance to Sharon, seeming completely disoriented, and the detective is still missing.

Tanya: Wait, was there a pool of blood?

Sheri: I think so. My dad didn't want to tell me, but I heard him talking to one of the deputies.

Tanya: That's creepy. Someone posted #BloodPoolKiller online. I missed you, but I was ok. I sat with Yasmin, so I wasn't alone.

She waited, staring at her screen.

Sheri: Ok. Did you have fun?

Tanya: Why would you ask that?

Sheri: Sorry. I don't know. I meant I hope it was a good meeting.

Tanya: It was. Are you ok?

Sheri: Yeah. I wanted to be there with you.

Tanya: We're good. You got me there. I'll talk to you tomorrow.

Sheri: <hugs>

She slipped her phone into her pocket and lay back against the side of the house, looking up at the stars. She couldn't shake what Yasmin had helped her realize. Her dad controlled both her and her mother. Most of his anger came from his time with the Navy. She knew they hadn't recommended him to continue in the Navy after his initial tour following Annapolis. She thought back to her 12th birthday party. He had quite a few beers and went off in a drunken rant, blaming his department head for not supporting him against false claims of abusive behavior and sexual harassment. He went on and on about how it was his bad luck to have a female department head who didn't know how things worked on a ship at sea. *And it ends up being my luck to have a misogynistic, abusive father who doesn't respect women.*

She took a deep breath of the night air, no longer smelling the dead animal. *Maybe the vultures cleaned it up.* She turned her head, looking toward the Vulture House. She couldn't see it from here, but they sometimes circled overhead. At least the birds never ventured into any other houses. *What was it about that house?* Everyone ignores it. She brought it up to her mom and said she didn't know what Tanya was talking about. How is that even possible? Someone should have bought it by now. The location was excellent. Unless, of course, it *is* haunted or cursed.

She got up, thinking of Sharon, and climbed back into her room, slid the screen shut, and sat down at her desk. She opened the search engine and typed *blood pool killer.* The local story popped up, as did a few hits on Reddit and almost a dozen pages of crime scene investigators. She jumped from article to article and read everything she could find on social media, which wasn't much. It could have simply been a coincidence. She should have let it go. It had nothing to do with her, and she needed to get to work on her college applications. She was drawn to look into the killings as nothing this big had happened as far as she could remember.

She closed the search engine and opened the Rice application. Writing essays was something she had been avoiding. She looked up the admissions requirements. Everything was done, except for the essays and writing prompts. She opened the document and stared at the blank page. She shook it off, typed all the essay questions onto the sheet, organized them neatly, and then sat staring at the first question.

Doubts crept into her head. Was she good enough? Would her dad actually let her go, or would he recommend a local school? She had SMU, TCU, and UT applications in her applications folder, all at the same stage. Putting her doubts aside, she read the list of questions and began typing. With Yasmin's words in mind, she became even more determined to break free and live her own life. She refused to let him control her, and once she was free, she would take her mom away from him. Maybe this was the motivation she needed to answer the questions about what made her who she was.

Chapter 12

Thursday Midday

"I love Tater Tots Day!" Tanya exclaimed, taking one and popping it into her mouth, smiling at Sheri.

"They have tater tots every day," said Sheri.

"I know that, but remember in intermediate, Thursday was Tater Tots Day. So, I get them on their proper day."

"So, they conditioned you well," Yasmin joined in, taking a seat at the table. She didn't have a tray or food, just the thermos she brought every day.

"No, not conditioned. It's a choice. Yasmin, do you want anything? I could add it to my tray."

"No, I can't eat this."

"The food's not bad. I guess if you're conditioned to like it." She looked down at the processed food along the serving line.

"I wouldn't know. My beliefs require a strict diet and fresh food from the garden."

"Oh, I'm sorry."

"Don't be. How would you know?"

"Excuse me, Ms. Janessy. After you get your food, can I speak with you?"

Tanya turned to see the music director, Mr. Bilby, expecting an answer. He was a short man, at a few inches over five feet, and a little extra around his waist. His billowy white hair along the sides of his balding head gave him the "mad scientist look." Maybe 18ᵗʰ century musicians were closer to the mark. He addressed every student as Mr. or Ms., which had become more challenging for him of late. Still, he adapted well to however they wanted to be called, except by their first name.

"Sure."

He nodded and went to sit at an empty table near the door to the teacher's lunch lounge.

Sheri leaned in. "Ooh, what's that about?"

"I don't know. I'll tell you afterward." Tanya looked over at her favorite teacher. While she loved all her subjects, Mr. Bilby had a disarming personality that made you feel comfortable in class.

She headed to the table with the teacher as Sheri and Yasmin went to another table across the room.

"Hi, Mr. Bilby. Is everything ok?"

"Of course! Have a seat, Ms. Janessy. This won't take long. I have great news."

"Ok."

"I was talking to the guidance counselor, and your name came up. She mentioned you planned to apply to Rice, SMU, TCU, and a few others." He smiled with excitement. "Guess what? I know the dean of the Shepherd School of Music, at Rice. I know you aren't looking to pursue a degree in music, which is fine, but he also oversees the Rice Symphonic Band, which is open to all majors." He clapped his hands and leaned back.

She looked at him, waiting for him to continue.

He looked at her in anticipation.

"Ok."

"I invited him to come to our fall recital. He's going to see you play. So, I want you to play a solo that will blow him away."

Tanya sat looking at him, mouth open.

He looked past her. "Pick something exciting and challenging. It'll be great. Afterward, I'll introduce you, and you can talk about the school, admissions, or whatever you like. It's exciting, right?"

"Um, just a few weeks to find and learn a solo?"

"Yep. I can't wait to hear what you pick. The sooner, the better. We can practice after school."

"Ok, I'll start looking." Her mind shifted to overdrive, thinking about her options.

"It's going to be great!"

He got up, smiling down at her, before turning. She swore he skipped a step on his way to the teacher's lounge. She had a pit in the middle of her stomach. What was she going to pick? She felt overwhelmed. She mechanically got up and joined her friends.

She plopped into the seat.

"What? Was it bad news?" Sheri asked.

"No. I mean, I don't know. He invited someone to see me play at the fall recital. He's giving me a solo."

"That's great, right?"

"I don't have one. What am I supposed to pick? It needs to be unique. I'm sure he hears people play all the favorites, and I have to learn it in two weeks." She crossed her arms in front of her on the table and buried her head in them. "I am so screwed."

Sheri moved around the table and rubbed her shoulders. "No, this is karma calling out to you. You've got this. You've been the first chair since freshman year."

Tanya lifted her head. "Ok, well, I've got to find a song like nothing he's heard." She looked up. Yasmin was leaning on her elbows, looking past them, and scanning the room.

She stopped and turned back to Tanya. "What about a Persian song? Many of the ones I've heard have been on the Ney flute. I'm sure they would be just as beautiful on the flute you play."

Tanya sat up, intrigued. "Do you have one in mind?"

"No, but I can ask my grandmother. She is very knowledgeable about our old ways if you are open to playing something like that."

Sheri put her phone down on the table and turned up the volume. The wooden instrument had an airy, husky sound to it, and the Persian music in the video was beautiful. Tanya closed her eyes, listening to the melody as the story of the song transitioned.

Tanya sat up, thinking. "I love it, and it would be different." She looked at Yasmin. "I mean that in a good way. It needs to be challenging too. I don't mean to push, but how long will it take? Two weeks isn't a lot of time."

"It's not pushy, I offered. I'll ask her tonight."

"You could call me; send a link and I can start learning it."

Yasmin sat back. "I can't. I'll bring it tomorrow."

"It's ok, I'll give you my number. Just text me."

"I don't have a phone."

"Oh, um, I'm sorry. You could bring it by if you want." Tanya quickly became embarrassed. She reached into her backpack and took out a pencil and notebook, writing her address and tearing it off. She handed it to Yasmin, smiling. "We could hang out." She looked up at Sheri. "All of us. It'll be fun."

Sheri moved back across the table, sitting next to Yasmin and picking up her half-eaten cheeseburger. "I'll check with my dad. It's my night to make dinner. Maybe I can come over after."

"Yay! It'll be fun."

"Yasmin, are you in?"

"I'll run home after school and see if my grandmother knows of a difficult, but pleasing, song." She looked at the address. "Sure, I'll come over. I might not have anything, though."

"Well, at least you can hang out with friends." She looked at them both, smiling. Yasmin looked hesitant. Sheri smiled back, but something looked off in her eyes. She'd ask later.

Chapter 13

Thursday Evening

Tanya got up from the living room couch to answer the door. The doorbell music played in the background. She opened the door to find Yasmin standing there. The evening had just begun, yet the sun continued to shine. It wouldn't get dark until after eight. "Hey, come in."

She stepped aside, holding the door. As Yasmin passed, she smelled a flowery scent.

"Mmm, you smell good. Is that lavender?"

"No hyacinth, it's close."

"I haven't heard from Sheri. Let me call her." She reached for her phone.

"I think I found a song."

Tanya stopped. "Really? What song is it? I can search for it."

"I doubt you'd find it. I asked the same thing. Our imam told me I wouldn't find it. I tried to look it up on my laptop at home, but nothing came up. I hope it's ok that I told him why I needed the song."

"Yeah, of course."

"He said that he had just the song. He would get in touch with a musician friend in Dallas."

Tanya beamed. "I can't wait to see it. I'm sure it will be something special." She hugged Yasmin. "Thank you!"

She felt Yasmin hesitantly hug her back before backing away. Tanya liked the hyacinth smell. "We can go out back and wait for Sheri if that's ok. Do you want anything?"

"No, I'm good. I ate earlier."

They stepped out the back door and descended the steps into the backyard. The rear deck was off to the left, under her room. Tanya waited for Yasmin to pick her seat before sitting in the wicker rocking chair across from her. A slight breeze blew through the backyard, blowing Yasmin's dark brown curls into her face.

Yasmin looked around the yard. "It's nice out here."

"Yeah, I haven't been out here much in the summer. Too hot. I used to ask my dad to get a pool, but he always said we'll look at it, maybe next summer. Here we are in my last summer, and there isn't a pool."

Yasmin furrowed her brow. She looked out at the yard.

"I'm sorry that was rude. It sounded privileged, didn't it?"

"No, you're fine. I thought I smelled something."

Tanya sat forward. "I did, too! I told my dad and he said something probably died in the neighbor's yard."

"It's not that strong."

Her phone rang. "Hey Sher, where are you? Yasmin's here, we're out back. I'm gonna put you on speaker." She held the phone out and touched the screen.

"Can you hear me?"

"Yeah, Hi, Yasmin."

"Hey."

"Are you coming over? My parents are at a dinner thing for my dad's work. We're just hanging out."

"I can't. My dad wants me to stay home. They think they found another blood stain behind the laundromat at the corner of Main and Cedar Ridge View. It's not fresh."

"Does he think there is a serial killer?"

"He wouldn't answer. He told me not to spread rumors and to let him know what was happening around school."

Tanya looked at Yasmin, worried. "Do you think we should be worried?"

"I don't know if I'd wander out anywhere at night. Three pools of blood, no bodies. At least we know it's not a vampire."

Tanya laughed, "Good one."

Yasmin sat forward, serious. "Have you seen a vampire? It's nothing to laugh at." Tanya got chills.

"What?" Sheri asked.

Yasmin started laughing. "I'm kidding. Vampires don't exist." She paused, seeing Tanya looking at her. "I mean, not anymore."

"Oh my god, you are freaking me out."

"I'm kidding."

"Sheri, you're there alone?"

"Yeah."

"Do you want us to come over?"

"I'm good. I set the alarm and locked everything."

"Ok, call me if you need me."

"I will."

"Bye, Sher."

Tanya set the phone on an end table. "What is going on around here?"

Yasmin slumped into her chair. "What do you think it is?"

"Honestly, I don't know, but it sounds like a serial killer." Tanya sat up, scanning the yard again. "Do you need to go before it gets too dark?"

"I'll be fine. From what you've said, it doesn't sound like they are targeting lone high school girls."

"Yeah, I guess." Tanya relaxed back into her chair.

The girls jumped at a crash inside. Tanya got up and went in, followed by Yasmin.

They entered the kitchen, and Yasmin held the door from banging closed.

"I told you not to embarrass me. You had to bring up the Navy. What if someone digs into the story now? Stupid bitch!"

Tanya looked down at her mom, lying on the floor. Mascara streaked down her cheeks. She had been crying.

Tanya rushed across the kitchen, bringing her hand back to slap him. He caught her arm. She felt pain as he squeezed, digging his fingers into her flesh. He leaned in, looking her in her eyes. "Don't get involved in things you aren't ready for, little girl. Do you understand?"

She made a soft whimpering sound. "Leave her alone!" she said through clenched teeth.

He looked past her to Yasmin, let go of her arm, and threw it down. "Help your mom up. She tripped coming into the kitchen. You know how clumsy she is. We'll talk about this after you show your friend out."

Tanya looked at her dad, who was looking at Yasmin. Was he afraid she would say something or report him to the police? She looked back and saw her friend's clenched jaw and piercing glare. She turned and moved to help her mom up. Yasmin let the door close and helped as well. Her mom stood up and straightened her floral summer dress. "I'll be fine. You girls go on." She saw the pain and embarrassment in her mother's eyes. "I'll be right back, Momma," she said softly.

Tanya looked at Yasmin, who looked past her at her father.

"C'mon Yasmin." She led her friend out of the kitchen.

Yasmin turned on her in the living room. "He can't do that. You know he pushed her down. He would have hurt you too if I wasn't there."

"I know. I'll take care of it. He'll go off and do his own thing."

"Does this happen every night?"

"No, usually it's just words. We'll be ok. I think I need to stay here with my mom. Will you be ok walking home?"

"After that, you're worried about me?"

"Yeah, you're my friend. I've been through this before. I'll be fine."

"But you shouldn't have to." She turned and went down the steps. "I'll see you at school tomorrow. I'll call to see if they found the music."

Tanya smiled subtly, glancing over her shoulder at the front door. "Thank you," she said before going inside.

Chapter 14

Friday, After Midnight

Tanya sat up. Her room was dark. She looked at the clock and it showed 1:34.

Krsssshhhk.

She looked for the sound, hearing a scratching outside her window. She got up and opened the curtains. Her breath caught in her throat. A large black vulture pulled the entrails from a small dog, blood splashing onto the tiles of the deck covering. Ripping the meat array from the carcass, it turned its head. The creature threw its head back, swallowed, and then glanced in her direction.

Fear gripped her. Jackson?

Krsssshhhk.

Spreading its wings, the enormous bird turned toward her. It had to be five feet across.

She screamed and stepped away from the window. She tripped on her desk chair. Turning to catch herself, she hit the floor.

Bap! The window cracked in a spiderweb pattern.

Something hit the window. She looked over her shoulder and saw the enormous bird rear its head and hit the window again.

Bap!

"Daddy!" She scrambled to her feet, threw open her bedroom door, and ran down the hall to her parent's door.

"Mom, Dad! Wake up!"

Bap! Bap!

She heard the shattering of glass.

Tanya pulled down on the handle to open her parents' room. They weren't there. The bed was empty.

Krsssshhhk.

The sound came from her doorway. She ran by, reaching in to close the door. The bird lunged toward her, his beak aimed at her wrist.

Slam!

She didn't bother to see if the bird had hit her. She turned the corner and ran down the stairs.

Death attracts vultures.

"Mom! Dad! Is anyone here?"

Bap! Bap! Bap!

The sounds were coming from different windows in the house.

She reached for her pocket to call Sheri and realized her phone was in her room. She could make it. It's just a few houses down. She took a deep breath and opened the door, running, jumping down the steps, and turning right toward Sheri's house. She looked back. Three vultures were sitting on her dad's BMW, the outside light shining down on them as if they were on stage. All of their eyes were on her. They jumped in the air and flew toward her. She pumped her arms, running as fast as she could. Something hit her in the back, throwing her forward. The birds were on her. In her struggle, she swung every which way she could, becoming more entangled by the moment. Trapped by the birds' wings, she felt them wrap around her, imprisoning her arms. She tried to scream, but no sound came out.

Opening her eyes, she sensed her heart racing as she struggled to escape. She was in her room. It was dark. The moonlight illuminated her surroundings through the window, allowing her to see that she was wrapped in her blanket and sheets. She calmed down enough to get an arm free and turn on the small lamp on her nightstand. She looked around. Everything was where it should be. She slipped out of the tangled linens and timidly peeked out the window. The moon lit the roof outside her room. The birds were gone.

She dropped back onto her bed, feeling her heart return to normal. After a few moments, she got up to get a drink of water. She was wide awake and didn't feel like going back to sleep. The time was 4:53, so she would likely be fine in class. She sometimes got up early to study for an exam or review her homework. She went downstairs to the kitchen and made a cup of coffee, adding three spoonfuls of sugar and enough milk to make the dark liquid a light khaki. She sipped it, tasting the sweet drink with a hint of the original bitterness. Jackson came into the kitchen wagging his tail, taking advantage of someone being up and willing to let him out. Her dad had said they would put in a doggie door, but that fell on the long list of projects that never got done. She turned on the backyard light and opened the door for him to go out in the dimly lit yard.

"In and out, Jackson, no playing."

He looked at her and ran into the backyard, sniffing as he ran in his chaotic zig-zag pattern and looked for a good place to go. The motion sensor lights didn't come on. Her dad said he had replaced the bulbs, complaining about the cost the entire time, but it didn't fix the problem. It's odd for both to go out unless there was a problem with the security system. Whatever, we'll see how long he takes.

She looked for Jackson, who had gone behind the tree in the back right corner.

"Jackson, let's go."

She heard a yelp and Jackson whimpering as he ran out of the dark corner across the yard at full speed. He didn't wait for her to say anything. He bolted up the stairs, past her legs, and disappeared into the house. She could hear him whimpering softly. Despite not seeing anything, she felt a sense of unease in her stomach as she scanned her surroundings. She backed up the steps, promptly shutting and locking the door behind her. She continued watching through the rear window, but nothing appeared. She went into the living room, following the sounds from the dog, and found him behind the leather loveseat and end table. He was licking his leg.

She kneeled next to him. "It's ok, boy. Let me look." She pulled him up onto her knee, looking at his front leg. She thumbed through his hair, careful not to put pressure on it, and found a small red dot. "Poor baby, did something happen to you out there?" She got up and went to the kitchen, bringing back a dog treat and giving it to him. He wagged his tail, crunching on the bone.

She went to her desk, powered up her laptop, and searched for vultures, symbolism, and omens. Articles explored the contrasting beliefs of Tibetans and Egyptians about birds, some viewing them as symbols of positivity while others associated them with death. Stepping back from religious meaning, vultures were generally viewed as positive within environmental circles because they helped stop the spread of disease from the dead. Despite her uncertainty, she found it fascinating that some Native American tribes viewed them as messengers, helping souls travel to the afterlife.

Why had they attacked her in her dream? YouTube experts and others gave dozens of reasons, but the theories were all over the place.

She didn't want to think about it anymore. She put her earbuds in, raised the volume, and turned on Spotify to free her mind from the memory. "Please Don't Leave Me," by P!nk was playing. Tanya stood from the desk and started getting her clothes ready for school. She wanted to know what her friends thought of the dream.

Chapter 15

Friday Morning

Tanya sat at the kitchen table, eating a blueberry yogurt from a cup.

"Honey, do you need me to make you anything?"

She took another scoop of the yogurt, feeling the tiny blueberries in her mouth, a slight tanginess beyond that of the yogurt.

"Tanya!"

"Sorry, what, Mom?"

"I asked if you needed me to make you anything. Do you want a snack? I brought home some cheesecake from dinner last night." Her mom smiled.

How does she do that? Pretend that nothing happened, or let it go? Tanya looked past her mom's smile to the look in her eyes. She hadn't forgotten. She wanted to make sure my day was good. Tanya got up and went to her mom, embracing her.

"Mom, I love you."

"I know you do, honey."

She let go and took a half-step back, turning her head to listen for her dad. "Why do you put up with him?"

"Tanya, he's not all bad. He tries. Sometimes, he just gets stressed and lashes out."

"Mom! He pushed you down last night. I saw it, and my friend saw it. He's a bully, and that is abuse."

Her mom's expression changed, getting serious. "I don't want to hear you talk like that. I'll deal with whatever comes my way, how I want. I'll protect you and keep you safe. Let's leave it at that."

Feeling defiant, she stood. "No. It is abuse, and he is using power and coercion on you and me to get us to behave exactly like he wants us to. It's not right."

"I don't need to listen to this. He has never laid a hand on you in your seventeen years."

Tanya held up her wrist, the deep purple bruise visible. "But he has you. When are you going to see it for what it is? What happens if it gets worse? Who knows what could set him off?"

"Tanya, drop it!" She shrank back at her mom's harsh rebuke.

She lowered her voice and lifted her chin in opposition. "I'm not going to. Even if you're unwilling to do anything, I won't sit around and let you get hurt."

Her mom lurched forward, her face within inches. "You'll do nothing of the sort. Let it go now before he hears us."

"Yeah, because he might lose his temper and abuse us some more. Mom, I love you, but you're mistaken. He won't change, no matter how many times he says he will." She felt her courage creep back in.

Tanya stormed out of the kitchen. Her morning recovering from the nightmare was in shambles. How could her mom not see the obvious?

Her dad threw open the front door. He wore his light brown suit. The door hit the doorstop and popped it out of the baseboard. It tumbled and rolled across the tile. He threw his bag and jacket on the floor next to the door.

"You're not going to believe this!" he said, moving past Tanya and into the kitchen. She followed him to the door of his office off the kitchen.

"What happened, Chris?" her mom asked.

"My car. Look at my car! Someone scratched the hell out of it, and it looks like a bunch of birds had a shitting frenzy in the driveway."

Tanya stepped back, covering her mouth and hiding her quiet laughter.

"What are you doing now?"

"Really, Kaitlyn, what would I be doing here? I'm pulling up the security videos from last night. At least two angles cover the driveway."

Tanya stood straight and stepped into his office to watch the videos. He set the time to midnight and let it play at eight times the average speed. About an hour in, a large black bird landed on the car's roof. The a second one, followed by three more. They looked to be crying out.

"What the hell. I didn't hear anything. They look like they are raising hell out there, but I didn't hear anything." Her dad shook his head at the mess.

The birds were walking on the car, jumping from the hood to the roof and the trunk, leaving their droppings all over it. Two birds flew off, and three remained. Tanya watched as the three birds moved to the driver's side, sitting next to each other on the car's roof. Their feet were opening and closing like they were flexing in anticipation. At once, they all took off, flying across the yard.

Tanya gasped. Her dream had become a reality.

"What? What did you see?"

"Nothing, Daddy. I had a nightmare about birds last night."

He pointed to the screen. "This explains all the shit on my car and the scratches, but not the front side of the hood. How the hell do I explain to the insurance company that big black birds attacked my car in the middle of the night? They'll think I'm crazy."

"You have the video."

"Yeah, I'm going to get some smart-ass that says this was an act of God and therefore not covered. This is bullshit. I gotta call in." He pulled out his phone and waved her and her mom away.

Tanya left his office and headed upstairs to get her bag. The visual of the three birds taking off across the yard erased her humor about her dad's car. It mirrored her dream.

Ding!

Sheri: Almost there.

Tanya: OK, I'm walking out now. You have to see my dad's car!

Tanya went outside, closing the door behind her. Sheri was walking up, not smiling. Tanya waved to her, looking over at the BMW. The video didn't do it justice.

"Oh my God, what happened?" Sheri asked.

"It's the creepiest thing. I had a nightmare about vultures, and this morning, my dad found his car like this."

"You dreamed this?"

"Not like this. I'll tell you when we get to school. I just want to. say it once. I was scared, and this is," she paused. "I don't know. It's creepy."

"You don't even have a tree nearby. I've only seen this when someone parks under a tree with nests. He's gonna have to go through the car wash two, maybe three times."

Tanya walked to the front of the car. At the corner of the hood on the left side, it looked like the metal was bent. "What did that?"

Sheri leaned in. "I don't know, but it looks like it was pinched over the corner. That's a big grip. I haven't seen a vulture that big."

"Me neither. Let's go. He'll be out shortly to take pictures for the insurance company, and he's already in a foul mood because something messed with his *baby*."

Chapter 16

Friday Midday

The four girls huddled around a square table in the back of the library furthest from the desk. Tanya had her laptop open to a website discussing the symbolism associated with vultures.

"It could go either way," Sheri said. "I think we should be optimistic and take it as a good sign."

"Yeah, but they attacked me in my dream, and then you saw my dad's car. That didn't look positive."

Yasmin snorted, "Seems positive to me."

Tanya shot her a surprised glance. She explained, "I was scared in the dream, but what happened to his car was funny."

Amara shook her head. "I think it's bad, definitely bad. Omens of death, and then tie all this to the blood pool killer. It's something bad for sure."

"Great. So I'm screwed? Because none of you have seen anything, and I'm the link to Sharon and the dream, and my dad." Tanya sat back. Her heart was racing as chills ran through her body. "I want to talk to your dad," she said, looking at Sheri.

"And say what? You've had bad dreams about vultures, and you know someone related to a missing person and a bloodstain? He knows the worst parts of all that, and believe me, he won't care about the dreams. Unless you suddenly become psychic and can identify the serial killer. That would be exciting."

"Not for me. I don't want to see any of this," Tanya said.

Yasmin sat back in her chair. "Maybe it's just an unrelated bad dream and a little karma."

Tanya didn't feel better. "I hope that's all. Has your dad said anything about the third blood pool?"

Sheri avoided eye contact.

"Sheri, what did he say?"

"It was the boyfriend of someone in the group. He was in the police database. They fought at the laundromat. There was shouting. The owner threw him out, and she hadn't seen him since."

"Sheri, were you going to tell us that?"

"I just did. It's the first time it has come up. I only went to one meeting. I don't know who's who. The name didn't sound familiar."

"She didn't talk when you and I were there."

"Wait, what meeting?" asked Amara, looking left out.

Tanya leaned in and whispered, "It's a support group for victims of domestic violence."

"Oh."

Sheri jumped in, "I talked her into going last week."

"You could have told me." Amara looked hurt. "You know I'm here for you, too."

Tanya looked around. "You're all helping me in your ways, and I appreciate it." She reached over and squeezed Amara's hand.

Yasmin got up. "I need to get home." She leaned over and pulled a lavender folder from her backpack. "Here is the music. I didn't want to forget."

Tanya cheered up, taking the folder. "It's my happy color!"

Sheri looked to the side and then smiled along with her.

Yasmin flashed a quick, tight-lipped smile. "I hope it's challenging enough. I can't wait to hear it. The composer wrote it for the Ney flute, but I am sure it will sound beautiful."

Tanya jumped up and hugged Yasmin. "Thank you."

Yasmin hesitantly hugged her back. "I'll see you all tomorrow."

Amara sat forward. "I'm not really in the mood for ice cream."

"Yeah, I don't think I can, anyway. My dad wants me in the house at dark."

Tanya turned to Sheri. "Does he think it's that bad?"

"I don't know. Without being specific, he hasn't said anything. He knows I would tell you both. He's always been protective. It's just us two."

Tanya looked down. "I don't even know how that feels, but I think it's only me and my mom."

Amara leaned in. "You have us all the way to college and beyond."

Sheri took her other hand. "Yeah, and now Yasmin too." She smirked and shrugged.

Tanya frowned. "C'mon Sheri. She's good. She's in the same boat as me."

Amara looked puzzled. "What do you mean?"

"Don't share this with anyone. She goes to the domestic violence meetings. So, someone abused her in the past or is currently. I don't know what it is, but she needs support, too."

Sheri nodded. "Ok, fine, you're right. I'll try to be better. Even when she goes and hangs out with my best friend."

Amara sat up. "Wait, I'm her best friend!"

They all laughed.

"Sheri, do you think your dad would be ok if we went to your house tonight?"

"I'm sure he'd love it, actually. Let me text him."

Tanya opened the folder and looked at the yellowed sheet of music. She smelled hyacinth when she opened it. She examined the sheet music, carefully flipping through the pages. "This is going to be challenging. Looks like I'll have a busy few weeks after school."

"Well, Yasmin's not the only one who wants to hear it. We'll all be there for you."

"Thanks," replied Tanya.

"Yep, we'll be there with big poster board signs, noisemakers, and a cheering section."

Tanya slapped her shoulder. "Don't you dare!"

"What? I thought you wanted support. Don't you want the director to see how awesome you are?"

Chapter 17

Friday Night

Shadows danced around her room as the light from a lone candle on her windowsill flickered. Smelling hyacinth from a burning incense filled her with calm. Tanya leaned over the sheet music spread across her desk, following the trail of notes with her finger, humming the tune. Reaching up, she adjusted the desk lamp to center its focus on the old paper. Continuing through, she smiled while following the transitions and ambiance created by the notes. Taking care not to damage the discolored paper, she picked up her flute and moved the pages to her music stand. She would probably copy it to clean sheets.

Tanya relaxed, took a deep breath, and began to play. The notes flowed, creating an ethereal atmosphere. Her fingers drifted over the flute, the notes pulling emotions from her as the music filled the room. She sensed a longing in her heart increase, accompanied by a building resonance. The shadows on the wall danced with the song as the wind whispered through the open window, as if aspiring to be a part of the growing image. Her fingers trembled as the weight of loneliness overcame her. The atmosphere broke when she missed a note.

She took a deep, calming breath. While playing, she had felt a sense of longing and discovery building within her. When she fumbled, interrupting the flow of the song, a sense of loss threatened to overwhelm her. She had never experienced such a strong emotional connection to a piece of music before. The song was beautiful. She couldn't read the writing underneath the notes, it looked Arabic. The lyrics were likely written in the composer's language. She would ask Yasmin if she knew what the story was. Regardless, she imagined it was a song about being lost and longing for something they could never regain. She took a breath and played through again. The song was difficult. It would take her until the last minute to be ready.

As before, the music embraced her, enveloping her in a blanket of emotions, shifting with the melody. She looked over the music stand into the darkness outside her window. She swore the wind swayed the trees in her backyard with the shifting tune. The tempo quickened, and she noticed her heartbeat racing to keep up with the music's beat. She was being warmly pulled into the song. She missed a transition, and the feelings slipped away once more.

"Damnit!" she exclaimed.

She began playing again, making it through the first third of the song before missing a note. Her heart was pounding. The need to get through the music was tangible. She felt like she was in an intense workout at the gym. Fatigue overcame her body and mind. The song was demanding, but not impossible.

Once again, she started and fumbled.

She let out a piercing scream.

She was short of breath, leaning over when her mom burst into the room. "Are you ok? What's wrong?"

"It's this song. I keep messing it up."

"And that's why you screamed like you were dying?"

"Sorry, Mom. I really need to get this down before the fall recital."

"And you will, dear. You always do. Take your time. You'll get it." She smiled. "I can't wait to see you perform. You play so beautifully. Please, no more screaming, ok?"

"Yes, Mom."

Her mom closed the door. She sat back, looking at the music. The desire to play again, to get it right, was pulling at her. Just as she straightened her posture and lifted the flute to her lips, her phone rang unexpectedly.

She looked at her phone. It was Sheri. "Hey Sher, what's up?"

"Jump on TikTok right now. Search for *BankingBros,* one word."

Tanya opened the website and found the stream. She scrolled back to the beginning and hit *Play.*

The host's voice was smooth and eager, typical for a streamer.

> *"It was crazy. This dark-shaped person, I don't know if it was a person or not, was leaning over something when we came around the corner from Brian's Burgers. Shout out for some phenomenal food, B-T-dubs. We yelled, checking to see if everyone was ok when they got up and ran off. I'm not gonna describe it. Look for yourselves."*

The screen shifted to the host, talking to his friends as they came around a painted white brick wall to a dark area. The scene went fuzzy as the image shifted to the back cameras, and you could see a dark figure. She heard someone call out. The form looked like a person. They didn't look toward the camera. It jumped up and ran off into the darkness. She felt her stomach lurch as they got closer and could see that the bottom half of a body lay on the ground in a large pool of blood.

"Oh my god, oh my god, oh my god. What was that? Was that a person running away?" asked Tanya.

"I don't know. My dad is on his way there now. Are you coming or not? Amara said she can't."

"Yeah, I got tied up trying to play the song Yasmin found for me."

"Do you want to bring it over? I don't mind, I'll throw my music on, and my dad will be out all night. I'd really like you to come over, please?" Sheri pleaded.

"Of course, I'm coming. Let me grab my things, and I'll head over." She thought about the music and decided not to bring it. Until she had it down, she didn't want to share it. She experienced the stirrings of the melody playing in her head once more. *What is wrong with me?*

"No. I'd rather hang out. I was getting frustrated. I want to be in a good mood. It's been a stressful week."

"Sounds good. See you soon. I'm going to order food. You want anything?"

"Pizza, extra cheese."

Sheri gave her a thumbs-up and hung up. Tanya put the music on the stand and put away her flute. She gathered her things, threw them in a small backpack, and headed downstairs.

"I'm going to Sheri's," Tanya called out.

Her mom came out of the kitchen. "Ok."

"Where's dad?" she asked, afraid he had disappeared again, going out drinking with his buddies.

"He went out earlier. Was meeting a few of his Navy classmates."

"Mom, are you gonna be ok?" She knew it could be a rough night, depending on when her dad came home. Hopefully, they wouldn't be out too late.

"I'll be all right. I'm going to relax and watch my shows until your dad gets back."

"Ok. Call me if you need anything."

"That's what I'm supposed to tell you."

"Yeah, well, you know."

Her mom smiled understandingly.

Tanya went out the front door. The darkness surpassed its usual intensity. She glanced upwards and noticed that two streetlights to the left were out, contributing to the somber and ominous appearance of the street. Luckily, she was headed in the opposite direction and the lights were on. A gentle breeze blew. The leaves made a scraping, rustling sound as they slid down the street, collecting along the sides.

The air was cooler. They finally got a break from the heat. It felt good. She would love to sit by Sheri's pool in the back, but the shadows between houses and bushes seemed off. She saw nothing strange. It just felt off, like almost sour milk.

Chapter 18

Friday Late Night

As the story continued to unfold, the girls remained glued to the news. The crowd surrounding the police cars was shouting questions. The laundromat was still open, several customers parked as close as they could, making their way through the crowd. They had ordered pizza, but Tanya lost her appetite after a single slice. Sheri had eaten three and was halfway through a fresh bowl of popcorn.

"This is crazy. I can't believe it's happening here," Sheri said in bewilderment.

Tanya nodded wordlessly as they replayed the video of the person running off. A local pundit and spokesman for the police was going over how they would identify the victim. He expected that the family would be notified before a name was released. The still frame image in the upper right of the screen showed the bottom half of the victim.

"This is Janet Liu, here with Sheriff Downes, at the scene of another grisly murder. Sheriff, what can you tell us?"

"Janet, I don't have much to share. There is an ongoing investigation. As soon as we have something, we will let you know."

"Sheriff, is it true that this is the fifth incident in what some are calling the 'blood pool murders'?"

"Again, this is an ongoing investigation. We don't currently have anything linking any murders together."

"This is the first crime scene you have with a body, correct?"

"Crimes occur every day. Just because someone steals a pair of shoes at Walmart and someone else steals a pair from a TJ Maxx doesn't mean we have a serial shoe thief. We will look at all the evidence and guide the investigations into the citizens' best interests."

"My sources tell me that your department has called the behavioral analysis unit of the FBI. Wouldn't that imply that you believe there is a serial killer on the loose?"

"I wouldn't say that. The fine officers of the Cedar Ridge PD will use all available tools."

"Thank you, Sheriff." Sheri's dad turned and walked away toward a crime scene tape line, toward the area obscured by a barrier to block cameras from seeing the body.

"The residents of Cedar Ridge should take precautions if you have to be out at night while the Blood Pool Killer is at large. This is Janet Liu from Channel Four News."

"Your dad is good."

"She said there were five murders."

Tanya nodded, "Yeah."

"I didn't feel scared before, but I am now."

"All the killings are in town, nothing out here."

"Probably too many eyes. Everybody has doorbell cameras now."

"Yeah, my dad has three in the front alone."

Sheri laughed, putting her hand up over her mouth. "It didn't stop the birds."

Tanya laughed before her smile turned into a frown. "True. It's funny, but it shouldn't be."

Woof.

"Just a minute, Benny," Sheri said as the yellow lab shuffled into the room. He was old, and his hips had been bothering him for years. He looked at both of them, his tongue out as he panted, waiting for someone to let him out.

Sheri got up. "I'll be right back."

"Wait." Tanya got up to go with her.

"Are you scared?"

Tanya thought about denying it, then shook her head. "Yeah."

"Me too."

"You know my dad. We'll be safe if anyone tries to break in."

Woof!

"Sorry." They went to the sliding glass door to the pool deck. The pool was lit, and the waterfall on the side poured over three feet of decorative rocks before splashing in the water. The underwater lights gave the pool a glowing blue aura, and the back deck lights illuminated the yard in a cool yellow.

Tanya sighed. "I love it back here. I could sit and listen to that waterfall all night."

The backyard lights flickered on and off, then dimmed before going out.

Tanya grabbed Sheri's arm. "Ow."

"Sorry." The backyard was still visible around the pool. The darkness at the yard's edge looked to be closing in on them.

She pulled Sheri's arm. "I wanna go inside."

The silence was eerie. Benny was almost invisible to the side of the yard, sniffing the ground.

"Ok, Benny will bark at the door when he wants in."

The girls went back into the house. Sheri slid the blinds closed over most of the door, leaving about a foot so they could see Benny when he was ready.

"We should be alright. Benny wasn't concerned about anything, and he barks at everyone walking in front of the house, even if they are across the street."

"Ok," Tanya said hesitantly. Not knowing what it was, she believed the darkness trailed behind her. She didn't want to tell Sheri. Her best friend would claim it was all in her imagination, just like her dreams.

Sheri went to the refrigerator and took out two bottles of cranberry raspberry juice, passing one to Tanya.

"I wish Amara was here."

"Strength in numbers?"

"Something like that." Tanya took a drink of her juice. "Did you turn off the pool lights?"

Sheri looked scared. "No," she said, drawing out the word and turning around. "Ok, now you've got me."

"What about Benny?" Tanya asked.

"You want me to open the door?"

Tanya slowly shook her head and started backing away. "Something doesn't feel right."

"Yeah." They backed out of the kitchen.

The darkness made her feel uneasy.

"Another murder in Cedar Ridge," the TV announced. The girls jumped. Tanya hit the edge of the closest table, knocking over a picture frame. It tumbled, the glass breaking when it hit the floor.

The girls screamed and ran upstairs. They threw open Sheri's door and went to the other side of her bed, kneeling behind in silence. Colors swirled around the room from four lava lamps. One on either side of the bed, one on the desk, and another on a shelf. They peeked over the edge of the bed, looking out the door to the hallway wall and listening. Tanya saw the picture of Sheri and her mother on the hallway wall. Her mother held her up in the air, her cherubic smile as wide as possible.

"The swirling is gonna make me sick," Tanya whimpered.

"Shhh, do you hear anything?" Sheri interrupted Tanya in a hushed tone.

"No," Tanya whispered back.

They waited for another minute before Sheri finally stood. "Our imagination is going to get the better of us. Are your parents home?"

"Yeah, my mom is."

90

"Do you want to go there? I'll text my dad."

Tanya thought about it. It could have been their imagination and coincidence that the lights went out. If they went to her house, her mom would be there until her dad returned, but that might be worse. She stood. "No, can we watch a movie up here? My dad is out with friends." She forced a weak smile. Sheri slumped her shoulders, seeming to catch the subtle meaning.

"Yeah, let's get my laptop, and then we'll stay here until my dad gets home."

Tanya and Sheri woke at the knock on the door. "Sheri, I'm home."

Tanya looked at the clock on the nightstand. The time was 2:40 in the morning.

"Ok, Dad."

"Did you let Benny out?"

"Oh my gosh, yes."

"I'll get him."

"Dad, are you ok? We saw you on the news."

"As good as I can be. Let me get Benny inside. He'll try to sleep out there all night and won't be able to walk around in the morning."

"Ok, Dad. G'night."

"Goodnight, girls."

They heard his footsteps as he headed back down the hall.

Sheri closed the laptop and set it on the floor. Tanya rolled over, facing away, and looked into the blue lava lamp. "Can I turn this one off?"

"I got it." Sheri picked up her phone and used the app to turn all four lamps off. The room was dark. They heard footsteps coming back down the hall.

"Sheri, can I come in?"

"Yes." The door opened slowly.

Her dad stepped in. He still had his sheriff's uniform on. His thick hair was slick with sweat and held the shape of his hat. His brown eyes looked sad, the bags under his eyes more pronounced. "Baby, Benny's gone."

Sheri bolted out of bed. "Did he get out? We need to go look for him."

"No, he's *gone.*"

Tanya sat up and saw Sheri's face. It changed from concern to realization that Benny was no longer with them. Sheri started to cry. Her dad sat down on her bed and put his arm around her.

"Can I see him?" she asked.

"If you need to. He's by the back door. I moved him from the yard. What happened to the lights?"

"I-I don't know, they went out. We got scared, came here, and fell asleep watching a movie. I'm sorry, Dad, he was all alone out there in the dark."

"Sheri, he was an old dog. We knew it was gonna happen. It's not your fault. I'll take him to the vet in the morning."

Sheri nodded and continued sobbing. Tanya was also crying, sympathizing with her friend and knowing she would feel the same if something happened to Jackson. She put her arms around Sheri and held her as she cried. As she held her friend, the song returned to her thoughts. She sensed the stirring emotions tugging at her heart. They cried for a while before exhaustion took them back to sleep.

Tanya rolled over, checking for Sheri. She was asleep on her pillow, her eyes still puffy from crying. She tried to get up without waking her friend.

"I never understood how people get out of bed in the movies, and the other person stays asleep."

"Sorry, I tried to be quiet. Are you ok?"

"I don't know. I want to go down and see him. He's been a part of the family for as long as I can remember. Dad brought him home when I was one."

Tanya sat down, taking her friend's hand. Sheri sat up and put her head on her shoulder. "Thank you for being here."

"I'm glad I was. That's what best friends are for."

"Let's go."

They got up and went downstairs. Benny was lying on a large beach towel inside the sliding glass door.

"He looks peaceful. I don't think he was in pain."

"That's good, Sher. Your dad said he would be happy staying out all night. He got to be happy."

"I know. I just wish we could have been with him." Sheri sighed, running her hands along his body. "You were a good boy, Benny."

Images of vultures flashed into Tanya's thoughts. They were fortunate that Sheri's dad came home and checked on Benny when he did. It would have been much worse if they had found him in the yard after the vultures did. Tanya shuddered.

Chapter 19

Saturday Morning

Tanya's phone rang. "Hi, Mom."

"Hi, Tanya. I know you probably wouldn't come home until later, but your friend Yasmin is here. She said she needed to see you. She's pretty upset."

"Ok, Mom, tell her I'll be right there." She hung up.

"Is your mom ok?" Sheri asked. "You have a look."

"Um, yeah. Yasmin is at my house and she's pretty upset. I think I need to see what's going on. Are you ok? I could bring her back here, or you could come with me."

"No, I want to go to the vet with my dad when he gets up. I'll be ok. Call me later. I'm going to sit with him for a while."

"Ok, Sher, I'm torn. I want to be here, but if she's upset, it could be, you know, from the meetings."

"I got it. Go make sure she's ok."

"Ok, love you."

"You too."

Tanya raced upstairs, changed, grabbed her bag, and headed home. It was a cool day, indicating they had entered the Texas weather window of days bouncing between the forties and upper eighties. It wouldn't settle into a typical winter until late November. The sky was overcast, and it smelled like rain. Orange and yellow leaves covered the lawns and street. She sighed, looking at her home's peaceful, serene setting in the fall, and dreaded what was waiting inside her house.

She opened the door. No one was in the living room. She dropped her bag by the stairs and headed into the kitchen. Her mom and Yasmin were sitting at the table. She smelled the fresh coffee, seeing a cup in front of her mom and a half-empty glass of water in front of Yasmin. Yasmin's eyes were red.

Tanya sat down next to Yasmin. "Are you ok? What happened?"

Yasmin leaned over and rested her head on Tanya's shoulder, sobbing.

Tanya turned and rubbed her back. Yasmin flinched at her touch, pulling away. Tanya gazed at her mom. "Take your time. You're safe."

Yasmin continued to cry for a few minutes, her head buried in Tanya's shoulder. Her mom looked at her and raised her hands in a questioning manner. Tanya tilted her head to the door and gave a forced smile. Her mom nodded and got up. "Girls, let me know if you need anything."

"Thanks, Mom."

After the door closed, Yasmin looked up at Tanya, perhaps building the courage to say what she wanted. "It's been two years since we moved to America from Iran. They approved us as refugees. We moved here from Philadelphia this summer." She paused, taking a deep breath. "My aunt brought me here. My father was not a kind or a good man. His place was as head of the family, and what he decided was law, under our beliefs." She paused.

Tanya held her hand.

"My mother was a strong-willed woman. In private, she would disagree with my father, who would then beat her for not obeying him. If my mother believed what he was doing was wrong or would hurt the family, she would not back down, no matter how much pain he inflicted. When I was thirteen, my mother challenged my father in public. He hit her and dragged her through our town, back to our house."

Tanya wanted to remain supportive, but could not withhold a gasp.

"I was not there to see what happened in town, I was working in our backyard." Yasmin became calm, watching it play out. "My father dragged my mother into the backyard by her hair and threw her down. I backed away, not wanting to bring his wrath to me. He told her she had brought dishonor to their home and embarrassed him. No matter what he tried, she refused to learn. He took a large blade, grabbed her by her hair, and swung the blade into her neck. He killed my mother in front of me."

Tanya held her breath. She couldn't imagine the horror. Memories flashed in her mind of her mother on the kitchen floor, in her room crying, and in the backyard. Could her father do that? She was afraid to answer the question.

"I ran away that night, back to my grandmother's home on my mother's side. She took me in and got me out of the country."

Yasmin sighed. "I live with my grandmother on the other side of the school district. We have little money. She works nights and I'm alone after school. I work in the garden out back because it reminds me of my mother, and it's less we have to buy."

Tanya looked into Yasmin's eyes. She was hurt, but there was a momentary sense that something else was off before she looked down.

"Did something happen?"

Yasmin sat quietly for a moment. "Yes. Our landlord has been seeing my grandmother. He has an old-world attitude. He was in our home, fixing a leak in our bathroom. I couldn't help but lash out when he broke something dear to me because of his clumsiness, telling him to be careful and respect our home. I know I shouldn't have." She looked into Tanya's eyes. "He took off his belt, pushed me down, and whipped me with the belt. I tried to be tough, to resist. When I didn't cry, he turned the belt around and hit me with the buckle until I did. I rolled into a ball and covered my face until he stopped."

"Oh my gosh, are you ok? Do you need to go to the hospital? I can get my mom. We should call Sheri's dad."

"No! It'll heal. I needed to talk to someone. When I called Diane, her voicemail picked up right away. I didn't know where else to go. The idea of going back scares me. I don't know what he'll do."

"What about your grandmother? Does she know?"

"Not about this, but he has smacked me before or pushed me into my room. She told me we sometimes have small prices to pay to survive. He has helped us with money, rent, and bills, and I think she's worried he could kick us out. We don't have anywhere else to go."

"Do you want to stay here? At least for a few days. Maybe everything will cool down," offered Tanya.

"Do you think your parents would mind?"

"Let me check with my mom."

Tanya got up and left to find her mom. She narrowly avoided tripping, stepping over Jackson, who was going into the kitchen. "Jackson!" He turned and sat down, looking at her. She nodded and headed down the hall by the stairs to the laundry room and garage. "Mom!"

"In here," she heard from the laundry room.

"Mom, Yasmin needs somewhere to stay for a few days. Can she stay here?"

"Well, I need to check with your father."

"Mom, he doesn't care. We'll stay out of the way. He's just going to watch football all weekend. He won't even know we're here."

Her mom wrinkled her brow, looking to the side. "Ok, fine. Is she going to be all right?"

She hugged her mom. "I hope so. This will mean a lot to her. Thanks, Mom."

She returned to the kitchen. Jackson was lying on the floor, staring at the back door. She stepped around him and opened the door, letting him out.

"My mom said you can stay here for a few days. Do you need to get anything?"

A frightened look crossed Yasmin's face. "No, I'll be ok."

"You're a little taller than me, but I have some sweats you can wear when you need to change."

Yasmin wrapped her arms around her, pulling her close. "Thank you."

Chapter 20

Saturday Morning II

"Oh, that smell." Yasmin's eyes lit up. "You got my scent—hyacinth."

"I did, I like it. It's helped me relax lately with all the stress and craziness." Tanya lit the incense, strengthening the smell in the room.

Yasmin walked to the windowsill, closed her eyes, and leaned over, breathing in the smoke from the incense. "It reminds me of home."

"I could put it out. I'm so sorry."

"No, it smells good."

"We can relax up here. I'll be here for whatever you need."

Yasmin sat on her bed and pointed to the flute. "Have you been playing the song?"

"Yes, I have. It has been an interesting experience. I can almost feel the music if that makes sense. It's like nothing I've ever played. It draws me in, and I get frustrated when I miss a note or make a mistake."

"I know little about music. I don't play, so I'm not a good judge."

"It's challenging."

Tanya picked up her flute, took a deep breath, and played the song. She looked at Yasmin as she started playing through the memorized opening and saw a smile cross her lips. The melody developed, becoming more intense. Maybe it was that she was playing for her friend and wanted to give back to her for the gift of the song, but she felt more connected to the music. The melody danced between octaves, countering itself as if in conversation.

Tanya looked at the scene of her playing music for her friend. The notes floated from the page around Yasmin and out into the world. She felt her breathing steady, seamlessly matching the amount needed to play softly or reach a crescendo. Tanya lost herself in the song when a wind blew through the window, sending the pages to the floor. An overwhelming sadness gripped her heart as she stopped playing.

"That was amazing!" Yasmin was beaming. "I would never have thought to hear that song again. It's been so long."

"I'm going to transpose all of this to clean music sheets. I don't want to damage these. But you liked it?"

"I do. You played it beautifully. I cannot wait to see you playing it on stage."

"It's strange, but I feel such an attachment to the song that it feels like my heart breaks when I mess up."

"I felt something in the music too. Thank you for letting me listen."

Tanya wiped the flute with a soft cloth and slid it back onto its stand. She gathered the music and put it back into order.

"Do you know what these words are?"

"I don't know the words. They look like a variant of Persian script. My grandmother told me the song is about a young woman who lost her true love. She wanders the land, trying to find out whether her love will wait for her in the afterlife or if she should move on. As she travels and becomes older and wiser, she falls in love again. She feels her heart torn between her original passion and new love and pledges her heart to her new love. She battles with her heart to break through the pain of letting go of her true love and fully committing to her current partner. Her feelings and memories surround her throughout the battle, allowing her to reflect on her life. In the end, she gives herself completely to her newfound passion."

"Wow. That is a lot. I can feel those themes in the music when I play. I don't know what it is, but I get so immersed in playing the song that it becomes part of me. Knowing the story helps make sense of it. I feel it. Is that weird?"

Yasmin smiled. "Not at all. Some elders in my sect talk about love and magic, being able to open portals to another plane of existence. I don't know if I believe them. Certain songs have the power to connect with people. I have a song that touches my heart. It's about a girl and her love, but I think of my mother because it was one of the first songs I heard when we arrived in the country."

Tanya smiled. "What is it? Do you mind?"

"You'll think I'm silly. It doesn't match my personality or what anyone at school thinks I'm like."

Tanya tapped her knee. "What is it?"

Yasmin looked away, embarrassed, then turned back. "Surrender."

"I'm not sure I know it." Tanya opened her phone and found it on YouTube, sending it to the speaker on her desk. The soft voice of Natalie Taylor came out soothing. The gentle music and soft tones called to the listener, her lover, or friend, to surrender to their feelings.

"I'm not familiar with the song, but it's beautiful."

"Yeah, I don't know why it reminds me of my mom."

"The lyrics could even be a third person telling the woman in the old song to surrender to her heart's desire."

"I hadn't thought of it that way."

A knock sounded at the door. Sheri opened the door and said, "Hey, first, how are we doing? I wanted to check on you both."

Yasmin looked at her. "Better. Tanya is a good friend."

"Yes, she is. Are you ok?"

"I should ask you that." Tanya looked at Yasmin. "Their dog died last night."

"Oh, I'm sorry. Was he sick?"

"No, he was old, though. The vet mentioned that there have been a few deaths this week. You know the Sans, across and back from you?"

"Yeah," Tanya answered slowly.

"Both of their dogs died."

"Aww the little shih tzu, Tik and Tok. They've only had them for maybe five years. When did they die?"

"Last night."

Tanya got goosebumps. "That's weird."

"Maybe something's going around," Yasmin offered. "I've never had a dog, so that I wouldn't know."

"Maybe. You'd better watch Jackson."

"I will. Do you want to stay for pizza?"

"I can't tonight." She raised her chin, looking down her nose at them, feigning importance. "I have a dinner date."

"With whom?" Tanya asked eagerly.

"Dad. We're going out to tell stories and celebrate Benny."

Tanya wrinkled her nose at the thought. "That's sweet."

"What? It's like a doggie wake, and I think it will help Dad. I haven't seen him sad like this since we lost my mom. He needs it."

"Aww, good daughter award."

Sheri shrugged. "I just wanted to check on you two. If things get," she lowered her voice, "tense, come down to my house."

"Thanks, Sher. I'll walk you out."

Yasmin waved.

When they got outside, Sheri turned on Tanya. "Is she ok? Was it bad?"

"I'll let her tell you when she's ready. But, yeah, it's a bad situation. She's gonna stay here a few days to let things cool off."

"All right. I'll text you later."

Tanya waved.

When she returned to her room, the window was open, and the screen slid up. She saw the long curls of Yasmin's hair in front of the window. Tanya climbed out and sat beside her. "This is my getaway spot. I'll sit out here for hours when I want to relax and look up at the sky."

"It's nice out here." She breathed in the cool afternoon air. "It's going to rain."

Tanya looked up at the clouds. "That doesn't seem like too difficult of a prediction. You can see the rain falling over there." She pointed.

Yasmin shrugged. "It's a gift."

Tanya sat forward, looking into the Burke's yard. Coolio was lying in the middle of the yard, facing the house. Fear gripped her heart. "Coolio!" She watched before calling the dog's name again. She heard the jingle of a collar and Jackson came from around the side of the house, facing the back fence. He carefully sniffed the air, making his way towards the wall. He stopped a few feet from the fence and lifted his head.

Rowf!

He waited a moment.

Rowf! Rowf!

He turned around, sniffing the air, then lay down, looking at the fence.

"Oh no."

"The dog?"

"Yeah, that's Coolio, the Burke's English bulldog. He's only three. I need to get Jackson in and let them know."

They climbed back in and went downstairs to the kitchen.

"Jackson, come!"

He jumped up, his little tail wagging, and trotted toward her, bounding up the steps, stopping to sit patiently in front of her.

She scratched behind his ears before shooing him into the house.

She pulled her phone out and scrolled through her contacts.

"Do you know them?"

"Yeah, I babysit for them every so often. They have an adorable little girl, Sadie."

"Oh."

"Mr. Burke, this is Tanya. I was looking out my window and noticed Coolio in the backyard. I thought you might want to check on him. It's Saturday afternoon. Bye."

She slid the phone back into her pocket. "It's not like them to leave him outside when they're out of the house. Maybe we should go around and check on them."

Tanya's dad came into the kitchen. He wore dark blue sweatpants and a grey and blue Naval Academy T-shirt. Glancing at the two, he made his way to the refrigerator for a beer. On his way out of the kitchen, he cast a quick glance back at Yasmin.

"I don't think he likes me," Yasmin whispered.

"Most of the time, I don't think he likes me either. I'm pretty sure he wanted a boy." She shrugged. "I'll be free next year. I really need to get out of here. I wish my mom would come with me."

"Maybe things will change as you get close to graduation once he realizes what he's going to lose."

Tanya looked at her, then at the door to the living room. "I don't know. I wish he would."

"I will never forgive my father."

"I don't know if I ever will, either. Do you want to come with me? I want to walk around the block and see if the Burkes are home."

A sound like pebbles falling on glass answered her as the rain started falling. "Great."

"You still want to go?"

Tanya kneeled and scratched behind Jackson's ears. "I'd want to know. He's a good dog. I'd like to know if something happened to Jackson. A dog is a member of a family. Look at it like losing a brother or sister."

Yasmin nodded. "Ok, let's go."

Chapter 21

Saturday Midday

They walked around the block. The heavy raindrops produced a steady beating rumble as they fell on their umbrellas. The heavy downpour picked up so fast that little rivulets of water had formed and carried the piled-up leaves in the street toward the sewage drains. It felt more like twilight than midday as the thick clouds blocked out the sunlight. As they rounded the corner of the block, she pointed at the red Marine Corps flag hanging in the rain.

"That's not normal. He always brings his flags in before it rains." Mr. Burke had explained flag etiquette to her right after hiring her as a babysitter, taking twenty minutes to talk about respect for the American and Marine Corps flags.

She stopped. "They aren't home. He would have brought it in out of the rain. Let's check the side gate. I can't stand the thought of Coolio lying in the back year getting drenched in the rain."

Tanya stopped at the streetlight just before the Burkes' house. "Look at these missing cat signs. Three cats are missing. I know one of them, also from babysitting. That one, the orange tabby, is declawed. What is going on?" The paper was peeling from the light post, ink running down the paper.

"How often do you come over here?"

"Not a lot, only when someone needs me to babysit."

"Maybe someone doesn't like animals."

"I hope it's not that. I'll let Mom know. We'll have to watch Jackson."

Yasmin nodded. Her curls were becoming more pronounced with the moisture in the air.

Plops of raindrops on their umbrellas picked up as the storm intensified.

"Let's hurry." Tanya walked up the driveway and to the side gate. It was unlocked. They made their way into the backyard and saw Coolio's body lying in the same position.

"Let's get him to the back porch. I'll let them know when I can get in touch with them."

They worked together to pick up the dog, its head lolling to the side as they carried him to the back deck. Tanya laid him down near the door and felt a tug at her heart, tears welling in her eyes. She kneeled and pet his still body, pushing the rain off his thin coat. "I'm sorry. I hope you're running around heaven."

"You really care for them, don't you?"

"I do. We've always had a dog. Before Jackson, we had Grant. He was a beagle my parents got before I was born. They're family. They provide love, comfort, and help when you're feeling down. Jackson has been with us when things were rough. He's a strong little guy."

Tanya put their coats and umbrellas in the closet. Yasmin followed her to the kitchen. Her dad was asleep on the couch, with SportsCenter playing on the TV. She let the door swing closed and went to the refrigerator. "I was supposed to order dinner. I'm sorry. Are you hungry?"

"I'm ok. Go ahead if you're hungry."

"I'll just make something here. Feel free to get something later when you need to eat."

Yasmin smiled. "I will. You said something before that I don't understand. You said you hoped the neighbor's dog was happy running around heaven. Do you believe animals go to heaven?"

"I hope they do. Heaven is supposed to be a happy place to get back together with family and friends. I hope our pets are there. I'd be sad without them." Yasmin looked like she was about to say something, but decided not to.

"I wish I could be that positive. I think we are destined to be reborn again and again, correcting the mistakes we have made."

"Like reincarnation?"

"Yeah."

"When do you get to move on?"

"I don't know. When you get it all right?"

Tanya looked toward the door that led to the living room. "I guess some people would take longer than others." She preferred the concept of heaven and hell. Some people were just bad people.

Yasmin shrugged. "It is similar to Buddhism or Hinduism. The goal is to become enlightened. My faith translates this as becoming true to your soul."

"How do you know what that is?"

"It's different for every being."

Tanya sat down across from Yasmin at the breakfast table. She had decided on yogurt. She ate a spoonful, tasting the tart yogurt with a hint of strawberries.

Jackson whined to go out.

"Ok." She got up and went to the back door to let him out. Lights were flashing around the side of the Burkes' house.

"Something's going on." Yasmin got up and looked out the window. "Do you want to see what it is?"

"Let's go up to my room."

As they entered the living room her dad looked over at her. "Hey honey, would you get me a refill?" He shook an empty beer can.

Tanya forced a smile and took the empty can to the kitchen. She returned with a full one, handing it to him. "Have you seen your mother? We're supposed to go out tonight."

111

"No. I think she went out." She looked at half a dozen cans sitting off the side of the end table. *It's a good thing, too, because you're in no condition to drive.*

"Figures. She better remember to bring back dinner. What did you girls eat?"

"Stuff from the refrigerator."

He grunted and opened the beer, reaching for the remote. "At least I'll be able to watch the games tonight without all the yapping."

Tanya nodded, still forcing a smile. *He hasn't talked to mom all day. It was probably a blessing to her you left her alone.*

"Something is going on at the Burkes' house. We spotted Coolio from my window. It looked like he was dead."

He sipped his beer and set it on the end table. "Maybe that will shut Jackson up. No more competition."

"Daddy!"

"What? That dog did nothing but taunt Jackson. You've heard him barking in the back. Pain in the ass to the entire neighborhood. I'm just saying we may get some peace in the evenings."

Shaking her head, Tanya stopped on the stairs. "What if it was Jackson?"

He mumbled something under his breath and chuckled to himself.

"I didn't hear what you said," Tanya called downstairs to her father.

"Nothing. We'd all be sad, of course." He rolled his eyes and turned back to the TV.

Tanya glared at him, then stomped up the stairs.

"Don't get mad at me. I'm just saying what everyone else in the neighborhood will be thinking."

Tanya didn't stop to reply. She continued to her room.

"He's not a good man," Yasmin said.

Tanya looked at Yasmin briefly, then went to the window.

Yasmin joined her. "Are you mad at me for saying that?"

Tanya looked at her again, then back to the Burkes' house. The lights were on inside, but most of the blinds were closed. The blinds on the sliding glass door to the patio were open, and they could see several police officers inside.

"I'm not mad at you. He's gotten worse. I'm afraid for my mom when I leave."

"Are you having second thoughts?"

"No," she said too quickly. "I have to get out of here. I'll talk to Diane on Tuesday about what support there is for my mom. Maybe there's a way to get her to see what's happening."

Yasmin nodded, staring at the neighbor's house.

Tanya glanced at her friend. Yasmin watched the people moving about in her neighbor's home. After what she had seen and experienced, this was likely nothing. Maybe they called the police because they think someone poisoned Coolio.

The rain had slowed from a downpour to a light drizzle. It wasn't late, but it felt like the middle of the night. A dark shape swooped down and landed on the backyard fence. After a moment, another vulture landed. Tanya pointed up. "Look, the vultures."

"Death is close," Yasmin whispered.

A chill ran down Tanya's spine, and she got goosebumps. "Why'd you say that?"

"The vultures sense it."

"They wouldn't even be here if someone would clean up the Vulture House."

Yasmin stepped back, turning toward her. "The what?"

"Vulture House. It's up the street toward school with all the vultures perched on it."

Yasmin looked up at the circling birds. "That's a bad omen."

Tanya felt a sense of dread. *Death is near. It's an omen, dogs dying.*

Knock, knock, knock.

Tanya screamed, her voice piercing the quiet of her room. Yasmin stepped away from her, turning.

"What's wrong?"

"Girls, are you decent?" her dad's voice sounded from the other side of the door.

"Of course we are. What do you want?"

"Sweetie, the police are here. They'd like to talk to you two." Tanya flinched at his attempt to sound endearing.

Tanya looked at Yasmin, a pit forming in her stomach. She whispered, "They know we went over there."

Yasmin was calm, whispering, "Yeah, to help them with their dog."

"They're not going to see it like that."

"We did nothing wrong," she declared her defiance.

"They don't know that."

"We'll be fine. Let's talk to them."

Tanya looked panicked. "Ok."

She returned her voice to normal. "Ok, Dad."

Chapter 22

Saturday Afternoon

Tanya and Yasmin came downstairs. Two uniformed police officers stood inside the door. Their cruiser was outside, the lights flashing through the front windows. "Evening, ladies. Your dad said I could ask you some questions." One officer looked at her dad. "Is there somewhere we could sit and talk?"

"Yeah, sure, come on in. You can use the dining table."

"Thank you." The officers followed them to the kitchen. Tanya noticed them looking around as they moved through the house, inspecting every little thing.

The officer sat down across from the girls, resting his arms on the table. 'Ortiz,' his badge read. His eyes were friendly but challenging. The short-sleeved shirt looked tight around his arms as his biceps flexed from being crossed. Tanya shook herself back. She didn't hear what he said.

"I'm sorry. Could you repeat the question?"

"Yes, ma'am. Your dad said your bedroom has a view into your neighbor's yard and the back of their house. Have you noticed anything unusual over the past few days?"

Tanya told them about seeing Coolio in the yard and wanting to let them know. Seeing they weren't home, they went into the backyard and moved the dog out of the rain.

"Did you check to see if they were home?"

"Uh, no, sir. Mr. Burkes's truck was gone and his Marine Corps flag was out in the rain. He never forgets to bring it in if he's home. I didn't think to knock."

He looked at Yasmin. "Ma'am, do you have anything to add?"

"No, sir."

Tanya leaned on the table. "Is everything ok?"

"I'm sorry. I can't say anything right now." He looked at his partner. "Do you have any questions?"

The other officer looked out the kitchen window. "You said you haven't noticed anything off in the last day. Would you have seen if the dog were in the yard earlier?"

"Yes, ma'am. I sometimes sit outside my window. My dog, Jackson, would get into a barking match with Coolio, their dog. Not in a bad way, more like arguing with friends. I would have noticed if he were out there. I'm sure he wasn't there this morning when I got up."

Officer Hendercriss turned to question Yasmin, "Ma'am, you said you're staying here for a few days. Do you mind telling us why?"

Yasmin looked at the officer. "I'd rather not."

"That's fine. Could you tell us when you arrived and where you were before that?"

Yasmin cocked her head to the side. "I came here this morning, maybe around nine, and I was home before that. Which is across town, about a mile on the other side of the school." She glared challengingly.

Officer Ortiz pulled two cards out of his shirt pocket, handing one to each girl. "Thank you, both. Call us if you remember anything else or notice something unusual."

Tanya took the card, rubbing her hand over the raised seal of the Cedar Ridge Police. She was going to call Sheri right after they left. "I will."

Officer Ortiz got up. "Do you mind if I take a look out back?"

"Sure." She let them out, watched as they looked at the Burke house, and then walked along the fence.

"If I could inconvenience you for one more thing. I'd like to look out your bedroom window if that's ok."

"Yes, sir. I'll take you upstairs." She led them to her room, letting them in. They looked around on their way to the window.

Officer Hendercriss nodded to the shelf with Smurfette. "I loved her growing up. That's a nice collection."

"Thank you."

Both officers took their time looking out the window.

"We're good. Thank you, ladies. We'll get out of your hair. Again, let us know if you think of anything."

"Will do, officer."

They led the police downstairs and showed them out.

When the door closed, Tanya looked at Yasmin. "What is going on? This is all a bit much for a dead dog."

"I don't know."

Tanya shuddered. "This is too much. I'm gonna call Sheri. She'll know."

"Will she tell you?"

"Of course."

Her dad was not in the living room; it was straightened up and the empty cans were missing. She grabbed her phone and returned to see what they could from her window.

"Hello."

"Sheri! The police were just here. Do you know what's going on?"

"Can you come down?"

"Yes, Yasmin is with me."

"Bring her over. Definitely don't come alone."

"Ok, we'll be right there." She pressed *End*. Fear crept into her chest, tightening its grip. "Something bad happened. I know it. She wants us to come down. Are you ok with that?"

"Of course. Maybe she can give us some answers."

Sheri let them in and swiftly closed the door. "Someone killed the Burkes," she blurted out before they could get out of their coats.

A shiver shot up Tanya's spine. "How? He was a retired marine. I know of at least three guns between the kitchen and the front door."

Yasmin and Sheri looked at her.

"What?" She looked at her friends. "He asked me if I knew how to handle a firearm. I didn't at the time."

Sheri put her hand on her hips. "And you do now."

"I do. He said that if I was going to watch his little girl, he wanted to make sure I could fully protect her. Oh, my God!" Her hand covered her mouth, her eyes widened. "Please tell me Sadie is ok." Tears welled up in Tanya's eyes. The happy little girl's face popped into her thoughts at the memory of playing games while babysitting.

Sheri shook her head, tears in her eyes as well. "Someone got to them all."

Tanya plopped down on the floor. "It can't be. Why is this happening? That house is cursed. The vultures are an omen of death. Something is wrong with it." She looked at Sheri. "You need to talk to your dad. He has to know what's going on. There's something evil there, spreading its tendrils into our neighborhood." Her emotions were a swirling wreck. Energy, anger, and sadness filled her. Something needed to be done.

Sheri grabbed her shoulder. "Tanya, calm down. Panicking isn't going to help."

"Ok, Sheri, so what are we going to do? Did you know the dogs are all dying? Not just Benny. Other dogs in the neighborhood, too. Did your dad tell you that? Why? And it's not just the dogs. Three cats are missing in the neighborhood as well. It's that house!"

Sheri let go of her. "Are you going to do anything about this?" she asked Yasmin, pointing at Tanya. "You seem pretty calm."

"Leave her alone." Tanya got up. "Maybe she's in shock. She's had a bad day too."

Yasmin looked at her friends, but didn't answer. After a moment, she got up. A flash of sadness crossed her face. "It's ok, Tanya. I'm going to go for a walk." Yasmin started for the door.

"No! What if the killer is out there?"

"With all the police around here? It stopped raining, so I should be safe. I just want to get some air. I'll come back to your house in a little bit."

Sheri nodded. "I'm sorry. Let me make you some tea. I didn't mean to be insensitive. It's all of this, Benny, the birds, and the murders. I'm not myself."

Tanya pulled away. "I don't understand! Why are you so calm? Don't you see what is going on?"

Sheri stepped forward with a concerned look. "Tanya, I do. But my dad's a cop. I see it every night. Every night he has to go out, I worry, and I'm worried now. I have to believe that my mom is looking out for him because he's had some bad days. Yes, something bad happened in our neighborhood. But bad things happen every day."

Tanya was trembling. How could she justify, break it down, and be so logical? Now isn't the time to be stoic. "Fine, make tea, and then I'm going home. I want to check on Jackson."

Sheri looked at Yasmin, who nodded and went out the door into the night.

Tanya's heart was pounding in her chest. "Ok, I need to calm down." She began breathing in and out, attempting to get her nerves under control.

"There we go. Let's go to the kitchen."

Tanya followed her there and sat on the small island in the middle of the room. She folded her arms and put her head down. She wanted to cry again, but she kept inhaling and exhaling with measured breaths.

After a few minutes, Sheri put a cup of chamomile tea in front of her. She smelled the relaxing scent and took a sip. Sheri had dropped an ice cube, cooling it enough to be drinkable.

"Mmm. Ok, I'm better."

"Are you sure?"

"I still think something is going on. But I'm willing to look at it logically."

"It's not linked to the blood pool killer. This was something different. Maybe a home invasion gone wrong. I felt scared, but my dad reassured me that it wasn't connected. I'll tell you if it is, ok? It's just something bad."

"I still think it's all connected somehow. A curse."

"There's no such thing, and you know it."

She sipped her tea. "You may be right, but you have to admit that statistically, you could be mistaken."

"I'm right, and if you're going to pull math into the argument, I'll concede that nothing is absolute. Have I ever steered you wrong?"

"No, but you could be nicer to Yasmin. I can't share her secrets, but she has had a rough life, worse than mine."

"Fine, I'll try. Are you gonna be alright?" Sheri's eyes were fixed on her as she sipped her tea.

"Probably. It's the vulture dreams. I haven't been able to sleep that well since my dad's car got messed up."

"Are you having more bad dreams? Or is your mind racing?"

"I don't know. I wake up in the morning, and I'm so tired, like I haven't slept at all. Maybe it's just a bad feeling." Tanya slumped back in her chair. "I think I'm gonna go home. I want to crawl into bed and go to sleep. Maybe this is a bad feeling." She set the cup down and twirled her finger around.

Sheri smiled at her, getting up to walk her to the door. "I'll see what I can get from my dad. I'll tell him about the other dogs. Benny's passing shook him. Maybe he'll look into it, but with this and the serial killer still out there. He may not have time."

Tanya sighed. "This is supposed to be our year. The last year of high school. The happy farewell. Have you talked to Amara?"

"Yeah, but it was a quick conversation. She's being cryptic about her parents and something at the mosque. Maybe you can call her tomorrow and get something out of her. Her mom loves you."

Tanya smiled weakly. "Yeah, ok, I'll try. We need the entire gang together."

She walked to the door and hugged Sheri.

"G'night, Sher."

Chapter 23

Saturday Night

Tanya lay in bed propped up on her pillows, watching a video showing gurneys being brought out from the Burkes' home and rolled to ambulances. One of her neighbors was live-streaming from their phone. She switched apps to the local news.

> *Initial reports stated the police believed it was a home invasion gone wrong. Upon entering the house, the unknown assailant came face to face with the father, a retired marine.*

The video showed his USMC picture.

> *An altercation ensued, resulting in broken furniture and blood spread through the first floor. The assailant then attacked the mother on the stairs before going upstairs and killing the couple's twelve-year-old daughter. Police are looking for a motive for the brutal murder. We'll keep you up to date on this breaking story.*

Tears rolled down her cheeks. Sadie was a sweet girl and tough, like her dad. They had always had fun when she watched their daughter. She looked up from her phone to the house, now dark. A thick cover of clouds hid the moon, making the night seem deeper and more foreboding than usual. She jumped up and closed her curtains. She checked the time on her phone. The time was just past ten, and Yasmin hadn't returned yet. She opened her bedroom door and stepped into the dark hallway. A sliver of light emanated from under her parents' room. Her mom had texted that she was helping her sister and may just stay over.

Tanya smiled. Her Aunt Karen was the opposite of her mom. She didn't like her sister's husband and let him know every time they were together. She was feisty, driven, and protective of her big sister.

Stealthily, she made her way down the hall to the stairs. A scraping sound from downstairs caught her attention, causing her to stop—goosebumps forming on her arms.

"Yasmin, is that you?" While she waited for a reply, she heard the scratching again. She swallowed, on the verge of running back to her room and locking the door. Peering over the banister, she searched for the source of the sound, but found nothing. Gradually, she made her way down the stairs and turned on the lights. Stepping off the landing, she didn't see anything. She checked the side windows by the door to see if Yasmin was outside, but the steps were clear. She turned on the outside light. *Of course, my dad wouldn't check to see if we were back.*

Tanya went into the kitchen, reaching in and flipping on the light before entering. Her eyes were heavy. Jackson was lying down, his paws on the wall, which was different, but he didn't seem alarmed. As she entered the living room again, she turned on the TV and stumbled upon a movie. She pulled a blanket from a basket and wrapped it around her. She lay on the couch, resting, so she would be here when Yasmin came back.

She picked a comedy, but felt too exhausted to laugh. As she watched, her eyes closed, following a deep yawn.

Ba-boom.

Tanya stood up at the sound that reminded her of a large kettle drum. In her living room, she noticed a difference. She turned around to take in everything around her. As she looked at the couch, she noticed herself peacefully snoozing, wrapped in the warm blanket. The TV was off. Shadows concealed the walls of the room, making them almost undetectable. The darkness swirled in shades of black. She tried to focus on the walls, but the smoky mist kept them just out of focus. *This is a dream.*

Ba-boom…Ba-boom, Ba-boom, Ba-boom…Ba-Boom…

The sound resonated through the house. Two heartbeats, one slow and steady, the other racing. She looked toward the stairs, and the sounds became visible as waves rippling upstairs and flowing down the stairs like a liquid. Someone was watching her. She could feel it. She spun around, searching the room, but she saw nothing apart from the swirling darkness.

Something was just beyond the mist. It wanted her to come closer. She backed away toward the stairs. She looked out the window and saw nothing. Darkness encompassed everything.

Ba-boom…Ba-boom, Ba-boom, Ba-boom…Ba-Boom…

As she climbed the stairs, she touched the sound flowing downward. It was a mixture of warm and cold, like two liquids preventing mixing. The temperatures locked in a battle, neither wanting to move toward the other. The sounds were recognizable. One was love, the other fear. She reached the top of the stairs. The waves were coming from her parents' room. She hesitated, afraid of what she would find. Attempting to call out, she found herself unable to make a sound.

She entered the room. A jaundiced yellow light illuminated her father as he leaned over her mother. Her father reached up to caress her mother's face with his left hand, looking into her eyes. Upon smiling, her mother's expression transformed to horror as her father's other hand ruthlessly stabbed her chest with a large blade. His left hand grasped her hair, holding her in place as she squirmed, trying to escape. He smiled as he slid the blade down her chest and across her stomach. Blood spurted into his face and hands. His smile never faltered. He lay the knife next to her weak body and reached into the long cut and her chest.

Tanya's paralysis broke. She attempted to back out of the room and found her way obstructed. She turned away from the scene, finding the black smoky mist had filled the hall behind her.

Ba-boom…Ba-boom.

She looked down, seeing the wave from her father crossing the room. Despite her reluctance, she couldn't resist the compulsion to look at her father. He stood frozen, his hand inside her mother, a look of pleasure on his face. A light glimmered on his bare back. With caution, she inched closer to identify what it was. She fought against the fear. She wanted to run, to wake up from this dream. As she moved around him, she saw what looked like a black cursive capital B surrounded and filled with thin patterns of blood. She felt a powerful attraction to the symbol, but everything else around her disgusted her.

As he turned to look at her, she stepped back, sensing the malevolence, his wicked grin frozen in place.

With a jump, she tossed the blanket and got up from the couch. She was cold. Sweat soaked her clothes.

"It was just a nightmare. Just a nightmare." Her heart was racing in her chest. She looked around the room. The shadows pulled to her like the mist.

"Please be awake." She tried to calm down when she felt a pinch on her arm.

Tap, Tap, Tap.

She jumped, almost screaming, and looked toward the window. Yasmin was looking in the side window by the door.

Tanya sprinted to the door and opened it, pulling Yasmin in and shutting it fast.

"Tanya, what's going on?"

"I had a nightmare. Everything is getting to me. I'm so tired."

"You're ok. I'm here."

"Where did you go? I was worried."

"I went back to my grandmother's and grabbed a few things."

"He could have caught you."

"I left my window open. They didn't hear me."

Tanya hugged her again. "I'm glad you're here."

"Me too. You need to sleep. You look exhausted."

Tanya slumped. "I am so tired. I need to shower and get some rest."

"Ok. We can talk about it in the morning."

Chapter 24

Sunday Morning

A knock at the door pulled her from a restless sleep. Tanya rolled to the edge of her bed and forced herself to sit up. Her body ached, her head was throbbing, and her arms felt like lead.

"I'm coming."

She opened the door. Yasmin was there, looking better than before. She had changed into a dark brown pullover shirt and light brown corduroy pants. She smiled, thin, almost imperceptible.

"Did you sleep? You have dark circles under your eyes."

"Not really. I tossed and turned all night."

"Was it the nightmare?"

"No. I heard Jackson walking around, wind and rain outside, and my mind was racing." She turned and jumped back in bed, pulling the covers over her head.

"Try to sleep now. I'll be fine."

"No, the sun's out. I need to be awake."

"Ok, get me when you're ready."

"Ok, a shower should do the trick."

Tanya knocked on the guest room door. Her long brown hair was still damp. She had on a V-neck, long-sleeved brown and white top and jeans.

"Yasmin?"

Her friend opened the door. "You want to tell me about the nightmare over breakfast?"

Tanya perked up. "Yeah."

She sat across from Yasmin at the table. Her friend had a cup of tea; it smelled pungent. "What's that tea?"

"It's a recipe my grandmother makes from the herbs in our garden. It's an acquired taste; do you want to try it?"

"Not right now," she said, scooping the last bite from her peach yogurt. "I don't think it would go with all the sweetness."

"Are you saying I'm not as sweet as you?"

Tanya looked up, shocked. "No, I, uh, meant—"

"I'm kidding. I know it's strong. You ready?"

Tanya got a cup of coffee, adding sugar and milk. She took a sip and repeated her dream, taking time to recall every detail. Yasmin listened, letting her get through the entire tale before saying anything.

"That's pretty vivid. I don't know if it was a dream. It sounds like a vision."

"What do you think it means?"

"You're worried about your mom? Our dreams sometimes echo what we experienced recently. Yesterday was a rough day."

"It was so real. What about the symbol on my dad's back? I've never seen it before."

"I don't know. I'd ask my grandmother, but you know."

Tanya sighed, sipping her coffee.

Bang!

They heard the front door slam.

"It's about goddamned time you got home."

"Let it go, Chris. My sister needed my help."

"Don't you walk out on me. Your sister's putting thoughts in your head, I know it. Don't think you can leave me. I take care of you and our daughter!"

Tanya jumped up and went into the living room. Yasmin followed.

Her dad wore jeans and a blue and gray flannel shirt. Tanya noticed his shotgun case leaning in the corner.

"What's going on?"

He turned and pointed at her, his face stern. "Stay out of it, Tanya."

"No, Daddy, leave her alone!"

He took a step toward Tanya, and her mom grabbed his arm. He threw an elbow back, catching her in the face. She screamed and went to her knees, blood running from her nose between her fingers.

Tanya was furious. She wanted to get him away from her mom. She ran at him, screaming, "Leave her alone!"

Her mom reached for the door, opening it, catching her husband in the back and causing him to straighten up and step toward Tanya. A shape filled the doorway. Pain erupted from her cheek as the back of his hand hit her across the side of her face. The world flashed white as she stumbled to the right into a table.

"I told you to stay out of it. You—"

She heard something heavy hit the ground near her. She turned to see Officer Ortiz, his knee on her father's back, twisting his arm around. "Sir, you need to calm down right now."

Tanya's vision shifted between blurry and in focus as she tried to look at her mom, who was kneeling again. Another police officer, Hendercriss, put a hand on Tanya's mom's shoulder. Her mom nodded, and the officer stepped through the door to help the other officer cuff her father.

Tanya looked back at Yasmin and saw her friend glaring at her father, a subtle anger in her expression.

Her jaw hurt. She opened and closed her mouth a few times.

"Miss, are you ok?" She looked up to see Hendercriss reaching to help her up. She took the extended hand and stood, almost falling over with dizziness. Yasmin moved to help, wrapping her hand around Tanya's waist and guiding her back toward the couch.

"This is bullshit. It's my house."

"Sir, you have the right to remain silent. I strongly recommend you use it."

Her dad spit on the floor. "She attacked me. Did you see that? Huh?"

Officer Ortiz clicked his mic. "This is Cedar Ridge, unit two-one. I have a male in custody for exaggerated domestic violence and assault on a minor." He let go of the mic button and looked at her mom. "Ma'am, are you willing to press charges?"

Tanya watched, expecting her to back down. Her mom looked at her, and she saw sadness in her eyes. "Yes."

He clicked the mic. "The victims intend to press charges. Request assistance at 2376 Hellman St."

"Copy, two-one. Two-six is in the vicinity and will assist."

He clicked the mic twice.

Ortiz helped her father, grabbed him behind the arm, and led him out.

"You better drop it, Kaitlyn. This is my goddamn house. I paid for it. I will put your ass out on the street, you bitch."

Her mom was looking down. She looked worried. Tanya saw Ortiz trip on the lip where the wood flooring from the living room and the tile from the entryway met. He fell forward, placing his shoulder into her dad's back, driving his face into the door frame.

"You did that on purpose!"

He steadied himself and took her father out to the patrol car.

Officer Hendercriss took their statements. The other officers showed up within a few minutes and helped. She heard them say that he had resisted getting into the car and had not stopped making threats the entire time. Tanya was sure the neighbors saw the police and her father being taken away.

"Mrs. Janessy, would you like to pursue a temporary restraining order? We can provide you with a hotline to call that will keep him away for about fourteen days until a full restraining order can be issued."

"Yes, I don't know what he'll do if he returns." Her mom swallowed.

Tanya reached over and took her mom's hand. "We'll be okay, Mom. This is the right thing to do."

Her mom agreed but avoided eye contact with the police. Tanya looked past the officers to Yasmin, who was watching everything play out. When she noticed Tanya looking at her, she flashed a reassuring thin lipped grin. This must have brought back horrible memories for her friend. Tanya felt sorry for her. The adrenaline of the moment was gone, and she felt exhausted.

"When will he be able to come back?" she asked the officers.

"At least a few days. Once the temporary protective order is in place, he won't be able to be near either of you. I suggest either arranging a time for him to come to the house and be escorted to gather his belongings, or you can pack them for him and have them ready when we bring him here. After that, he'll be required to stay away and not have contact with either of you."

Tanya squeezed her mom's hand.

"Are you both sure you don't require medical attention?"

"I'm ok," her mom said.

"Me too," Tanya added.

"We'll get out of your way. The next few weeks will be stressful. Because of the other incidents in the neighborhood, we'll have an increased presence. Call us if you need to."

"Thank you," her mom said and showed them out.

Tanya waited in the kitchen with Yasmin. "I'm sorry you had to see that. I'm sure it was hard."

Yasmin nodded.

"I don't want to leave my mom alone. Are you ok if I call Amara and Sheri over?"

Yasmin shook her head. "Of course. Whatever you need."

Chapter 25

Sunday Afternoon

Tanya sat on the couch in the living room, cross-legged on the sofa. She had a cup of jasmine decaf tea in hand, blowing on it. Sheri sat to her right on the loveseat, also relaxed and drinking a cup of tea. Tanya had offered a cup to Yasmin, but she declined. She sat at the end of the long couch, facing Tanya and Sheri, running her fingers over the blue fabric of the couch backing.

Knock. Knock.

Amara opened the door and rushed in, moving towards Tanya and hugging her. "Are you ok?" She leaned back, looking at the side of her face. "Ooh, that's bruised pretty bad."

Tanya hugged her back and reached up to touch her face. "It doesn't hurt as much now. I think we'll be ok. My Aunt is coming over later to check on us."

Amara sat, then looked between Tanya and Sheri. "Oh, I need my tea." She ran to the kitchen, returning a moment later with her cup.

Tanya looked at Yasmin. "I told you. It's our plotting and planning tea."

All three girls lifted their tea toward the other. "What are we planning?" Amara asked, blowing her tea before taking a sip.

Sheri reached over and gave her leg a playful slap. "We're here to help Tanya get through this."

"I know that. I meant, what are we doing right now?"

Sheri gave her a sideways look.

Tanya set her tea down on the end table. "You can help by telling us why you're so distant this year. We hung out all summer, and now that we're back in school, we don't see you anymore, except at school."

Amara smiled. "I know. I'm afraid to say anything." She looked at her friends, lingering a moment longer on Yasmin.

"Do you need me to leave?" Yasmin asked.

"No, you're with us. It's just that my father is not happy with my schoolwork."

Sheri tilted her head. "You have straight A's."

Tanya nodded.

"Not that. It's my test scores. He says they should be better. My applications are in, but he wants me to keep taking the tests and updating my scores until they decide."

"So you're studying?" Tanya asked.

Amara sat back. "Tutoring, every afternoon." She looked at her phone. "I have just over three hours. It's exhausting. But worse, you're right. I miss you all, too."

She took a longer drink of her tea. "But that's me. Tanya, girl, we are here for you."

Tanya let her head fall back to rest on the back of the couch. "I don't know what's going on. I'm stressed about my applications, the recital, my mom, my dad, Jackson, the neighborhood, all of it."

Sheri reached over, patting her hand. "Tell her about the dream."

Tanya sat forward. "It was so real. I don't think it was a dream. It felt different. It's like I knew it was a dream, but other stuff was weird." She remembered the dream in vivid detail. It lingered in her mind like a memory. Her friends waited until she finished before saying anything.

Amara spoke first. "That sounds like a dream mixed with a vision and astral projection."

Tanya replied in shock, "Astral projection? You mean leaving my body?"

Sheri joined in, "You said you looked down and saw yourself sleeping."

"Sometimes powerful spirits or the divine use dreams to send messages to us."

Amara looked to Yasmin. "You think a spirit sent her a message?"

Yasmin shrugged. "Maybe. They don't have to be exact. Sometimes symbolism is used to get a message through."

"You had the dream last night. Maybe it was a premonition. Your dad was going to do something to your mom, I mean not like in the dream, and you saw the worst, so that you would react." Sheri added.

"You're saying that a spirit gave me a heads up so that I could save my mom."

The girls shook their heads emphatically.

"What about the symbol? I've never seen that before." She picked a paper up from the end table, handing it to Yasmin, who looked at it and passed it to Amara.

"Hmm. It looks like calligraphy."

"Yeah, a slanted capital B."

"No. Yes, this looks like it, but what about all these squiggles in and around it? Yasmin, you've seen this before, right?"

Yasmin took the sheet of paper back. "Yes, I see how it could be. But what could it mean?" She returned the paper to Tanya, who set it on the coffee table.

Amara turned the paper to look at it from different angles. "It's hard to tell. We should look it up."

"I did. There weren't any matches."

"Can I borrow this?" She took a picture with her phone.

"Sure. It's stuck in my head. The symbol is clear as day, but I don't know the shapes of the bloodlines underneath."

"Look at this." She turned her phone around for the others to see.

Tanya nodded. "Yes, it was like that style, though most of the swerves and writing were inside the openings of the symbol. Outside, the red looked more like blood splatter."

"If you see it again, try to get some of the writing inside."

"Amara!" Sheri exclaimed. "I hope she doesn't see it again."

"Of course, all good dreams would be nice. I'm just saying that if she does, we might see if there is a message there."

Yasmin chuckled. "Maybe there won't be another message. Maybe her actions were driven by the message she received, and she's safe now."

Amara nodded. "Let's hope so."

"I think it is a cool-looking image, though."

Sheri looked at her. "What do you mean?"

Tanya shrugged. "There's something about it I like. If you could see it like I did, it would make a nice tattoo."

Sheri sat back. "Whoa. Who are you, and what did you do with my best friend?"

Yasmin subtly adjusted her posture.

"What? Maybe without the blood splatter, change the color to a lavender. Maybe it would look nice."

Amara sneered. "I'm with you," she nodded to Sheri. "I don't know about that. I don't even know where you'd put it. Maybe on a guy."

Tanya shrugged.

Sheri shook her head. "I don't know where this came from. You've never mentioned getting a tattoo before."

"I'm not saying I want to run out and get a tattoo."

"Oh, ok."

Amara scooched forward on the couch, leaning her elbows on her knees. "How's the song coming?"

Yasmin smiled. "It sounds beautiful, so moving."

Tanya blushed. "I need to work on it more. Everything that's going on has me completely off my routine." She thought about playing it the day before, how it took her away from everything happening here. "I won't let this take away from my chance at Rice. I'll have it down before the recital."

Sheri smiled. "I like your confidence. I can't wait."

Jackson came in from the kitchen. He strolled into the room and jumped on the couch, nuzzling Sheri for attention. Her expression changed, her eyes becoming sad.

"I'm sorry, Sher. I can put him out back."

She smiled weakly. "I'll be alright, and he needs his loving." She scratched behind his ears, and his back leg started kicking. "That's your spot, isn't it, Jackson?" He pushed up, licking her cheek.

"The vet said we would have the toxicology report back tomorrow or the next day. My dad called back to inform the vet about the other dogs. He's worried that someone may have poisoned them because of the timing and the small area."

Tanya shifted on the couch, turning more toward Sheri. "He thinks someone might be poisoning dogs in our neighborhood?"

"He doesn't know, yet. Even with the Burkes' murder, no one saw anything unusual."

Tanya shuddered. "Something is going on in our neighborhood."

Amara nodded. "I thought you were jumping to conclusions, but now, all of this makes it seem like there's something wrong, maybe a curse."

Sheri looked at her, astonished. "Now you think there's something wrong with the Vulture House? None of us have seen anyone enter or come out of it."

Amara nodded. "There are too many coincidences. You should get your dad to go in there. Vultures are omens of death. There's probably a dozen bodies buried in the backyard."

Sheri shook her head. "Let's go look."

Tanya tilted her chin up. "The sheriff's daughter wants to sneak into someone's house, breaking in?"

Sheri shrugged. "I don't know about that. No one lives there."

Yasmin shook her head. "I've seen enough of the police for a while. Maybe we watch the house this week to see if anyone is going in late at night."

Sheri pointed at Yasmin. "There's a good idea. Let's watch. If we see something, then we can tell my dad."

Tanya laughed. "Only if they're carrying bodies in and out of there."

Sheri leaned forward, hunching her shoulders and waving her arms like a storybook witch. "Oooh, maybe that's where all the bodies are from, the serial killer. They could be right there, just six houses away. Sitting in a macabre BBQ pit in the backyard set up for the killer's glee."

A chill ran down Tanya's spine. "Ok, let's change the subject. I don't want to think about it. Let's set up a watch or something."

Amara started to say something, then sat back.

Tanya saw her. "What, Amara? You were going to say something."

"Nothing. I'll help, too."

She looked at each of them. "We should stick together or be with someone else, just in case."

"Wait, didn't the serial killings also have witnesses? It didn't matter. Only that video from those guys on TikTok caught anything useful. There were probably too many for whatever it was to take them all."

Amara shook her head. "Unless it's an evil spirit or something."

Yasmin stared at her with a puzzled expression. "What do you mean by that?"

"You know, an evil spirit, maybe someone possessed. They left that person's legs there. Someone or something cut him in half. That sounds evil to me."

Yasmin nodded, but said nothing.

"I think we need to pay attention to everything that's happening. There is something dark going on here.

Amara nodded. "I'm going to talk to my imam. Maybe there are wards or something."

Sheri laughed, "Like holy water?"

Amara shot her a look. "You're not taking this seriously, Sheri."

Sheri shook her head. "I said I'm in. I offered to walk down there right now."

Tanya watched the debate between her friends. She didn't want to go. The house gave her an uneasy feeling. She could feel it in her chest every time she walked by. It felt like someone was watching her. An image of her dad looking at her from inside the front windows flashed into her head. "I don't want to go down there. I think we're inviting too much trouble."

Yasmin got up. "If it's ok, I need to check on my grandmother. I'll be back later."

Tanya got up. "Of course. Do you want me or us to go with you?"

"No. I can get in and out without them knowing. If my grandmother is there, I'll talk to her."

"Alright."

Tanya walked her out and went back into the room. "I need a snack."

Amara perked up. "Mmm, I could eat something." She looked at her phone. "I've got a few more hours."

Sheri got up, and the trio went to the kitchen.

Chapter 26

Sunday Night

Tanya held Jackson's leash, giving him a little room to walk ahead of her and Yasmin. His tail wagged eagerly as he crossed back and forth in front of them, not entirely pulling the leash. She hadn't taken him on a walk in months. He ran to every tree, post, and vertical surface near the edge of the sidewalk, inspecting each one and claiming some as his own when the urge hit. His adventures tonight were spotlighted from the lens of a bright survival flashlight.

They crossed the street, heading toward their school. The street looked different. Several more streetlights were out, which made the distant light cast long shadows down the street and eclipsed other areas in darkness. Yasmin looked unfazed. Tanya tried to keep a smile, but she was scared they would be caught in the dark by whatever was casing the neighborhood. Of her small circle of friends, Amara was coming around to her belief that there was a curse or something as sinister. She appreciated the support. Of course, Sheri, as the sheriff's daughter, would lean toward cold facts.

Tanya shivered, though the night was only a cool sixty degrees. It was more from fear than temperature. She looked ahead, counting the lights on in the houses on this side of the street, leading to the dark area of the Vulture House.

"It's dark ahead. Have you seen the Vulture House?"

"I don't know that I've noticed it." She looked behind them and then back up the road. "It all looks the same to me. Suburban houses all in a row."

"I suppose. When you say it that way, I guess it doesn't look as menacing."

"Do you think anyone else is thinking as you are? That there is something evil or a curse?"

"Probably not. Most of the people on this street stick to themselves. They probably didn't know the Burkes, or that someone was murdered so close to them. They are all safe in their homes, oblivious to what goes on in the neighborhood."

"Do you really think this place is cursed?"

"I don't know. I mean, I see Sheri's point. It just feels like it is, but it could be bad luck or my imagination looking for links."

Yasmin walked in silence beside her.

Tanya shined the light ahead, sweeping it across the suburban landscape. The yellowed grass of the yards seemed to glow when the moon peeked out between the clouds. The moonlight shining through the barren branches of cover from the overhanging trees provided an eerie feel to the night.

She heard the scraping of something heavy being rolled. She shined the light up the street to see one of her neighbors rolling their trash bins out. He positioned the recycling bin and rolled it next to the designated spot. Tanya moved the light across the road ahead of them. "That's the Vulture House." She swept it across the street forward of them and onto the edge of the semi-abandoned house.

"It looks like all the others."

With a swift motion, Tanya directed the light towards the roof, where several dark shapes sat in the moonlight. Several large black birds swung their heads toward the girls, their eyes glowing in the light.

"It's the only house I've ever seen with vultures making it their home."

Krsssshhhk. The lone call rang out into the night.

144

The birds leaped into the air. Tanya swung the light around, looking for the vultures. A cool sweat trickled down the back of her neck. She heard wings a moment before a large shape dropped out of the sky close to them. She ducked and turned on the light in time to see the blurred form sweep over them. The sound of wings surrounded them.

Yasmin ducked, looking around for more of the birds.

Tanya was swinging the light around, looking up, when she heard the yelp from Jackson, who came running back to them, two red stripes across his back.

"Yasmin, we need to run." Tanya picked up Jackson as a vulture grazed her arm. "Go!"

They ran down the street near the trees, trying to get as much cover as possible. They crossed the road and ran up the steps when they neared her house. She set Jackson down and reached into her pocket for her keys. Yasmin watched for more birds.

She got the door open, and they were inside the house again.

"They shouldn't do that. Vultures are supposed to only eat carrion," Tanya gasped, out of breath.

"Maybe it was the light. They didn't react until you shined the light on them."

"Oh my gosh, do you think so?"

"We were fine until then."

Tanya looked at the light. "I guess so. I'm sorry, I didn't know they would do that. I need to check out Jackson." She picked up the little dog and took him to the kitchen. "I thought they wouldn't go after living animals."

Yasmin looked at Jackson in Tanya's arms. She touched the scratch on his back, getting a little blood on her hand. Jackson whimpered. "I think there are some that do, and he's small." Yasmin leaned closer to look at Jackson. "It doesn't look too deep."

Tanya spread his short fur around the cut and looked at the wounds with her fingers. "It's not that bad. He's being a baby. Aren't you Jackson?" He started trying to lick her face, his tail wagging quickly. "See, he wants sympathy and probably a cookie."

At the word, his ears popped up, looking at her with a tilted head. She had said the magic word to garner his full attention. Tanya took him to the sink, got a wet paper towel, and dabbed at the cuts. They were superficial. She took out a dog treat and handed it to him as she set him down. He grabbed the bone, walked over to his padded bed, which he rarely used, and lay down, crunching his treat.

"I won't shine the light on the birds next time."

"Probably a good idea."

"If you weren't there to see it, I'd probably think it was the house sending the vultures after me."

"Remember what you said in the library? Some cultures believe vultures are good omens, taking the souls of the recently dead to the afterlife."

"If that's true, I think they were looking for a little snack before they got to escort duties tonight."

Tanya stopped. "The vultures are here, in our neighborhood."

"Yes."

"And there are quite a few."

"Yes."

"Well, good or bad, they must think there is plenty of food around here. A lot more."

Yasmin tilted her head, nodding.

"I need to warn Amara and Sheri."

Chapter 27

Monday Midday

"Ms. Janessy!"

She turned to see Mr. Bilby winding his way through the crowd of students. "How are you doing? I heard about your neighbors. I'm so sorry."

Tanya nodded, unsure of what to say. Rumors were circling the school about the serial killer. She had been asked if she saw something because the police were at her house. She had been getting strange looks all day. It was a mix of pity, fear, and curiosity.

"I wanted to offer you the chance to skip the solo if you are not up for it. I can't imagine what you are going through."

Mr. Bilby looked at her, strands of white hair sticking out to the side. He appeared sincerely concerned.

"I'll be fine. I've been practicing. I'll be ready."

"Well, let me know. We have two more concerts, and I don't want to put undue stress on you." His expression changed from concern to excitement. "What's the song? When can I hear it?"

"I'm still working through it. I don't know the song's name, but it is beautiful. It's a Persian song. Ancient, I believe. I'd like it to be a surprise if it's ok." She hoped he wouldn't press. She hadn't been practicing as much as she should and didn't want him to be worried.

He smiled. "You know I rarely allow that, but I trust you, Ms. Janessy. By the way, I talked to my friend. He has confirmed his attendance. I've been talking you up and he's eager to hear you play."

"Thank you so much for inviting him."

"It's my pleasure. You keep working on that song. I look forward to hearing it. I'll see you in class."

"Yes, sir."

He nodded, turned, and shuffled back through the students. She smiled. Mr. Bilby was one of her favorite teachers. He always gave her the impression of being a warm-hearted grandfather, sitting in a rocking chair, telling stories about famous musicians. She would miss him next year.

She got to her world history class just before the bell sounded. Yasmin's seat was empty. Tanya hadn't seen her friend since they got to school. Her worry intensified as she remembered the incident with the bullies. She could take care of herself. It could be her grandmother came to check on her. She looked out the windows at the dark sky. The weather was cloudy. Not too dark, but the wind had picked up. It wasn't supposed to rain until later. She enjoyed watching the leaves blow around the field on this side of the school. Today, she watched the branches of the trees sway in the wind. The wet leaves stuck to the ground, creating a depressing, wet scene. Tanya looked at Yasmin's empty seat before focusing on the lesson.

Tanya dipped her French fry in ketchup and then mustard before eating it. The noise level increased today. More kids were present, though she wasn't sure how many were eating. Glancing upwards, she noticed them avert their eyes or lower their gaze to their food.

"Just ignore them. Most are idiots believing every rumor that swirls around," Sheri told her.

"Which rumors? That I saw the Burkes get killed or something else?"

"Something else. A few people have asked me if my dad arrested your dad as the serial killer." Sheri looked nervous.

"What!"

"I said no, but I'm not about to spread your business all over the school. They don't need to know what happened."

Tanya leaned in. "That explains all of this." She swirled her finger around. "Are they going to follow me, too?" She dropped her voice to a whisper. "I don't need them crashing the meeting tonight."

"Are you sure you still want to go?"

"I do. I want to talk to Diane and tell her what happened with my dad."

"My dad wants me to go straight home and text when I get there."

"I'll be fine. Hopefully, Yasmin will show up. I haven't seen her since this morning."

Sheri looked at her, then looked up and waved.

Tanya turned to see Amara and Yasmin coming toward them.

Amara sat next to Tanya, and Yasmin sat next to Sheri. Amara sat back in her chair and looked around at the other students as if holding court. She had a thin-lipped smile, her raven hair in a long, thick braid. Their stares were turned away as they got the message to ignore the group.

After taming the crowd, Amara scooched her chair up to the table and lowered her voice. "I have some news."

Tanya looked to the side, whispering back. "Is it about me?"

"Not just you. Yesterday, my tutor informed my father that I lacked focus. When I spoke with him, I expressed my concern about you and everything that's happening."

"Amara!"

"I didn't say it was all about you, specifically. I said it was everything going on in the city. He didn't get as upset as I thought. But he took me to see our imam. I went through it again—"

Yasmin snorted, "What did he have to say?"

"He asked questions about you, the birds, and the murders."

Tanya looked at Yasmin and then back to Amara. "What did you tell him?"

Amara looked down at her hands. Her confident look faded. "I told him what happened this weekend about the murder, your dad, and even the pets."

Tanya looked at her friend. She knew she had broken their trust.

Amara leaned in. "I know you might be mad at me, but listen. He thinks that there is something evil near."

Tanya sat up, shocked. "He believes us?"

"Yes, and he says we have to be careful because there are too many coincidences around us, or you three." She looked from Tanya to Sheri and Yasmin.

Sheri shook her head. "It's just bad luck."

Yasmin shook her head. "I agree with Sheri. It's bad luck, not evil spirits and whatever."

Tanya shook her head. "I think it's something dark."

Sheri looked at her with confusion. "Tanya, it's fun to talk about the occult, evil, and spirits, but look at it scientifically."

Tanya turned on her, "Don't do that, don't dismiss me. I know what I feel!"

Sheri raised her hand. "Sorry, fine. You're right. I don't know how you feel."

Tanya looked around the table. Her mood had gone from blah to disappointment. They were supposed to be here for her.

"I need to go to my locker before class. I'll see you all later. I'm gonna study in the library after school before the meeting tonight."

Sheri shook her head. "If you think there's evil, do you think you should attend those meetings?"

Tanya shrugged. "I won't be alone." She looked at Yasmin.

"No. I'll be there," Yasmin replied.

A loud rumbling came from the large windows. The wind had gusted, and they could see people coming back inside. Their loose clothing was blown almost horizontally by the wind.

Chapter 28

Monday Afternoon

Tanya sat in her usual spot at the back of the library. Instead of focusing on schoolwork, she had her attention elsewhere. She had found a couple of books on hauntings, possessions, and the ghosts of Texas. While thumbing through them quickly, she found nothing that sounded similar to the situation they were in. She searched through the books on the library app but found nothing on vultures and the paranormal. Rather than the typical turkey vultures she had grown up seeing, she identified the birds as black vultures.

She felt frustrated, grabbed her phone, and typed in the address of the Vulture House. Before she could get through, she saw Yasmin enter the library and go to her little table.

"Hey," Tanya greeted her.

"You've been busy." Tanya turned a few of the books over, looking at the titles. "Did you find anything?"

"No, lots of info on hauntings, not much on evil places. I was about to search for the house address to see if anything bad happened there."

"Let's go to the meeting. Get your mind off of this."

Tanya placed the books in the return bin on her way out.

Tanya and Yasmin left the school and walked over to the church building. They went to the meeting room and straight to the refreshments table. Yasmin poured a cup of hot water and pulled a packet from her pocket, emptying the contents into the cup and stirring it in. Tanya smelled the bitter liquid and wrinkled her nose.

She spooned a third serving of sugar into her coffee and reached for the French vanilla creamer.

Yasmin looked askance at her coffee. "Maybe we should both be brave and trade drinks."

Tanya raised her eyebrows and took a sip, letting the smell of the bitter-sweet liquid complement the taste. "Maybe, but not tonight." She opened her eyes and moved to the side. "There aren't as many people."

Yasmin nodded, narrowing her eyes and looking at those in attendance.

Diane approached them and said, "Girls. I'm glad you made it. I've gotten a few calls from people saying they're scared."

Tanya looked from Yasmin to Diane. "I had to come. Something happened at home."

Diane's eyes quickly shifted to her cheek and back to her eyes. "Do you want to talk about it?"

"I do. I want to share what happened."

Diane patted her arm. "Do you need anything?"

"Not right now."

"Ok, you let me know. We'll start in a few minutes if you want to find a seat."

Tanya and Yasmin crossed through the middle of the circle, going to the other side, facing the doors.

When the last group reached their seats, Diane moved into the circle in her regular position near the dry-erase boards.

"I know some of you have noticed that a few of our regular participants are missing." Diane paused, letting a few whispered conversations die down.

"I know that you've seen the news. Someone has been assaulting people in our community. Sharon was a witness to one of the first attacks, and the victim from the video, I am sure you all saw, was her boyfriend. Three other people have disappeared. The missing people are people who knew the ladies missing from the meeting tonight."

"What are you saying?" a middle-aged redhead asked. "Are we being targeted by the blood pool killer?"

"What's going on?" another shouted.

"Why didn't you cancel the meeting? You put us all in danger."

The lights went out. The room was so dark she couldn't see anything. Tanya heard screams on either side and chairs crashing to the floor.

"Yasmin!" She reached to her right. The seat was empty.

The lights flickered back on. Yasmin was lying on the floor.

Screams erupted again. The woman who had spoken up was sprawled on the floor across the circle, her torso torn open from her throat to her groin. Blood flowed around her, down the sides, onto the floor. Tanya's heart skipped a beat and felt like it leaped into her throat. She couldn't scream. She reached down to grab Yasmin and run for the doors and caught Diane staring at the body, blood on her hands.

"Let's go!" Tanya pulled Yasmin up and started to run toward the doors. She slowed when the lights went out again. Something large hit her, knocking her down, and she lost grip on Yasmin.

"Tanya!" she heard her friend say. She couldn't see anything. The echoes of the lights prevented her eyes from adjusting. "Yasmin! Yasmin!" She pushed herself up and started crawling in the direction she had felt Yasmin get pulled. She felt around on the floor and put her hand on something wet and sticky. *Blood! Oh my God, it's blood.* She stopped moving and started to back away. Something hit her in the ribs, knocking her breath out. She heard a cry as someone hit the tile floor near her. A light appeared. Someone pulled out their phone. She reached for her phone. The light flew, spinning, and a wet, meaty sound hit the wall.

Tanya's imagination took off. That was an arm. Something cut someone's arm off. Her stomach lurched. *No! I will not get caught here!* She tried to remember where she was and where the doors were. Tanya couldn't see anything, though the light globes had faded. Her ribs hurt. "Is someone there?" she called out. She heard whimpering to her left.

The lights came back on, and she saw a handful of women down, not moving, staring whichever way they had fallen. She noticed Yasmin rise and move in her direction. Tanya looked to where Diane was before. The counselor was on her knees, and blood stained the bottom of her face. Tanya tried to stand and slipped in the blood on the floor, falling back and hitting her head. She saw stars.

The lights went out. *Find the doors to get out.* She shook her head, trying to clear the fuzziness. Tanya thought she knew where the door was and started inching toward them. Yasmin was coming toward her. She glanced back to where she had seen Diane and froze. She saw eyes, red and yellow, looking right at her. Two burning coals pierced the darkness.

She heard another scream. Someone must have seen the eyes. She got up and moved toward the door. She felt someone grab her arm and slide down to take her hand. "Tanya?"

"Yes. Did you? Did you see Diane?"

"Something knocked me out of my chair. Let's get out of here." She pulled Tanya. Tanya heard the doors slam open against the hallway wall. She stood up, let go of Yasmin's hand, and ran down the hall toward the main doors.

They hit the doors at a full run, throwing them open as they burst into the night. Tanya pulled her phone out and dialed 9-1-1.

The hall outside the meeting room wasn't as dark, with lights from outside coming through the windows. When they reached the glass double doors, they pushed them open and crossed the street toward the football field. "What is the nature of the emergency?"

"Someone attacked us at the Cedar Ridge Community Church by the high school. People are dead. The person is still inside. Send someone now!"

"Ma'am, please try to stay calm. We are directing units to your location. Can you tell me your name?"

"Tanya. Tanya Janessy. There's blood. Something attacked us!"

"Ma'am, was the person armed?"

"I think they had a knife."

"Ok, a unit will be there in less than a minute. Are you safe?"

"I don't know. I don't know. We ran across the street to the high school."

"Try to get somewhere safe, well lit. I will stay on the line with you until the officers arrive."

Tanya started crying.

She saw the flashing lights of the police as two cars pulled up in front of the building.

"The police are here. You need to send an ambulance."

"Tanya. I have contacted the officers on the scene. Do you think you can make your way to them?"

"Yes."

"Ok, Tanya, an officer is waiting for you. An ambulance is on the way. It will be there in about five minutes. Try to get to the officers."

Tanya stopped and looked back. The lights for the building were on. She watched as two police officers entered the building and started moving down the hall, visible through the windows.

"Let's go. The police are waiting for us."

Yasmin shook her head. "I can't go back over there. I don't want to see it. I-I-I. The blood, I keep seeing my mother. I can't."

"We need to tell them what happened."

"You go. I'll wait here. Give me a few minutes to calm down. I'll try to come over." She sat down against the stadium wall. Looking down into her lap.

"Ok, I'll be right over there. They'll want you to tell them what you saw."

"I know, I will. Just not right now."

Tanya stared at Yasmin. She got up and headed back toward the police. She made fists as she went, trying to stop the trembling.

Her stomach turned in knots as she approached the street. *What if it gets out? I'm walking right back toward the danger. But the police are here. I should be safe. But the blood.* She looked down at her hand. The blood was drying. She shook her hand. Realizing where she was. She stopped in the street. *I can't go back. I can't.* She looked at her hands. There was blood. She had someone else's blood all over her. A hand grabbed her arm. She screamed.

"Tanya! Tanya, you're safe. I've got you." When she looked up, she locked eyes with Officer Hendercriss.

As she threw her arms around her, a dam broke. With tears streaming down her face, she collapsed. "I saw her. Diane had blood on her hands and her face. I think it was her. Her eyes glowed like fire."

"Tanya. Calm down. Breathe slowly." She was unaware of the two EMTs helping her to the back of one of the arriving ambulances.

"The eyes, they glowed. Diane. Blood."

"She's in shock. We'll check her out," said one of the EMTs.

Tanya became aware of a blonde woman looking into her eyes, asking her something. "What?"

"Tanya, my name is Beth. Are you hurt? Is this your blood?"

She shook her head. "It was on the floor. It was dark. I crawled through it. I don't know her name. She was mad. The lights went out, and someone cut her."

"Tanya, is there someone we can call?"

"My mom. I have my phone." She pulled it out of her pocket and dropped it when the screen lit up.

"It saw the light from the phone. It attacked the light."

"What did? What attacked you?"

"Diane. Diane attacked us, but why? Why would she do that?"

"Relax, Tanya, Drink this, it's water."

Tanya did as asked. The second EMT, an older man with short, black, graying hair, handed her the phone. "Tanya, can you call your mom to come down here?"

Tanya nodded, looked up at the man, and took her phone.

She hit dial on the phone.

Around her, more police cars had arrived, accompanied by ambulances. Officers had their guns out, keeping the EMTs back as they entered the church building.

"Hello, honey."

"Mom, please come get me. There's so much blood."

"Where are you?"

"I'm at the church across the street from my school."

Chapter 29

Tuesday Morning

Knock, Knock, Knock.

Her mom opened the door, peeking in and holding a tray. "Tanya honey, I made you lunch."

"I'm not hungry, Mom."

"Sweetie, you need to eat something."

"Don't call me that! Don't treat me like a little girl."

Her mom nodded apprehensively, "You're right. I'm sorry."

"Stop it! Just stop it! Why are you so submissive? Why do you put up with all of Dad's crap? Why are you taking this from me? Be a parent! Be my mom. I'm not looking for sympathy from you. I want your support."

"I am supporting you. I made lunch. I let you rest."

Tanya glared at her. It's the same. The same as when Dad was here. She's so passive. Does she need approval? Tanya turned away, looking out the window and pulling the covers up.

"I'll eat later." She let the anger creep into her tone.

Her ears caught the sound of the door closing. She stared out the window at the overcast sky. She attempted to sleep, but her night was restless, haunted by nightmares.

Tanya shifted, staring at the ceiling. She had to go back to school. She could only imagine what the rumors would be. Poor Tanya, more bad luck, more murders. The recital was three days away. *I need to practice. I need to get out of here.* She opened her phone, swiping through social media. The police hadn't found Diane. Someone killed four women. Six others were suffering the same catatonic state as the two serial killer witnesses. The police and media were now saying that the investigation had taken an unexpected turn, with Diane being the primary suspect, wanted for questioning. Despite what Tanya had told the police, no one had witnessed her doing anything. People were spreading rumors on X that someone had sent the toxin used to put people in a coma to the FBI forensics lab. Crazier stories implied Diane was a CIA operative gone rogue, using top-secret neurotoxins designed for soft assassinations.

"People will look for a conspiracy anywhere."

The police had searched the building with no luck. The SWAT arrived from Dallas Police after the local sheriff's department had secured the perimeter around the building. She didn't know how long it was before they had entered, or what else happened after Yasmin and she escaped.

Sitting upright, she looked around. As she got out of bed, she took a moment to look in the mirror. She had tangled hair and the dark circles under her puffy eyes stood out. She glanced at the food tray her mom had placed on her dresser. Cranberry juice and a small plate of her favorite berries—strawberries, blackberries, and raspberries. She took a bite of the berry mix and looked at her flute resting on its stand.

"After my shower." She tried to push the images from her mind, but they kept creeping back in when she didn't expect it. With resolve, she focused on the music. She was not in the mood to put up with mistakes. She would master and memorize that song and show everyone she was ok.

Tanya dried her hair and put it in a large twirled bun on the back of her head. She took the tray downstairs and stopped to scratch Jackson behind the ears when he sat at her feet in the kitchen.

Making coffee, she filled the large mug and went upstairs. With a sip of the hot beverage, she tasted the bitterness. She didn't want the sweet sugar and milk mixture to mask the bitterness. *That's my problem. Everything has been hidden.*

She set the coffee down on her desk, picked up the flute, wiped the instrument down, and rolled her lips, making sure they were moist. Tanya felt comfortable with the first two-thirds of the song, but the last part was tricky. She flipped the pages of the music to the desired section.

She played the previous part in her head. The melody's airy, ethereal portion dropped an octave, creating a sense of foreboding and a promise of action. She felt the music as she played. Her anger and fear from the attack fueled her desire to get through the song. She played fervently, effortlessly transitioning between the sections, jumping back and forth as if in a discussion or plea for help.

She missed a flat and stopped playing at the sharp break in the flow. With a renewed determination, she flipped the pages back and started again. As the song filled the room, an ominous feeling filled her. The clouds outside darkened as the air in the room grew thick. Cautiously, the music flowed from her flute, fearful of missing another note. Her fear turned to an image of Diane standing in the room, blood on her hands and around her mouth. She was biting the victims.

Another mistake derailed the song.

"Damnit!"

She began again, playing with determination, her breaths punctuating the notes, enhancing the song's flow. It sounded better. She let the forcefulness drive her. She continued, pushing through the decision point. The agreement or acquiescence of the request comes with the determination of her will. The music took on a life of its own. As the notes rose off the page, they flowed into the air, circling her. She lost herself in the tune, feeling the music press down on her. The feeling was welcome, partnership, and a new world of possibility. Apprehension welled up inside her, and she attacked the music, escalating the tempo and perceiving the music as her fingers glided over the keys on the flute. She turned the last page and built through the climax before dropping to the soft overarching melody masterfully weaved throughout the song. As she stopped playing, she could feel the tension in the room release. Making no mistake, she finished. Drained from the back and forth, it was as if she had endured a battle of wills or a physical contest. She had pushed through. With confidence, she knew she could play the entire song. Her performance would leave the audience in awe. It would be like nothing they had ever heard. Still, she felt disconnected. Something was missing, and she couldn't figure out what it was.

Chapter 30

Wednesday Morning

Tanya left her house earlier than usual. Sheri wouldn't be along for another fifteen minutes. She wasn't ready to talk to her. Sheri should have called. She crossed the street. Uncertain of what to expect, she walked towards school with her eyes down. She had entered the school year wanting to enjoy her senior year with her friends. Each of them had been pulled away by everything that was happening. Maybe this was a more realistic ending to her childhood—a fresh break.

As she walked, she felt a little longing in her heart. Amara, Sheri, and she had been friends since elementary school. There had been difficulties, but nothing like this. She missed them and held that against them. She needed them to believe, support, and be there for her, and they weren't.

Honk!

She jumped, looking up to see her dad's BMW parked on the wrong side of the street ahead of her.

She slowed as the door opened and he got out. He was wearing a gray suit with a white shirt and no tie. His hair was styled to the side, and she noted the scent of the gel he used to keep it in place.

"Tanya, I heard what happened. Are you ok?"

She reached up, touching the side of her face where he had backhanded her. She looked around. The street was empty. "Daddy, you're not supposed to be within a hundred yards of us."

"I know. I just wanted to see how you and your mom were doing. I saw you on the news."

"I'm doing fine."

"Tanya, I'm sorry. I shouldn't have done that, but you attacked me."

"Unbelievable." She turned to move around him, but he stepped in her way. She had an unsettling sensation in her stomach.

"If you could talk to your mom, I could come home. I'd be able to protect you. You know that. I've always kept you safe."

Krssshhhk.

She jumped, looking past her dad to the house across the street. No trees were blocking her view of the vultures perched on the roof. She looked up and observed five more circling. She felt someone grab her arm, and she screamed, yanking away on reflex. The hand let go.

"Honey, it's me. Did you hear what I said? Are you ok? I've got a meeting with your mom and a mediator later. I'm going to do better. I promise."

Tanya didn't believe him. He had said the same thing to her mother before. Each time, he failed to keep his promise with something worse than the last. The image of him slowly turning his head, smiling, his hand in her mother's chest, flashed into her head. She jerked away, stepping back into the grass. The large black birds were watching her. Who was next? Who were they waiting to take to the afterlife? There had been so much death already.

"*Krssshhhk,*" a bird called out, stretching its wings to the side, looking like an angel of death.

"I-I've got to get to school." She turned away and walked up the street. She wanted to run from her father and the vultures. Fear threatened to overtake her. Breathing was difficult. She walked fast, almost jogging.

"I'll see you later, Tanya."

She couldn't determine if it was a threat or his way of concealing everything, but she didn't care. Tanya wanted to get away. At the main intersection, she looked back and saw that her dad was gone. She turned around to cross the street and almost ran into Yasmin.

"Yasmin, where have you been? I was worried. Did you talk to the police?"

"No. I walked home."

"Are you ok? What happened?"

"Nothing. My grandmother was angry; she didn't know where I was. Then she said I was a woman and could care for myself. She's not going to worry about my coming and going."

"That seems harsh."

Yasmin shrugged.

The crosswalk lit up and they started walking. Tanya could feel the stares as she got closer to school. Yasmin looked around. "They're whispering. They don't know what to think. Confused little lambs."

"I choose to ignore them."

Yasmin stepped to the side, looking Tanya up and down, a determined look on her face.

Tanya continued, "I'm not going to give them or the little rumor mills what they're looking for. Poor little Tanya, breaking down and running away."

"Good for you!"

Tanya looked toward the school. "Besides, we're just as likely to die here as anywhere else."

Yasmin grinned slyly. "That's true. Poor little lambs."

Tanya and Yasmin walked into the school together, eyes focused, not reacting to the whispers as they passed.

"I have to go to the office. I'll see you at lunch."

"Ok." Yasmin headed for the stairs to the second floor.

Tanya entered the office, and it got quiet. Tanya refused to look around, feeling the eyes of faculty and students alike watching her. She approached the desk. "I'm supposed to see the assistant principal."

The woman smiled thinly, nodding and picking up a sticky note. "You can go in."

Tanya entered the small office. Knick-knacks, awards, pictures, and student gifts decorated the small office. No horizontal surface beside the desk escaped. More of the clutter covered the sides of her desk. Despite the chaos, Tanya could see a pattern in the placement. Everything had its place. Mrs. Adams stood, walking around the desk to sit in the front row of chairs, indicating she should sit in the other.

She wore her light brown hair in a bob. Her eyes were kind, and she looked to be forcing a smile. "Tanya, I was so sorry to hear about your ordeal. How are you doing?"

"I'm doing as well as I can, I guess."

"How is everything at home?"

"What do you mean?" She couldn't know what was going on with her father. She must have heard the rumors.

"Are you ok? I can only imagine the stress you are currently going through."

"I'll be all right."

"I wanted to let you know that we're here to support you in whatever you need. We have spoken to the police. They're going to increase their presence on campus."

"That's good."

"Do you feel you're ready to come back? If you need time to work through your feelings, the district has available grief counselors. Just let us know."

"Ma'am, I've got to deal with all of this and move on, or it will drag me down. Thank you for the offer. If I need something, I'll ask. I just want to get back to normal."

"Ok. I understand you're supposed to perform at the recital this weekend. No one would blame you for stepping aside."

Rage boiled up inside of her. "No!" She took a breath. "No, ma'am. I have worked hard for this and want to do it."

Mrs. Adams jumped at the outburst but recovered from Tanya's request. "Ok, I look forward to hearing you play. I'll let you head to class." She looked at the clock over her door. "There's enough time, you won't need a note. Please let me know if you need anything."

"I will, ma'am, thank you, and I'm sorry for my outburst."

Chapter 31

Wednesday Midday

Tanya took longer than expected at her locker. She waited until the crowd in the hall dissipated, students leaving for their next class or lunch. She looked toward the cafeteria and saw only a few students lingering behind. Lost in thought, she strolled down the hall, her eyes downward, focusing on where she was walking. By the time she got through the line, the constant noise of clashing voices filled the place. She saw Amara and Sheri at one of the small round tables near the windows. She selected her food and politely acknowledged the cafeteria workers as she made her way through the line before heading to her friends' table.

"Amara, Sheri."

Amara looked up. "Hey, are you ok?"

"If another person asks me that, I'm gonna lose it. I'm at school, so I'm fine."

"You know we're just concerned about you."

Tanya nodded, picking up a small fork full of mashed potatoes. Her frustration boiled over. "Were you *really* concerned? Because you didn't call yesterday or come to see me. Were you at home with Daddy's tutor?" She took a bite of mixed vegetables from her plate.

"That's harsh, Tanya. Of course, I care. You're my friend!" Amara sat back in her chair, crossed her arms, and looked to the side. She looked hurt.

"Hey. I stopped by this morning to get you." Sheri set her fork down on the lunch tray.

Tanya didn't answer. She felt torn and angry with her friends. She didn't want to hurt them, but it was frustrating.

"I'm glad you're here," Sheri insisted.

"Are you? Are either of you actually worried? Why didn't you stop by to check on me yesterday?" Tears were rolling down her cheeks.

A pained look crossed Sheri's face. "I wanted to, but my dad—"

Tanya dropped her fork on her plate, pushing the tray back. "Your dad? Your dad what? Wouldn't let you stop by or text your supposed best friend, nothing?"

Sheri looked away.

"How many times have I stayed at both of your houses?" She paused. "More than I can count. They know we're friends. I could have died, and your excuse is that your dad wouldn't let you, or recommended against it, or some other lame-ass excuse."

She pointed at Sheri. "You haven't been there since you took me the first time. You didn't know any of those women. Betty, Melanie, Gabrielle, and Samantha. Those names mean nothing to you, do they? But I know their names because I was there when they were killed. Three people made it out of there. Me, Yasmin, and Diane escaped, but they haven't located Diane yet, so she's the primary suspect. We could all be dead right now."

She noticed the stares coming from around the cafeteria. No one said anything. Tanya didn't look around. She looked between Amara and Sheri. Both appeared hurt and ashamed. She felt guilt creep in, but she pushed it down.

"I can't rely on either of you. You don't realize it, but you're as trapped as I am by my dad. I guess it's as good a time as any to find out what our friendship is worth." She looked at Yasmin, picked up her tray, and walked out, dumping the tray in the trash.

Tanya stepped into the hall and fell back against the wall. Her tears continued to fall. Sound erupted from the lunchroom as they reacted to her words. Although she didn't want to care, she was aware that her outburst would contribute to the spread of more rumors. She refused to become a victim. Wiping her eyes, she made her way to class.

The rest of the school day was a blur. She tuned out everyone and remembered nothing anyone said to her. None of her teachers called on her, which made the day a little easier to deal with. She left the school and looked down her street in a daze. Most trees had lost their leaves, making the road look gloomy. She didn't want to go home yet and headed to the side of the school with picnic tables. Sometimes, the school clubs would meet outside. She hoped that the dreary weather would keep them away.

Few people were outside. She picked a table furthest from the doors. There were plenty to choose from. She had gotten lucky for once this year. No, that's not right. Introducing Yasmin into her friend group had been a lucky move. The images from two nights before flashed in her head—the dark, light, dark, light, and all the blood. Yasmin was there for her in the end. She was the one bright spot lately. The evil of her father scarred another broken soul. They were now connected by a horrific tragedy. Yasmin's life experience was worse. She had seen her father kill her mother just because she disagreed with him. Tanya thought of her mom lying on the floor of the kitchen. She saw the look on her friend's face. Yasmin had glared at her father, her jaw muscles clenched. A beep from her phone interrupted Tanya's thoughts. Her mom would get worried if she didn't call soon.

Startled by a car horn, she looked up from her phone. She thought of the morning talk that her dad had said about meeting with her mom. She couldn't let that happen. Her dad wouldn't change. She saw it in his eyes, the same manipulation he used on her mom. She called.

"Hello, honey."

"Mom, I saw Dad on the way to school this morning."

"Where?"

"A few houses down from ours."

"He shouldn't be there."

"I know. He said you were meeting with a mediator."

The line was silent.

"Mom?"

"That's not entirely true. We are meeting with a mediator to work things out for a divorce."

"Oh, thank God."

"I'm sorry I didn't tell you. I thought you'd be upset."

"I'm not. He's bad for us. I was worried you might let him back in. I know he's my dad, but he's not a good person. Mom, you deserve someone that will treat you right."

"He wasn't always like that."

"Mom, don't make excuses for him. I've been reading the materials from the domestic violence support group. He manipulates us."

"I don't know. It's been like this since he had to get out of the Navy."

"Mom, you've heard him talk about his days at Annapolis. He was angry, the same as on the ship. It was always someone else's fault. He doesn't respect women."

"Don't you worry about me."

"Someone has to."

"Will you be home soon?"

"I'm about to leave."

"Ok, be careful. Love you."

"Love you too, Mom."

Chapter 32

Wednesday Evening

Seated at the kitchen table, Tanya dipped chocolate chip cookies into a small glass of milk. Besides yogurt, it was her go-to snack for comfort, but it provided no solace today. She almost allowed a slight upturn of her mouth as she noticed Jackson's head moving in tandem with her hand bringing the cookie from the milk to her mouth.

"You little beggar." She broke a piece off, making sure it didn't have any chocolate chips in it, and handed it to him.

Her phone buzzed.

> Dad: I know what you did!

She stared at the screen, debating whether to answer the text.

> Tanya: I don't know what you're talking about, Dad.

> Dad: You turned your mother against me.

> Tanya: I haven't talked to her yet.

Dad: She told the mediator she wanted a divorce.

Tanya: That's her choice.

Dad: Don't you lie to me!

Tanya: I don't need this right now.

Dad: You and your mother are going to regret this!

Tanya: Is that a threat, Dad?

Dad: No! But you better talk to her. You two need to find somewhere else to stay. That is my house. I paid for everything.

Tanya: We'll see.

Dad: Don't you get smart with me. You're going to end up just like your mother, a weak, dependent leech, sucking the life out of some poor guy.

Tanya: I'm blocking you.

Tanya blocked her dad's number. She felt a slight hint of regret and worried they would have to move. Maybe this would help convince her mom to follow her to whatever school she got into. Her mom could find an apartment nearby. For a moment, she smiled before her sour mood took over. She dunked another cookie in her milk, while scrolling through her phone. There was nothing new from the police. She had seen two patrol cars on her walk home, so Sheri's dad was at least doing that.

Tanya thought of her best friend. She saw the hurt in Sheri's eyes when she went off on them at lunch. Maybe she had been too hard on her friends. She took another cookie out of the package and dipped it in her milk for a few seconds before biting off the soft milk-soaked side of the cookie. They had been friends for so long and had survived a few fights, but this was different. This was real. It wasn't about liking someone, disagreeing on a movie, or any other dumb reason. She could have died. Someone else's blood had covered her hands.

Still, Sheri was listening to her dad and staying safe. Tanya had no way to know. The same went for Amara. Schoolwork was everything to her parents. She sighed. Yasmin was there, though. Tanya wanted to call her, but she didn't have a phone and didn't want one. She would need one. Eventually, everyone did.

Jackson whined. He was at the back door, looking expectantly at her after giving up on getting another bite of a cookie.

"I got you." She got up and opened the door. She was about to walk away but noticed the dark shapes sitting on the back fence. Jackson ran out into the yard, barking at the birds. Fear shot through her. She lunged for the pantry door, opening it and grabbing a broom before running into the yard.

She uttered a piercing scream and swung the broom in the air. The birds looked at her and then took off into the night sky.

Krsssshhhk.

"Oh my God, Jackson, are you trying to get eaten?"

He looked up at her, his tail wagging.

Tanya shook her head and looked up at the sky. "You better hurry so we can get you back inside."

"Arr, Arr, Arr," he barked at the back fence where the birds had gone. An act of defiance, and he began sniffing around the yard.

Tanya realized the clouds had parted just enough to let a glimmer of moonlight through. Her dad hadn't gotten around to fixing the lights. She felt uneasy.

"Let's go, Jackson."

The darkness crept closer. She spun at a noise from the side of the house. Her eyes darted around. Her mind filled with images of what had been hidden in the darkness at the church. She felt pressure on her chest.

"Jackson, let's go." Her eyes searched for the dog. When she spotted him, she ran over and grabbed him. He gave a little yelp of surprise. She ran through the back door, closing it and twisting the lock.

She looked out the window, her breathing heavy.

"I'm ok, I'm ok. The police are outside."

She closed the curtains to the patio and all the windows around the house.

Her mom said that she would be late. She had applied for a job at a restaurant. They closed at eleven, and then she'd help wrap everything up. After checking the front door to ensure it was locked, Tanya went to her room.

She closed her bedroom door and locked it, shutting the curtains and turning on all three lamps. She did not want the faintest shadow, if possible. Tanya sat at her desk and opened her laptop. She searched the local news and found a story from earlier about the continued search for Diane. The spokesperson said that they were following several leads. She had trusted Diane. They all had. Something had made the woman snap, taking advantage of victims, lulling them into a false sense of security, and then using them. Tanya felt sick to her stomach at the betrayal of trust. She recognized her trauma, but she couldn't understand the other's pain. Violence and abuse affected each of them. As she thought once more of the women who were killed, tears welled up in her eyes. She swallowed and set her focus on the determined resistance. She did not choose to be a victim. Her emotions shifted to anger. She would not be controlled by anyone else. Her life was hers.

With the laptop closed, she turned her attention to the sheet music. As her emotional roller coaster continued, she smiled. The music drew her in. She could feel the melody inside her. With her flute in hand, she turned the pages back to the beginning. She began the song and felt the now familiar change in her emotions and the atmosphere in the room. She longed to share the song with the entire assembly.

Ding!

Sheri: Hey, I'm sorry. I really want to talk.

Tanya stopped playing and read the message. The urge to play caught her attention. She lifted the flute, then set it down in her lap.

Tanya: Me too. Can you come by early?

Sheri: Yeah, of course.

She switched her phone to silent and set it down. She didn't want to think of anything else but the song. The melody rolled through her thoughts.

Chapter 33

Thursday Morning

Tanya stood inside the door, her jacket and boots on. The clouds were thick and looked like they would burst at any moment. When she saw Sheri come up the steps, she opened the door and stepped out into the cool, dark morning.

"Hey."

"I miss you."

Tanya nodded.

"Look, my dad is protective, but I should have been there for you."

"Sher, I was selfish. If you and Amara had been there, it could have been worse. You don't know how bad it was. I haven't slept much since. I keep seeing Diane and the dead people. If it weren't for Yasmin, I don't know if I would have made it out."

Sheri looked ashamed. "I'm glad that she was there. I don't know what I would do if I lost you."

"I'm glad she was there, too. I don't want to lose you either." Tanya felt her heart warm. She smiled.

"Amara is upset. She had something she wanted to tell you. Before," she let the words hang in the air.

"Before I let the whole school know how upset I was?"

"Yeah. Let's get her and we can talk before school."

"Ok."

They started up the street, and both were quiet as they walked, looking down and watching the ground pass under their feet. Tanya looked up in time to see a blue BMW go by. She turned to watch it speed by her house and bend at the corner.

"Was that your dad?"

"Yeah, he's upset. They're going to get divorced."

Sheri shook her head.

"It's all right. He's not a good man. My mom deserves better."

"I know. It's just more crap for you to deal with."

"That's what friends are for, right?"

"Yeah."

Tanya stopped to look at the Vulture House. "The birds are gone."

"Good, maybe whatever death omens they were bringing with them have moved on."

Tanya looked at the house, not feeling anything. "You believe in death omens now?"

Sheri shrugged. "I have a reliable source, so maybe I can consider the possibility."

Tanya smiled and leaned over, bumping her shoulder.

They passed the next few houses, turning in toward Amara's house. Tanya always loved how vibrant the flowers looked, even after a week of cold temperatures. Amara's parents spent most of the weekend outside tending to the colorful flower gardens. "I love their flowers; they never have a down season. It's always so colorful."

The door opened and Amara came out. "Sheri called me. How are you feeling?"

"As good as I can. I'm still terrified of the dark and see the images everywhere."

Amara reached inside the door, picked up her bag, and threw it over her shoulder. She wore skinny jeans, knee-high brown boots, a brown jacket, and an off-white turtleneck. Her hair hung over both shoulders.

"It's not fair."

"What?"

"You always look gorgeous."

Amara smiled and turned around. "I know. I'm torn between becoming an aerospace engineer or a supermodel."

Tanya rolled her eyes. "Sheri said you had something you wanted to tell me."

They started walking toward school.

"Not just you, all of us, Yasmin, too. My dad heard what I was talking about with our imam and lost it. He started telling stories from when he was little of similar things happening in my grandfather's town. He said there were unexplained deaths, bad luck, and sick animals. It went on for most of the season before it stopped."

Tanya nodded. "How did they get rid of whatever it was?"

"He doesn't know. He remembers his grandmother bringing home small red tassels, like from the ends of Persian rugs. She told him they were special, blessed against evil. He said she made everyone carry one with them."

Tanya thought about it. "That sounds like magic to me, or superstitious occultism."

"Hey, I've been with you on something bad being in the neighborhood."

"Does he know where to get these tassels?"

"I don't know. They talked about evil and our decisions, inviting Iblis into our hearts. Before you ask, Iblis is Satan to Christians, the same concept."

Tanya walked in silence. "So, the devil is in our neighborhood?"

"I don't know about that. But it might be an evil spirit trying to do bad things."

"Let's not let our imaginations run all over the place. While the Devil in the neighborhood would be bad, remember that you told the police that you saw Diane attack those women. I support you, but I'm leaning more toward psychotic serial killers. Has anyone investigated her past?"

Tanya shrugged. "I assume the police are, and the media. The thing is, no one is saying anything, and she's hiding somewhere. For all we know, she's watching us right now, waiting for her revenge because I identified her."

Sheri looked around. "I didn't think of that."

"It's been two days. She could have driven to either the coast or Mexico by now," Amara added.

"I wish," Tanya said with a sigh.

"Amara, what about the vultures? Did they say anything about that?"

"Not really. I may not have stressed it."

Tanya turned, walking backward and looking at her friends. "Well, they're gone today, so maybe that's a good sign."

Sheri shook her head. "Or it could mean that there are plenty of souls to escort because Diane killed more people."

"Are you serious or mocking the situation?"

"C'mon Tanya, they're birds, not supernatural beings. A dead deer on the highway probably has their attention."

"I thought you were going to support me."

Sheri shrugged. "Support doesn't mean blindly following. I'll listen, but you need to respect my opinions, too."

Tanya raised her voice. "I respect your opinions, even though I think they're wrong."

Sheri was about to retort, but Amara was shaking her head. She looked away across the street.

"Don't forget this affects all of us. You still have your dog. Unlike my dog and the others, your dog wasn't poisoned."

"Poisoned? What are you talking about?"

"We got the report from the vet on Tuesday. The vet told my dad that Benny and several other dogs in our neighborhood, including Coolio, showed signs of botulinum toxin."

"Someone poisoned them?"

"According to her, it can be found in mushrooms and other natural places. So it could just be a random strain of fungus that blew in and spread in our yards."

Tanya walked in silence. Poisoned—She would look it up. If it occurred naturally, she and Jackson were fortunate. If someone tried to kill all the dogs, why was Jackson spared? It made little sense. It had to be something natural, which didn't rule out bad karma. She wanted to bring it up, but didn't feel like arguing with Sheri. She didn't know what was wrong with her friend. They didn't see this the same.

Tanya looked over at Sheri before looking down at her feet, plodding along. Sheri fixated on the school. *She's likely stewing because she knows I'm right. She'll come around.*

Tanya looked up when they got to the main crosswalk to school. Yasmin's regular spot under the tree was vacant. She looked around but didn't see her. She'd try to catch her in the hall between classes.

Chapter 34

Thursday Midday

Tanya sat in calculus class, listening to the teacher cover the basics of implicit differentiation. She was trying to get her mind off of everything going on by working through the homework assignment for the night. She was halfway through the problems when the lights went out. Her heart jumped as fear gripped her. The room didn't get dark. The light from the windows was enough to illuminate the room despite being overcast. After a moment, the lights came back on. She could feel the adrenaline coursing through her veins.

Ding, ding, dong, ding, ding.

"Teachers, please dismiss our senior class for assembly in front of the school. All members of the class of 2025, please report to the flagpole." Tanya looked around, wondering what was going on. She waited for the others to leave before falling in behind them. She looked for Yasmin, but she hadn't shown up for school. The students filled the halls. Most of their classes were on the second floor. She looked around and spotted Sheri. She slowed and picked her way through the mass of students to meet her.

"What's going on?"

"It's the homecoming drill."

Realization hit Tanya. It was a drill the local schools ran every year in the week of homecoming. The school would select a few student role players to act out a car accident from driving under the influence.

She had heard about it before; it was supposed to help students visualize the harm that could be done. There would be police, EMTs, and grieving parents to talk to the students. It worked. The number of accidents was down since they started doing it.

"I wonder who they got this year," Sheri leaned in to talk over the noise. The selected students were sworn to secrecy, which allowed others to experience the impact of seeing their friends "dead." Tanya stopped. She didn't want to see. Searching for an escape from the moving crowd of seniors, she glanced around. She had seen enough death.

"I don't want to do this," her voice was shaky. She felt flush as panic set in. "It's not Amara, is it? Or Yasmin?"

"Ok, stay back here. I'll go see."

Sheri left her near the flagpole, her view of the accident blocked by students.

"I see Amara across from us, but," she lifted on her toes, which did nothing in the crowd of taller students. "I don't see Yasmin."

Tanya took in a deep breath. "Good. I think she's not in school today."

"Maybe you shouldn't be either. You know they would probably let you have time off. You haven't had time to grieve properly."

"No, if I miss, they won't let me play at the recital."

"You don't need to play if you need rest."

"I don't need rest! I need to play."

"Ok, don't bite my head off."

"Sheri, I know you care, but I don't want to be babied. I'm here, and I'm fine. You can stop worrying about me."

The police officers on the scene described the accident, and several guest speakers went through their prepared speeches. The question on her mind was whether anyone would speak about the victims of the attack at their funerals. Ignoring the thought, she tried to listen to the EMT talk about speed and seatbelts.

Tanya couldn't pay attention. She didn't plan on attending homecoming, which was the following week. All she cared about was the recital Saturday night.

After half an hour of speeches and discussion, the teacher dismissed them to their next class. Tanya couldn't focus on any of her afternoon classes. *Something must be wrong.* She worried about Yasmin but didn't know where she lived or how to contact her. She went to the main office at the end of the day and asked if she had called out sick. They told her student information was releasable only to family members.

She waited for Sheri in front of the school. Students swarmed around her, with some side glances, but not as many. Their attention span was brief, and a YouTuber had likely lured them away, talking about the latest challenges they should try, uploading their attempts on TikTok or whatever. She enjoyed watching the short videos, but wasn't as pulled in as much as others. Her parents were oblivious and didn't talk about it unless something made the news.

"Hey, you waited for me."

Tanya turned to see Sheri walking up, hair held back by a light blue headband. Her blue sweater vest, over an open white collared blouse, exposed her mother's pendant. "I did. I was looking for Yasmin, too."

"I haven't seen her either."

"I hope she's ok."

Sheri started walking toward the crosswalk, Tanya at her side. "Amara got her parking spot."

Tanya nodded.

"So we shouldn't have to walk anymore. No more creepy house."

"That'll be good." She looked around while waiting for the crossing light.

"Tanya, hello." Sheri waved her hand in front of her face.

"What?"

"You're off in your own little world. What's up? Talk to me."

"It's everything going on. I'm worried about Yasmin. What if Diane got to her?"

Shari looked down as if the realization just occurred to her.

"She's a killer. If she's the serial killer, that's hanging over my head. I hope your dad catches her. Until then, though, I'm going to be worried. Add the drama with my dad, and I just want to go to sleep and let this nightmare pass."

Sheri put a hand on her arm.

"Could you mention Yasmin to your dad? The office wouldn't tell me anything because I'm not family. Maybe he could have someone check out her neighborhood."

"I will. Let's go." She hooked her arm in Tanya's, leading her across the street.

"Look." Tanya pointed to the houses around the empty house. She counted in her head. "Twenty-three vultures. If that's a sign, we're screwed."

"It's just a coincidence."

Tanya felt her skin prickle as she walked by the house. She looked at Sheri, who looked at the home but seemed unaffected. She wanted to shake her and ask how she didn't feel like someone was watching them as they walked by, how she felt the urge to go into the house. It was useless. She didn't believe it. Tanya looked again, seeing a window on the second floor open, the white curtain moving with the wind. The birds watched as they passed, not making a sound. Tanya felt they were waiting for something.

Tanya veered off at her house, looking at her mom's red car parked in her dad's spot in the driveway. She needed to ask her mom what they would do with the house and everything. If they had a spare moment, she would talk to her this weekend to recommend she move near her college. The house was too much for them.

"Text me if you want to hang out."

"I will if I can. I need to rehearse."

"You're going to be amazing. I can't wait. You know I'll be right there in the front."

"I know."

Chapter 35

Thursday Evening

Tanya's mom laughed, which was a significant change in the house. Jackson was running around the table, his little tail wagging.

"So you got the job?"

"I did. I'll start on Monday."

"That's great, Mom!"

Tanya took another fork full of twirling spaghetti.

They heard the front door open and someone walking heavy footed toward them. Tanya jumped up and grabbed a large knife. Her mom went to the door, pushing it open. She stepped back as her dad came through, looking at them. "Well, this is a nice, quaint, family dinner."

Tanya blurted out, "You're not allowed to be here."

He dismissed her, "Shut up. I just need some things from my office."

Tanya stepped forward, holding the knife by her side.

He turned around and walked back into the kitchen. "What are you gonna do, Tanya? Kill your father?" He stepped close and smacked her forearm. She dropped the knife. Struggling, she fought to keep control. Her heart was racing. He kept his eyes locked on hers and kicked the knife across the room.

Her mom stepped between them. "Leave her alone, Chris."

"Or what Kait?"

Tanya backed away as her father turned and went down the short hall to his office.

She sent a quick text.

> Tanya: Sher, my dad is here. Please tell your dad I can't call.

"Go up to your room and lock the door," her mom whispered to her.

"No, Mom. I'm not leaving you alone with him," she kept her voice down.

She heard him rummaging through his desk drawers.

"Kait, did you go through my drawers?" He came out of the office with a small bag. He walked up to her, putting his finger in her face. "Don't you lie to me. Did you go through my desk?"

"No! There's nothing in there I want."

"Don't go through my shit. You two will be out on the street when all of this is done."

He turned to leave.

"Ass."

He spun around and turned on Tanya.

She stepped out, fighting the urge to run. "What? Are you going to hit me again? You're an Ass!"

He glared at her. The muscles in his jaw were working. She held his gaze.

Ding.

He grabbed her phone and read it. "Fuck!" He threw her phone against the wall.

He ran out of the kitchen and out the front door.

As he drove off, she heard his tires squeal.

Despite her heart still pounding, she relaxed. She went to her phone. The screen had several cracks across the face. It was frozen.

She set it down and went to her mom. "Mom, are you ok?"

"I'm fine. Don't antagonize him. I'll call the police. You don't know what he's capable of when he gets this mad."

"I texted Sheri. I think she told her dad."

Her mom looked back toward the front door. "I haven't seen him this mad since you were one."

"What happened? Why is he angry all the time?"

"They forced him out of the Navy. Coming out of the Academy, he had visions of having his own ship. When they encouraged him to leave the service, he spun out of control. He lost his dream. I was worried about him. He talked about getting back at his department head and another officer for blowing an incident out of proportion."

Tanya was curious. She hadn't heard the story of why her dad was forced out. Every once in a while, he would get in a drunken rage about the Navy and their '*bullshit policies.*' "What was it? Do you know?"

Her mom nodded and looked away to avoid eye contact. "There were accusations of sexual assault while he was at the Academy and again on deployment."

Tanya felt ill. Her father was a monster. "Were they true? Why did you stay with him?"

"You were one. I was afraid to be a single mom. He constantly told me I'd never make it. That I would be a failed mother for putting you in danger. We needed his benefits to cover your appointments."

Tanya's disgust turned to rage. "Did he do it?"

Her mom nodded, "He claimed there was no evidence, and there was none regarding his time at school because it wasn't reported. But on deployment, there were pictures."

"Oh my God! Mom!" Her eyes filled with tears at the thought of what her mother had endured.

Her mom sat up. "When we went to mediation, I told him about the pictures and told him that if he contested the divorce, I would release the pictures to everyone."

Tanya covered her mouth, looking at her mom.

"Mom, I'm so sorry."

"We'll be fine. It feels good to tell you. I know he's not a good man."

"He's evil."

A knock at the door interrupted them. The flashing blue lights came through the sheer curtains by the door. Her mom got up, answered the door, and let Officer Hendercriss in.

"Are both of you ok?"

"We are. He left several minutes ago."

Tanya nodded in concurrence.

"He violated the protective order. We'll take care of it if you're willing to give a statement. Do either of you fear for your safety at this time?"

Both women shook their heads.

Not from him, but I do from the serial killer on the loose. "What'll happen to him?"

"If we can prove that he violated the PO, they will charge him with a misdemeanor, impose a fine, and he could spend time in jail."

Tanya sat up. "We have security cameras." She pulled up her phone and saw the cracked screen. "He threw my phone. Mom, pull it up in the app."

Her mom pulled the footage from the cameras, showing the timestamp on the video.

Officer Hendercriss pulled a card out of her shirt pocket. "If you could send that footage to the email on the card. I'll add it to your statements."

Tanya let her mom describe what happened while she tried to restart her phone. After a few minutes, she forced a restart. She opened her texts and sent a quick one to Sheri. The content of the messages from the past two days became garbled, displaying as random characters and empty boxes.

Tanya: Thank you!

She waited a few minutes while her mom showed the officer out. Sheri didn't reply. Maybe she'd call later.

Chapter 36

Friday Morning

Tanya sat on the steps in front of her house, waiting for Sheri. Glancing at her phone, she checked for notifications. She was late. She sent another text and didn't get a response. Tanya got up and walked down the short path to the sidewalk, looking toward Sheri's house. Her dad's car wasn't in the driveway. Maybe her dad gave her a ride. She turned toward the school. The covered path to school looked like winter had come early, with most of the leaves already off the branches that intertwined from both sides of the street. Maybe she should ask her mom for a ride. She slowed, looking up the street. "You'll be fine. It's daylight," she told herself, and started her walk to school.

At school she went to Amara's locker among the bustle of the halls. Amara closed her locker and turned to go to class, not seeing her approach.

"Amara."

She turned. "Hey, Tanya. Are you excited? I can't wait for tomorrow night." She leaned in and whispered, "My imam says he will loan me a few wards against evil. He's going to bring them by my house tonight."

"That's good," Tanya faltered. "Have you seen Sheri? She didn't come by this morning, and Yasmin is still missing. I'm getting worried."

"Oh, did you miss Sheri's text last night? She sent it to you and me."

"I didn't see it." She showed Amara her phone.

"Oh. What happened?"

"My dad."

Amara grimaced. "Are you ok? Did he do anything?"

"Not to me. He broke the protective order, though. The police are looking for him."

"Oh. I'm so sorry."

"Did Sheri write back after she said she saw Yasmin?"

"No. Let's catch up at lunch. We need to get to class."

Tanya looked up at the clock. She'd need to push it to get to class on time. "Ok."

Tanya was worried about entering the cafeteria. She sped through the serving line. She looked for her friends and found them at a different table than their usual one. Yasmin and Amara sat at one of the round tables near the windows.

Tanya set her tray down and sat next to Yasmin. "You had me scared. Where have you been?"

Yasmin forced a smile. "My grandmother got sick. I had to take care of her." Her eyes had a slight sunken appearance, and her skin had a pallid look. "I spent the first hour in the office on the phone with my grandmother, trying to get them to believe me."

"Are you ok? You're looking like you may have caught something."

"I don't feel well. Whenever my grandmother didn't need me, I've been staying in bed. I haven't been eating enough."

Amara scooped a spoonful of sliced fruit, and a questioning look crossed her face. She swallowed hard. "Sheri said she saw you yesterday evening. She sent us a text that she was going to go talk to you."

Yasmin's expression shifted, and the exhaustion appeared to fade. "When was that? I haven't seen her. She must have mistaken someone else for me. Like I said, I've been at home," she stressed the last part.

Amara nodded. "Probably."

Tanya lowered her voice, "Amara said that her imam has found some charms to help ward away evil. He's going to deliver them later. That's good news, right?"

Yasmin looked to Amara, her expression neutral. "Wards?"

Amara nodded. "He and my father talked about everything going on, and my dad said he'd seen something like this when he was a boy, back in Iran."

"What do they think it is?" Yasmin pressed.

Amara looked aside. "They didn't say specifically, but it is supposed to be potent."

Tanya watched the exchange. Amara looked uneasy. She looked around to see if anyone was listening. "Really? Are you sure?"

Amara looked at her. "Yes, I'm sure. All they said was evil spirit." She was hiding something. Maybe she didn't want to share, or she was embarrassed about a portion of her faith that dealt with mysticism. Tanya would try to get it out of her later.

"Better news is that the fall recital is tomorrow night. We'll see our very own flutist play an amazing solo."

Tanya blushed. "Shh." She looked around.

Yasmin held her gaze on Amara a little longer before shifting to Tanya. "I can't wait to hear you play. I'm going to be right up front."

"That's what Sheri said."

"We'll all be there," Amara chimed in.

"Well, my mom is coming too. I asked Mr. Bilby to save four seats for all of you, so your names will be on the chairs."

"What time does it start?"

"Seven."

Yasmin got up. "It is going to be life changing, I'm sure of it. I'm going to get ready for class. I'll see you all later." She smiled at Tanya and looked at Amara before leaving.

"Bye, Yasmin."

"I think I'll go by Sheri's house after school. Maybe she's sick."

"Wouldn't she text?"

"I don't know. Maybe she's really sick."

"I hope not. I'll let you know."

They got up. "What are you doing tonight?"

"I'm going to go shopping with my mom. She got a new job and wants to pick up some work clothes."

"That's awesome. It should be a great break from all of this. I'm sure you're practiced out."

"Not yet. I love the song, but they pulled us out of our classes for a dress rehearsal."

Amara smiled at her. "Call me tonight."

"I will."

Chapter 37

Friday Evening

Tanya looked out the window as her mom searched for a close parking spot. She caught sight of a blue BMW following them. Fear grabbed her heart. Her mom slowed and the car passed. An older woman was in the passenger seat. As her mom circled, she spotted two more cars like her father's. The license plates were different.

She was relieved when her mom found a spot close by the main entrance.

"Look at that, a little vulturing, and we got one."

"What did you say?"

"A little vulturing and—"

Tanya glared at her mom. "Why would you say that?"

Her mom laughed it off. "It's the correct term. I came across a meme on Facebook. Cars circled a parking lot repeatedly, passing open spots further out, hoping for closer ones. Like vultures."

Tanya undid her seatbelt. Maybe she wasn't ready to be out. She was jumping at everything. No, she'd be ok at the mall. Plenty of people around. Tanya shook her head. "Ok, let's go."

"I'm excited. I haven't bought work clothes in years."

Tanya looked around as they walked toward the entrance. A parking light went out. Tanya looked over and saw someone staring at her. A tall person looking over the tops of the parked cars. She closed the gap with her mom, grabbing her arm. The light flickered back on. She eased up, realizing it was an office chair in the back of a truck bed. Tanya shook her head and tried to slow her breathing.

They went inside and she relaxed at the sounds and smell of late October. Pumpkin spice, fresh cookies, and bright fall colors filled the animated mall. She followed her mom. She felt uneasy. Her eyes darted back and forth around the stores and shoppers, looking for a threat. She felt someone was watching her, staying just out of sight. She took out her phone and typed a quick message to Sheri.

> Tanya: Hey Sher, I missed you today. I hope you're all right. I'm shopping with my mom. I'll try to call when I get home.

She watched the screen, expecting a quick response while her mom looked through the hanging blouses. She clicked Amara's name.

> Tanya: Amara, I'm checking to see if my texts are going out.

Amara: Looks good. What are you doing?

> Tanya: Hanging out with my mom at the mall.

Amara: Could you bring me a giant cookie?

> Tanya: Really?

Amara: No. Unless you want to.

> Tanya: Have you heard from Sheri?

Amara: No

> Tanya: Thanks

Amara: NP, chocolate chip.

Tanya looked up and didn't see her mom. She looked around and walked between the racks. She found her kneeling, going through a small stack of folded pants. "Those look cute."

"Honey, I don't need cute. I need professional."

"Ok, Mom, professionally cute."

Ding.

Unknown: We should meet.

Tanya looked at the number. It was a 312 area code. Why was that area code familiar? She couldn't remember why.

Tanya: Who is this?

Unknown: You'll figure it out.

Tanya: I don't know anyone from 312 area code.

Unknown: I think you do. We need to meet… again.

Tanya: I don't think so.

Unknown: I have a question for you.

Tanya: What?

Unknown: Now that your mom is alone, do you think she'd like to hang out with Betty, Melanie, Gabrielle, and Samantha?

Tanya stared at the screen. She felt the sweat on her palms, a tickle on her neck, and a vice tightening in her heart.

Tanya: You're sick! That's not funny.

Unknown: It's a little funny, but I'm serious. We need to meet.

Tanya: I'm done with you.

Unknown: Not yet… but soon.

Tanya blocked the number and moved close to her mom. Her mom found a few outfits but wanted to try another store. She started to calm down. Her eyes scanned the store. For what, she didn't know—anything out of the ordinary, a stalker, or something off, but nothing revealed itself.

They left the first store to walk across the mall to the other big department store. The mall was busier than she expected. It wasn't like Christmas when all the schools were out, and everyone was rushing around, panicking to find gifts, but there were quite a few people.

"Honey, what are you looking for? You're twisting and turning and look completely distracted."

"I don't know. Something feels off."

"Tanya, we're safe here. Look at all these people." She sighed. "I knew I shouldn't have brought you out. This is too much too soon."

"Mom, I wanted to come out. I'm just nervous."

Her mom leaned in. "Well, if it makes you feel any better, I have one of your dad's pistols in my purse."

Tanya's eyes went wide. "Mom! Do you know how to use that?"

"I haven't shot one in a while, but I was pretty good when I was younger."

"You never told me that."

Her mom shrugged. "A mom has to have some secrets, and I don't want anyone messing with my baby."

Tanya smiled. This was a different side of her mom. She liked it, confident and assertive.

They walked through the mall, bypassing the food court, despite the assault of pumpkin-spiced everything. They finally gave in and stopped at a Black Rifle Coffee Company shop, getting their pumpkin-spiced latte, which was good, albeit with more of a coffee bite. As they left the shop, Tanya froze. Diane was looking at her from behind a display. Tanya felt like her blood had frozen. Fear gripped her, holding her muscles locked in place.

"Tanya, are you ok? What's wrong?" Her mom followed her gaze and saw the person staring at them. She wanted to run but couldn't. The area was teeming with people. What if the lights go out? All these people will die.

"M-m-mom. It's her," Tanya's voice was weak and trembling. A stern look appeared on her mother's face after she pointed to where she had seen Diane. She hurried to the other store. She went behind the display, but the person didn't turn away.

The head lifted; her mom held the display up to see it was a mask.

Tanya breathed a sigh of relief and felt her muscles relax. Her mom walked back to her and took her by the arm. "Sweetie, I'm good for now. I'll come back this weekend. Let's get you home, ok?"

Tanya nodded, looking down at her coffee. She didn't want to look around. She was seeing things. A tear ran down her cheek, causing her to feel emotional. Her mom led her down through the heart of the mall to where they had come in. She didn't look up or around, even when a local group started playing songs from the center of the mall. She wanted to get home.

Chapter 38

Friday Night

Tanya went to bed with all the lights on, music playing, and her door locked. She felt better that her mom had a pistol and was comfortable with it. She hadn't gotten the courage to ask her for one of the others to keep in her room. If things kept going wrong, she may. She rolled to her side, pulling the covers over her head, blocking out the bright lights. She had a hard time keeping her eyes open. Every time she drifted off, her mind would wander, conjuring images of the dead women. She wanted to rest, but didn't want to fall asleep. Tension filled the air. Something was approaching, and she couldn't stop it.

Arr, Arr, Arr, Arr, Arr.

She didn't want to go downstairs. Her mom must have let Jackson out. The silence hanging in the air after his barking reminded her that the Burkes and Coolio were gone. The closing back door caught her attention. She drifted off as Bruno Mars sang in the background.

Sitting upright, she looked around. She had heard a noise outside her door. A scraping sound. She looked around her room. Every light was on. She waited to see if she would lose power and go into a panic. After a few moments, she tossed off the covers and got up. Smurfette sat watching as she put on her slippers and got up.

"Mom? Is that you?" She waited for a response, but none came. The hour was growing late. She was probably asleep. She picked up a small marble bust of Athena, goddess of wisdom, wrapping her fingers around the head, the square edge base on top. She looked at Smurfette. "Sorry, I need someone with a little more weight."

She unlocked the door and cautiously opened it, peeking into the hallway. The hall was dark, as was the downstairs. She looked toward her mom's room. No light peeked from under the door. Patiently, she waited and listened. She heard nothing. She thought about going downstairs to make sure everything was ok, but decided against it, shutting and locking her door. Returning Athena to her desk, she glanced up at the shelf nearby and let out a scream.

She backed away and collided with the edge of her bed, lost her footing, and ended up falling onto the floor. The miniature busts had morphed into the heads of her mom, Sheri, Amara, Sadie, and the women murdered at the meeting. Blood trickled down from the little heads and pooled on her white desk, slowly spreading. The heads turned to look at her. Tears of blood dripped from their eyes. Their little mouths moved, trying to say something but only producing a wet gurgle.

Her eyes flew open, and she sat up. Her pajamas were sweat soaked. Tanya looked at her shelf and spied the Smurfettes all in their place. She got up and changed clothes. She considered going to the bathroom but decided against it. Lying back down, she shifted her gaze towards a spot on her wall to the right of her window, where an orange threaded dreamcatcher was hanging.

"Useless."

She closed her eyes and tried to sleep. Her heart was still coming down from the fright. Her mind raced, thinking about her friends, mom, and tomorrow night's recital. She thought about the song and felt peace wash over her. As she played the music in her head, her room faded away. In her mind, the song was being played in the desert by a bard or minstrel entertaining travelers at a campfire. Instead, she found herself in a large tent with an open view of the surrounding oasis, the desert just beyond. Beautiful colors adorning pillows, sheer fabric, and deep red short tables surrounded her. Fresh fruits and vegetables garnished trays of silver and gold. The smell of hyacinth, jasmine, and lavender fought for dominance. A warm

210

breeze blew through. All of this had been prepared for her. She felt safe. The song's melody floated on the wind, not overbearing but delicately wafting about. Tanya felt welcome.

By the time she woke up, it was already mid-morning. Compared to the past two weeks, she was relaxed. She didn't recall what she dreamed about after waking from the nightmare and didn't care. She got up and went downstairs. She found a note from her mom letting her know that she had headed to the mall, wanting to get there when the stores opened. The scent of coffee reached her and filled the room.

Tanya sat down at the table and poured herself a bowl of cereal. She took a drink of her black coffee. The bitter taste was more welcoming than she remembered. Jackson was lying next to the back door, sleeping and chasing something in his dreams. The sunlight came through the blinds, cutting thin, bright lines across the floor. She opened the curtains and blinds on the window and the back door. The room lit up. It was beautiful outside. She reached for her phone. If it were in good condition, she'd know she was dreaming. She wasn't, the cracks spider-webbed across the screen.

She had forgotten to turn it back on after getting home. Maybe Sheri had texted her. She scrolled through her texts, which was a pain because of the cracks in her screen. Nothing. She had received a text message from Amara stating that the wards would be dropped off in the afternoon. She would bring them to the recital.

Tanya knew she should be nervous about playing, but she wasn't. Something about the song and playing it for her mom and friends calmed her. Maybe she'd walk down to Sheri's and check on her later. She felt warmth across her foot and looked down to see a ray of sunshine on her toes. She spooned another bite of the chocolate cereal into her mouth. The sense of dread from the night before was gone.

Chapter 39

Saturday Night I

Tanya waved to her mom as she drove away from the school. Her mom would be back later for the performance. The musicians came early to set up, relax, and play through their music, whatever helped them calm their nerves before the show. The sky was clear, blue, and changing to orange as the sun moved toward the horizon. They lucked out with a warm fall night in Texas during October.

She went to the rear of the music room and found her spot. As a freshman, they placed her at the back of the music room, next to the area where the chairs were stacked. She didn't mind. It had been a rite of passage. When she took the first chair in her sophomore year, she continued to warm up and prepare in the back. It reminded her of the hard work she had put in over that first year. It wasn't often that a sophomore moved up quickly on a popular instrument. As she thought about her musical journey, she smiled. It was a source of happiness in her disrupted life.

She opened her flute case, took each piece out, and cleaned them with a rod and cloth. Then, she glided the soft cloth across the instrument, ensuring its cleanliness by removing fingerprints and smudges. She repeated the same with the other two parts. She slid the pieces together and then raised the flute into position, running her fingers across the keys, making sure none of the springs had popped out of place or broken.

Taking a quick look around the room, she surveyed her surroundings. The other students were doing similar routines. She began her warmup exercises. When she practiced at home, she had reduced the number of times she did them, but she never skipped them before a performance. She enjoyed school, but she loved playing the flute. It was one thing that no one, at least here, was better than her. She played through the scales and parts of the song she wanted extra practice with.

Mr. Bilby entered the room and made his way around the other musicians, stopping to give each further encouragement.

"Ms. Janessy, I heard you in the hall. It sounds wonderful."

"Thank you, Mr. Bilby."

"I wanted to introduce you to Bernard Merryman, the gentleman I spoke about. He's running a bit late. Make sure you stay afterward."

"Yes, sir. I will."

"It's a packed house. Let's have some fun."

Tanya nodded. He said the same thing at every performance. His use of the term 'packed house' sometimes demonstrated artistic interpretation. She checked her phone. There were no messages. Hopefully her mom, Sheri, Amara, and Yasmin found their seats. She was worried that she hadn't heard from Sheri.

At a quarter to the hour, Mr. Bilby came back into the room. "Alright musicians, it's time to take our places. Go out and put on a fantastic show." She got up and put on her lip balm. She checked the mirror to ensure her curls were set and her hair hung evenly around. Everyone was told to wear black and white. She had chosen a sleeveless, long black dress. For white, she had borrowed her mother's pearls. Tanya turned from side to side, watching the dress swirl outward from her ankles. She wouldn't be doing that during the performance, but it had been something she enjoyed from when she was little.

With a deep breath, she made her way to the performance hall. It was the auditorium with modifications. Mr. Bilby wanted to share how he convinced the superintendent to make a few modifications to help improve the sound quality. She went up the steps to the stage and found her chair. She glanced at the other musicians. The expressions ranged from relaxed to downright terrified. They'd be fine if they just played the music in front of them.

The curtain rose to applause from a packed room. Mr. Bilby had been right. The room filled up with almost every seat taken. Tanya looked to the front, where her reserved seats were, and saw four empty seats. Her heart sank. She bit her lip and took a deep breath to focus herself. Her determination ensured that it wouldn't ruin the night. She would play her heart out. Tanya relaxed and looked up at Mr. Bilby, who had raised his baton, holding it in position. A calm came over her. She raised her flute to the ready position.

At his movement, the band launched into the first theme, *Star Wars*, led by the brass sections. The woodwinds propelled the melody to support the song as it surged forward. They flowed into the swirling sounds of the flutes, clarinets, and their string instruments in setting up the conclusion and transition into the bassoon-led opening to *Jurassic Park* and through building excitement toward the adventurous *Raiders of the Lost Ark*. The trumpets countered the low supporting bass of the deep string instruments and sousaphones. They fed off the enthusiasm of the audience's expressions when they recognized a tune. The first soloist stood as the band transitioned out of their song. The tenor sax began, flowing from the dulcet tones at the theme's end and merging into Van Morrison's "Tupelo Honey." Tanya rested, letting the music lift her. She looked past the empty seats to the audience, swaying with the rhythm. The brass led the band into the slow, deceptive opening to the *James Bond* theme. In transition, the drums shifted beats, keeping the adventurous theme going as she led the flutes through *Mission Impossible*, the rest of the band dropping into support. They paused, letting the silence hang. She could feel the anticipation. Mr. Bilby enthusiastically directed the French horns into the opening of *Superman*. The audience applauded as the orchestral song led them through the superhero's journey. As the song rose to the triumphant conclusion, a lone violin sounded slow and tantalizing. The soloist picked up the pace of the *Queen of the Damned* theme and brought the audience to the edge of their seats. Tanya visualized the song being played around a campfire by a traveling gypsy band. A dancer started with a gradual pace before escalating to a frenzy of twirls and jumps.

Starting with the low tuba, the timpani joined in to begin a slow buildup, taking us on a terrifying orchestral journey through *Jaws*. The audience was caught off guard when the thrill of *Jaws* flowed in the excitement and emotional flow of *E.T.* They continued the magical theme of the music, transitioning into *Harry Potter's* rise and fall adventuresome melody, carrying the audience into another world. The electric guitarist stood and started into the theme from *Top Gun* as her solo. Tanya smiled. Tracy played and moved from the side to the front of the stage. She wore tight leather pants, knee-high black boots, and a vest; her fingernails were painted white. She seized control of the crowd and moved with the ballad, playing her rock concert.

The violinist stood and took control of the song, moving into the *Godfather*, which could have been her second solo if not for the accompanying strings and behind-the-scenes bass. The violin faded, and the brass retook control in a slow buildup to *The Lord of the Rings*. It was a welcome slowdown in the journey, allowing the clarinet lead to stand out as he played the melody. Most of the band put their instruments down as the piano played the staccato alternating notes from *Forrest Gump*. Tanya swayed with the song, waiting for their time to join the journey. The trombonist stood and took off on a wild ride, inspired by the solo from Pixar's *Soul*. He also played in the jazz band and continued the theme from the movie in a three-minute improvisation that grabbed the audience's attention.

The brass stepped up to take the lead from the trombonist before the rest of the band joined in the return to adventure in *Back to the Future*. Tanya played her harmony effortlessly, raising in a crescendo toward the dark shift to the haunting *Psycho* with the punctuated staccato supported song, building a sense of dread. As the strings took over, Tanya glanced up to see Yasmin sitting in her seat. Their eyes locked for a second, and Tanya felt energized. The music slowed and faded, moving into the last song for the band, the theme from

Titanic. Tanya set her flute in her lap, allowing the second flute, Emory, a junior, to lead the song.

As the band faded, Tanya stood and began the slow introduction to her song. As she played, she felt the power of the notes penetrate her heart and soul, filling her with energy, and taking hold of the audience. She felt light on her feet, lost in the ethereal melody that permeated every corner of the performance hall. The notes floated off the page and spun around her. She swayed with the music, turning in a slow rhythmic dance, a celebration—the atmosphere in the room filled with energy. There were no other sounds as she moved through the ancient song. She felt the pull, drawing her toward a new world filled with a gleaming city of brass. The audience faded away. Colors swirled around, long bolts of sheer cloth obscuring her view of what drew her into the heart of the song. The opportunity rose before her. All she had to do was trust in the music and give in to those who called. She played, a longing rising from below, billowing vents of a dark mist, moving with the flow of the melody. She resisted the pull, playing the music, putting her heart into it, increasing the tempo. Her fingers moved of their own accord, meeting the demands of the notes as they appeared. Still, she fought against it, sensing herself being compelled towards an unknown summons. The swirling colors parted. A dark being stood before her, ancient, wise, and demanding. She was beautiful. Tanya felt herself drawn to her eyes. She wanted to resist, but they pulled at her. The vision faded, and she saw Yasmin smiling up at her from the front row. Tanya let go of her inhibitions and gave herself to the song, feeling it wrap around her like a soft blanket, fresh from the dryer.

The last note faded. The audience was silent, mesmerized. She peered out, wondering if something was wrong. The audience erupted in applause. They were on their feet, clapping and cheering their support. The rest of the band stood and bowed. Tanya felt elated. Yasmin was here. When she looked at her friend, she experienced something new. They felt a strong bond between them. She couldn't wait to get everything put away so she could talk to her. The applause continued.

Chapter 40

Saturday Night II

Tanya felt exhilarated. The performance was fantastic. The solos were great, and she felt empowered by the effect of her song. As she left the band room, she spotted Yasmin down the hall, leaning against the lockers. She wore black slacks and a dark gray blouse. She smiled, her flowing curly locks framing her dark brown eyes.

"Tanya, you played amazingly. I have never heard that song played with so much heart."

Tanya hugged her, hesitating, before she felt Yasmin's arms around her. She pulled back. "I wish I could share my feelings when I play the song. Tonight was magical, even though I was afraid to share. I could feel the music. It flowed through me. It was as if the music was pulling me into a magical swirl of all my senses. In front of me stood a breathtaking city of brass. I could feel it drawing me closer. I got scared, but then I opened my eyes and saw you, and I felt safe. Oh, my gosh. I am so excited. I almost forgive everyone else for not showing up."

"True to my word, I am here."

"Thank you so much." She placed her hand on her heart. "It really means a lot to me."

"Ms. Janessy! Ms. Janessy!"

She turned to see the diminutive form of Mr. Bilby waving to her, walking beside a very handsome man. His guest wore a black suit and

219

a dark gray tie with hints of deep red. His hair was short, combed back and to the side, and he wore a smile that would have given George Clooney a run for his money. To say the man was handsome would not be doing him justice.

"Tanya, right? I'm Bernard Merryman." He flashed a warm smile. His eyes held her in place.

"Nice to meet you, sir." She reached out to shake his hand.

"Bernard, please. And you are?" He turned to Yasmin.

"I'm not with the band. I'm Tanya's friend, Yasmin."

He offered his hand. "Yasmin, that is a beautiful name. Did you enjoy the recital?"

"I did, particularly the amazing flute solo." She looked at Tanya and smiled.

"It was breathtaking." He looked back at Tanya. "I often feel moved by music, especially when it is beautifully played. But to give you your due, the emotional connection I felt was incredible. Where did you find that piece?"

Tanya took Yasmin's arm and felt a tingle in her fingers. "Yasmin. Her grandmother had it."

"It is a remarkable piece, unique."

Yasmin smiled, glancing down at Tanya's hand, then up to her. "She wanted something challenging. I thought it was an excellent opportunity for her to introduce a sampling of my culture with her classmates."

"Thank you for sharing that song and a portion of your culture. Tanya, I understand you are applying to the University?"

"Yes sir, I am. I'm still working on my application."

He reached into his coat pocket and pulled out a card. "Call me. We can talk about your interests. If all goes well, you can use me as a reference."

She squeezed Yasmin's arm. "Thank you, mister, um, Bernard." Calling him by his first name felt odd, but he had insisted.

He looked at Yasmin. "And what are your intentions at the end of the year?"

"I'd like to travel. See more of your country and then others. Someday, I'd like to return to Iran."

"I wish I had done something like that when I graduated. Some of my peers took time to travel, backpack, and experience different cultures. I've traveled since then, some for vacation and some for work. You've inspired me with your song. I have a desire to search for other songs that elicit emotion and imagination. Thank you."

Yasmin nodded.

"Ladies, thank you for your time. Well done, Ms. Janessy. I'm afraid Mr. Merryman will miss his flight back if we don't get on the road."

Tanya watched the pair depart.

Yasmin leaned in, "He's very impressed with you."

"Do you think so? I know he liked the song."

"It was you. Everyone felt you in that song."

Tanya looked around, worried. "I need to call my mom. She dropped me off and said she would be here. She wouldn't miss this."

Tanya turned her ringer on and dialed her number.

"Hey sweetie, how was it?" her mom was slurring her words.

"Mom, are you ok?"

"I'm so sorry I missed it. I'm at the hospital."

"Mom! Why didn't you call me?" Her eyes were wide. She turned to look at Yasmin. "What happened?"

"Someone hit me."

"Who hit you?"

"No, no, not me. The car. I got rear-ended. The airbag is tough. Did you know how fast they come out?"

"Mom, are you hurt?"

"Not right now. They gave me meds."

"Where are you?"

"Texas United Methodist."

"I'll be there soon."

"I'm so proud of you. I caught the livestream. I really wanted to be there. You know I love listening to you play."

"It's ok, Mom, just rest. I'll be there soon." She heard the click as the call ended.

She called for an Uber and the app displayed a five-minute distance.

"Your mom was in an accident?"

"Yes, someone hit her car, and the airbag deployed. It sounded like she was out of it. I need to get to the hospital."

"Do you want me to come with you?"

Tanya's mind was racing. She was fidgeting. "Would you mind? I could really use the support."

"Of course."

They walked out of the school as the black Toyota Corolla pulled up.

The hospital was probably less than ten minutes from the school, especially at this time of night. Tanya watched out the window, focusing on the lights. Her mind had wandered back to the night of the murders with the alternating bright lights of the streetlights and the dark areas in between.

Tanya turned to Yasmin. "Thank you for coming with me. Do you need to use my phone to call your grandmother?"

"No, I'll call her if it gets late."

"Okay." She held her gaze for a second. Something in her eyes evoked part of the song. Something unknown is behind the veils of color. She shook it off and returned to focusing on the lights. She hoped her mom was ok, and that she hadn't suffered any serious injuries. The timing was horrible. She was supposed to start her new job on Monday.

Chapter 41

Saturday Night III

Tanya and Yasmin entered her mom's room in the ER. The space was small. It had all the equipment needed for short-term treatment but not for extended stays. Her mom was lying in the bed, under the knit hospital blankets, with her right arm in a sling, her left lay on the bed with an IV drip. Cuts and a bruise marred her face, particularly her right eye. The nurse had dimmed the lights, and the heart rate monitor beeped consistently, which was good. Two chairs stood to the side. One had her mom's clothes and purse on them. The air smelled sterile with a hint of alcohol.

"Mom," she called to her, moving to the side of the bed and taking the hand with the tubes. Her mom was asleep.

A nurse came in. She wore dark blue scrubs, had her black hair pulled into a tight bun, and wore a smile on her face. "Are you the daughters?"

"Yes." Tanya glanced at Yasmin quickly.

"I'm Genny, the attending nurse. We've got the results from the X-rays. She suffered a concussion, and a broken radius, one of the bones in the forearm. The other looks ok. We sedated her before resetting the arm."

"It might be a little while before she wakes up. There is a patient guest area by the nurses' station, where you can get coffee, hot chocolate, and small snacks."

"Thank you."

Genny pulled the curtains around the door and left them alone.

Tanya pulled a chair next to the bed.

"I'm going to see if they have a cafeteria. I'm starving."

"Ok, it will probably be a while. Would you mind grabbing me some coffee when you come back?"

"Whatever you need."

Yasmin stepped behind the curtains and let herself out.

Tanya sat, holding her mother's hand. "Hey Mom, I'm here. You get your rest. We'll be here."

Tanya lifted her head off the bed, taking a moment to remember where she was. She felt her mother squeeze her hand. Her mom was looking at her. "Hey, honey."

"I'm sorry, Mom. Did they find out who did it?"

"No, I didn't see the car that hit me. They must not have been paying attention. I was pulling into the driveway, and I got hit. I think the car spun into the front yard and hit the tree. The airbag popped out, disorienting me. My head and arm were killing me. I dialed 9-1-1, and here we are."

"The car kept going?"

"I didn't see them. I was on the front steps when the ambulance arrived."

Tanya didn't like it. No one drove around her neighborhood fast. The neighbors knew the sheriff lived on the street, a residential area.

"Mom, I'm going to step out to make a call. Do you need anything?"

"No, Honey. I'm ok for now."

Tanya kissed her mom on the cheek and left the room, walking toward the patient guest area. Off the side was a small space for kids. Wire puzzles, wooden Thomas the Tank Engine toys, fixed wooden tracks, and a small collection of children's books adorned the tables. She went inside, closed the door, and made a call.

"Hello, Tanya."

"Hey, Dad."

"What do you want?"

"No one showed up for the recital tonight. Mom dropped me off, but she didn't come back. Have you talked to her?"

"No, and why are you telling me this?"

"Daddy, I'm scared of all the murders. I'm the last one here at school. Everyone else left. I know you're mad. Can you come pick me up?"

"That violates the protective order. I'm sorry, not allowed."

"Dad! I don't feel safe."

"I'm sorry, but I can't."

Code blue, fourth-floor cardiology. Code blue. Emergency personnel report to Cardiology.

She stepped away from the large glass windows, moved to the back corner of the room, and raised her voice. "I'm scared. It's not safe. Please come get me."

"I can't. My car is in the shop."

Tanya felt her temperature rise, her face flushed. "I knew it was you."

"What are you talking about?"

She decided to lie. "I saw you on the doorbell camera. You hit Mom's car in the driveway. I saw you."

"You might want to recheck the cameras. There isn't any footage." He laughed, mocking her.

"Don't try to play me, little girl. I know your mom's in the hospital. You think you have me walled off, but I have all the passwords. I canceled the security service, by the way."

"You're lying."

"Am I? I don't know. Where else would there be a code blue? I'm not stupid. But, apparently, you are. So, for the record, in case anyone is listening, I don't know what happened to your mother. My car is in the shop, and my little bitch of a daughter is a liar."

Tanya was furious. He was responsible. She knew it. "Well, Dad, Mom is ok. She'll be out soon, and if you try to hurt her again, I'll take the thumb drive and release everything on every social media platform I'm on. Mom told me what you did! You're a monster!"

The line went dead.

Code Blue. Third floor ICU. Emergency team two report to the third floor ICU.

What was going on? She left the children's area and returned to her mom's room. She stepped around the curtain. They were disconnecting the monitors while raising the bed. Nurse Genny was getting all the cords in order and unlocked the brakes.

"We will be back shortly. The bone is in a good position. The doctor wants to get a cast on for at least six weeks."

"And then, how long before we can go home?" her mom asked.

"It should be within the hour."

Tanya nodded.

Another nurse came in and helped her mom get into a wheelchair. They took her out, leaving Tanya alone. She needed to talk to Sheri's dad. There had to be evidence that her dad was guilty. Where was Sheri? It was unusual to have a day go by without hearing from her. She wanted to call her or Amara, but stopped when she saw it was just before midnight. At least she didn't need to get up tomorrow. She would get up, check on Mom, make sure she was set, and then go down to Sheri's house.

Yasmin came into the room and handed her a cup of coffee. "I know you like it sweet."

Sheri lifted the lid and smelled. It smelled like old, sweetened coffee. It was better than nothing. She took a sip. The temperature was warm, slightly above room temperature. "Thank you."

"The cafeteria was closed."

"Did you find anything to eat?"

"Small snacks."

"Good." She sipped her coffee again. "I called my dad."

"Why?"

"Just the way my mom described what happened."

"What did he say?"

"He didn't admit it, but I'm pretty sure he hit her car."

Yasmin shook her head. "Bullies."

"Yep, and he's the worst kind. He is acting like no one will hold him accountable. He can do whatever he wants and get away with it."

"There's karma."

Tanya snorted at her coffee. "I don't buy it. Look at my past few weeks."

"There's time for it to get better."

Tanya didn't react except to stare ahead. "I don't know. Something is wrong."

Yasmin nodded, "Intuition."

"Yeah, intuition. I can feel something is off, out of balance."

Yasmin said nothing.

The door opened, and Genny wheeled her mom back in. "They set the cast. Her doctor talked to her and said she could check out when ready."

"I'm ready."

"How's your head, Mom?"

"I have a massive headache hiding just behind the painkillers. But I'm ready to be home."

They checked out and took an Uber home.

"Yasmin, do you want to stay? It's late to walk home."

"Thank you, Mrs. Janessy. It is late. I think I should stay if that's ok."

"Of course."

Tanya was happy that she had stayed. She felt better with her nearby.

The driver pulled up to the house. Her mom's car was across the sidewalk against the tree. The front lights showed where the tires had dug into the grass as the car spun around. Glass from the car's broken windows covered the sidewalk, starting from the driveway. She looked down at Sheri's house. The Sheriff patrol car was parked in the driveway. If something were wrong with Sheri, he'd be searching for her. He wouldn't rest. *Why hadn't she called?* She felt sad that her best friend had missed the performance.

"Honey, can you help?"

Tanya rushed to her mother's side and helped her up the steps and into the house. Inside, she got her mother upstairs and into bed. Afterward, she came downstairs, looking around. The picture of her mom and dad at Myrtle Beach was missing. Someone had opened the drawer in the end table under the lamp.

"What's wrong?"

"I think someone was in here. A picture is missing, and a couple of drawers aren't closed. I think my dad came back after they took my mom in the ambulance. He would have known I'd be at the recital."

"What do you think he was doing?"

"Looking for something my mom has that he doesn't want to get out."

Yasmin looked at her, tilting her head slightly, then let it go.

Exhaustion washed over her. She suddenly felt heavy, drained of energy. "I'm so tired. Are you ok if we go to bed?"

"Of course. I could use some sleep."

Tanya showed her to the guest room just past her room and ensured she had morning towels. Then she went to her room and slipped out of the dress. She changed and fell asleep before her head hit the pillow.

A dark form stepped out of the shadows and stood at the end of her bed. Eyes of fire watched her sleep. The being tilted its head at a sound from outside the door. It stepped back into the shadow, melding with the darkness and fading from view. Tanya grunted something and adjusted her position before falling back into a deep sleep.

Chapter 42

Sunday Morning

Tanya sipped her black coffee and spooned yogurt into her mouth. She felt rejuvenated. Yasmin sat at the end of the table. The smell of her bitter tea wasn't as strong as before.

"Are you gonna go home?"

"Yes, eventually. Do you want me to go?" Yasmin said, a smile that looked more like a smirk flashed briefly, then disappeared.

"Well, I'm going to Sheri's to talk to her dad about my father. I'm sure it was him that hit my mom's car. There has to be something we can do. We're done with him."

"Maybe the serial killer will get him."

Tanya laughed a little. "He's bad, and I want him gone, but I don't know about him dying." She looked off into the distance. "It wasn't always bad. There were good times."

"You're justifying his behavior."

Tanya snapped out of her memories. "You're right. I am. He just needs to let us go."

Yasmin got up. "I think things will get better." She walked to the window and looked out. "The winds are changing."

Tanya got up and walked to her side. "That's such a cliché saying." She smiled.

"Perhaps, but winds are powerful." She turned around. "If you're ok, I think I will head over to my grandmother's."

"I'll be fine. Mom is resting upstairs. I'll check on her before I go." She reached out and touched Yasmin's arm, and a spark jumped across, popping. "Oooh, it must be fall."

Yasmin nodded.

Tanya waved to Yasmin, who headed up the street toward school and beyond to her home. She flipped the hood up on her blue sweatshirt. Her hands were in the front pouch to stay warm. Texas' weather was cool today, not quite cold. The neighborhood was dead for a Sunday morning. She looked down the street past Sheri's house and then back over her shoulder and didn't see anyone. The Sheriff's car sat in his driveway. The inside was devoid of any light. It was late in the morning. They could be out in his truck. As she climbed the steps to the front door, she paused. A sense of unease overcame her. She felt stirrings of fear beginning to knot her stomach. She stood at the front door, trying to discern what was giving her pause.

Timidly, she pressed the doorbell. She heard the chimes sounding from inside. She noted the lack of Benny barking in the background, as he had been friends with Sheri for as long as she had. Maybe that was it. The camera to the right of the door blinked green, letting her know it was recording. When it was installed a few years back, she would lean over and make funny faces. She waited. The house was quiet.

She punched in the code Sheri had shared and opened the door.

"Hello! It's Tanya," she called out. She listened, but there was no sound whatsoever, not even the alarm indicating her to input the security code. Someone should be home. She went to the living room, and the TV was on at a local station. "Hello! Sheriff, it's me!"

Apprehension started creeping in. Something felt off to her. She went into the kitchen. Everything looked normal. She returned to the front of the house and slowly climbed the stairs, pausing every few steps to listen. A fly buzzed by her head. She smelled a sweet, metallic scent as she reached the top landing. She looked toward Sheri's room. The door was open.

"Sheri? Are you in there?" She started to go that way, but looked to the right toward her dad's room. The door was destroyed. Large pieces or wood had spread into his room. The edge of the door still clung to the hinges. Someone had torn it apart. She turned down the hall, creeping forward, gradually becoming aware of more buzzing. As she approached, she saw the red stain soaked into the bed.

Her heart pounded in her chest. She didn't see a body. The silhouette of a person in the blood. Beads of sweat formed on her forehead. Her stomach twisted inside. In her retreat, she stumbled on the carpet. She pulled out her phone and called 9-1-1.

"Hello—"

"Murder. I think there was a murder. I'm at Sheriff Downes' house. There's blood, so much blood."

"Ma'am, you said Sheriff Downes' home?"

"Yes."

"Are you alone?"

A chill shot through her body. Fear took control. She couldn't move. The killer could still be in the house. Tears forming in her eyes, she turned her head to look over her shoulder. She closed them. She couldn't look. What if they were there? She opened them and the hall was empty. Three holes stood out on the wall to the left of the door.

She looked back toward the bed. A pistol lay on the floor.

"There's a gun. I think it's the sheriff's on the floor."

"Ma'am, can I get your name?"

"Tanya, Tanya Janessy."

"Ok, Tanya, have you touched the gun or anything else in the home?"

"No."

"I've dispatched officers. A patrol car should be there momentarily. Are you alone?"

"I don't know?" her voice came out as a whimper.

"Stay calm. Officers have arrived. Do you have somewhere safe to go while they search the residence?" She saw the flashing lights coming through the bedroom windows.

Tears were streaming down her cheeks. "No, I'm in the door of his bedroom."

She heard the front door open.

"Police. We're coming in!"

She held still. "I hear the police."

"I told them where you are."

An officer appeared. A second was right behind him. They had their weapons drawn. The older officer, his eyes calm, raised his hand to her and raised his finger to his mouth. The second officer approached Sheri's room and entered. She made her way into the hall and against the wall as the older officer, Garcia, came through. She watched, holding her hand over her mouth, trying not to make a sound, as he moved through the room and cleared the closet and the bathroom.

"Tanya, are you ok?"

"Y-y-yes." She wanted to run.

He reached up and keyed the mic hanging on the dark blue shirt. "Report."

"Upstairs clear."

"Downstairs is clear," came from his radio.

"Ma'am, I'm going to take you downstairs. Are you able to answer questions?"

She nodded emphatically.

She sat on the couch in the Downes' living room, her eyes red and puffy from crying. Officer Garcia sat in a stiff wooden back chair he had brought in from the kitchen. Tanya had relayed the story of Sheri missing, seeing the Sheriff's patrol car in the driveway, and wanting to

234

check on her friend. They told her they didn't find any other blood. The forensics team was on site, going over the crime scene. She cried again, knowing something must have happened to Sheri.

"Did you find anything from Sheri, her phone, a note, or anything else? I haven't seen her since Thursday. I thought she was sick," she pleaded.

Officer Garcia looked at another officer, who shook his head. "We haven't found anything."

Tanya looked up. "I need to tell Amara. We were all best friends. Can someone go with me? It's up the street."

Officer Garcia nodded, "Sure."

Officer Hendercriss stepped forward, looking at Tanya, her blue eyes sympathetic. "I'll take her." Tanya looked up. "Thank you."

She got up, walked to the patrol car, and entered the front seat. The neighbors were out now. Three patrol cars, an unmarked black sedan, and the coroner's truck occupied parking spaces along the street.

"Why is this happening?" She felt the world spinning around her.

They drove up the street. Tanya felt a sense of dread as they neared the Vulture House. The dark birds covered the roof.

"Do you see that?"

The officer slowed the car, looking at the home. "What is going on there? I've never seen so many vultures in one place."

"There's evil here."

The officer shook her head. "The only evil is what people do. We'll find out who did this."

As they approached Amara's house, a white Honda Accord pulled into the driveway. An older man with a moderate white beard and graying hair exited the car. He wore a long-sleeved white shirt and dark gray slacks. A skullcap adorned his head. He stopped and turned toward the police car.

Hendercriss got out, as did Tanya. "Sir, have you talked to the residents?"

"I talked to them on Friday. I am Imam Yusuf Ahmed Al-Fortwani. We were supposed to visit yesterday, but they didn't confirm the meeting. I came to check on them."

Tanya looked at the house. The familiar sense of dread crept in. She covered her mouth.

"Are you alright?"

Tanya shook her head, tears falling again. "Our best friend is missing. Her father is dead."

Hendercriss spoke up. "We don't know if he is dead. We are running tests to see who the victim was."

The imam listened intently. "May I ask whether there was a large pool of blood?"

Hendercriss adjusted her stance, facing the imam. "How would you know that?"

"The other killings in the news. I talked to Amara. I am sorry, you must be Tanya."

She nodded.

"We need to see the Qadir's. They could be in danger."

Hendercriss looked from the imam to the home. The house was quiet. She looked around the yard and reached down toward her weapon. "Get back to my car."

Tanya and the imam did as she asked. Hendercriss keyed her radio. "Sergeant Garcia. We're at the Qadir residence. Something doesn't feel right. Request backup."

"Copy. We have a car on the way. I'll divert them to your location."

Hendercriss moved across the lawn and up the steps to the porch. She knocked on the door. "Police! Is anyone home?"

No response came. She reached for the door, turning the handle. It was unlocked. She opened it cautiously.

"This is the police. I'm coming in." Hendercriss disappeared through the doorway.

Tanya heard the siren of the approaching patrol car.

Hendercriss came back outside and hurled over the railing.

"No!" Tanya ran toward the house. Hendercriss tried to grab her, but she sidestepped and burst into the sitting room. She tried to stop and slipped on something wet. She fell back hard, but avoided hitting her head. Everything seemed to slow down. She tried to get up and felt the familiar stickiness on her hands. Her mind flashed back to the community center. *Blood!* "No! Amara." She scrambled to her feet, grabbing an end table to steady herself. Splattered blood covered two walls of the room and the entryway. Seeing Amara's body, she immediately put her hand to her mouth to cover it. She was wearing the clothes from school on Friday. Her head was missing. The others were the same. Her parents and older brother's bodies were there, all missing their heads. Someone had drawn a bloody symbol on one wall without blood spatter—the slanted B. On the couch under the character, the dead eyes of Amara's father stared back at her.

"Audhu billahi min ash-shaytan ir-rajim. *I seek refuge with Allah from the accursed devil.*"

She backed away, reaching out to steady herself on the imam's arm. "That symbol. I saw it in my dream."

The imam looked at her and said, "This place is cursed. You and I need to talk. When the police are done, call me." He handed her a card. He was concerned and afraid, but his demeanor was calm.

She nodded in shock. Someone had cut Amara's father's head from his body and used it to create the symbol on the wall. The dark red blood streaks stood out on the white wall. She felt hands take her by the shoulders and move her out of the house.

"This place is cursed," he said again.

It wasn't cursed. It was evil, and it was all around. Her friends were dead. Tanya felt numb, her muscles moving only because the officers helped her outside. She had a hazy awareness of the approaching sirens. Everything went dark.

Chapter 43

Sunday Midday

Tanya felt a terrible burning in her nose as she recognized the ammonia smell. Her eyes widened as she turned away.

"She's awake."

Tanya sat up, shaking the fuzziness out of her head. "Where am I?"

Hendercriss stood next to her as Imam Yusuf was off to the side. He looked pale, shaken. His hands caught her attention. He involuntarily opened and closed his hands. Not at once. His fingers move as if each wanted to work together to grasp something but refused to work simultaneously.

"Tanya, how are you feeling?"

She shook her head hard. "Are they all dead?"

"I'm afraid so."

"How could this happen? Why?"

Hendercriss looked at her, shock and pity still showing in her eyes. "I can't answer that. I recommend you see somebody, or this will eat you up." The officer looked at her with sympathy.

Tanya nodded back.

"When I returned from Afghanistan, it took some time before I could adapt to life here again. Little things are going to trigger flashes of memory. It could be a smell, a picture, or something you don't expect." She looked into Tanya's eyes. "We'll do everything possible to find the person responsible for this."

"What do you mean by that? I've been telling my friends for weeks something wasn't right. There's something dark here. They didn't believe me. Several dogs in the area died mysteriously. It was a botulinum toxin. The Burkes got killed, and now the Downes and the Qadirs." She waved her hand toward the other houses. "What about all of them? How many others could there be? And there's that house down there. The house with vultures on it. Why, of all the houses, why that one, and why do they stay? There isn't that much roadkill. I asked Sheri to talk to her dad, the Sheriff, and she didn't believe me. I asked Amara to," she saw the imam shaking his head behind her. "There are too many bad things happening. There's a curse around here." She was frantic, her eyes wide.

Hendercriss nodded. "Sometimes, it's easy to link similar but unrelated events together. You can create a feeling that you are in an epidemic of misfortune. Most of the time, there is a logical explanation." Tanya started to protest. "That being said, it could be something else completely."

Tanya rolled her eyes. "It's easy to dismiss everything, but what if there is a curse? How do you fight that?"

"That's out of my league. Listen, I'm going to call you later to see how you're doing. Are you ok with that?"

"Yes. Thank you, Officer Hendercriss."

"Just call me Haley."

Tanya looked up at her. Another first-name adult. "Thank you, Haley."

She watched Haley walk off to talk to a few others.

Tanya swung her legs off the gurney. "Am I ok to get up?"

The EMT taking off her blood pressure cuff, nodded. "If you don't feel dizzy, you should be ok. Let me help you, just in case." He held her arm as she tried to stand. She did, without a problem. "Take it easy. Make sure you're feeling alright."

She hopped down and went to Imam Yusuf. "Why didn't you want me to tell her about Amara's feelings?"

"Did you see the symbol on the wall?"

"Yes, it looks like a slanted capital B."

"Yes. I thought it was something else when Amara told me everything you described to the officer. Amara's father talked about a similar occurrence in his village when he was a small boy. I believe what we are dealing with is a Ghūl."

"A ghoul?"

"Ghūl. They are a type of Jinn that eat human flesh."

Tanya recoiled. "There has been nothing like that."

"There has. We've seen it on the news. The large pools of blood."

"You say that they eat flesh. Even when I saw the sheriff's bed, there was a lot of blood. Where are the bodies?"

"I'll need to do more research. Keep my card. I will get in touch with you."

"Wait, what about me? I feel like it's all closing in on me." She felt panic. "I don't want to die." She resisted the urge to run home and lock herself in her bedroom.

"If it is a Ghūl, they are tricky, but not different from a deceitful or evil Jinn. They have a reason for what they do, and to make themselves visible, they must believe in their cause."

Tanya felt pain in the muscles in her back. *I need to take something. My back is killing me.* "What can we do against a Jinn or Ghūl? Aren't they magic and supernatural?"

"Not like you've seen in the movies."

Tanya looked back to the house where they were bringing out the bodies. "Why here, though?"

"It's difficult to understand the mind of a being like them. We have stories and myths. I will look into them and contact others I trust. Do not believe what you read online. The ghoul is an ancient creature, but is not the mindless devourer of corpses that lives in graveyards, most Western stories would have you believe."

"What about my friend Sheri? There has been no evidence of her, no blood."

"I don't know. Perhaps the Ghūl is holding her for another purpose. There seems to be a motive for both deaths today. The sheriff was investigating the murders, and Amara had contacted me about receiving wards. Someone tipped it off."

"Could it appear as someone else?"

"They are skilled shapeshifters, thought to take on the shapes of animals and humans."

"How are we supposed to kill it?"

"I don't know that we can."

Tanya felt pressure on the back of her head. She turned, seeing no one there. Someone was watching them. She whispered, "I think it's watching us. I can feel something dark, hidden, waiting to see what we do." She felt the world closing in on her. Her breathing sped up. "I'm going to talk to my mom. Get out of here."

"You may not get away."

Tanya looked at him. A chill ran down her spine.

Chapter 44

Monday Morning

Tanya opened the door to let Jackson in. She had stayed home from school, not ready to face her classmates. The weather outside was chilly and cloudy. She remembered the car accident drill from a week ago. This was worse than she imagined. Her friends were gone, their families were gone, and her mother was hurt. She felt alone, no longer protected by her circle of friends.

"Jackson!"

He trotted in the door as if nothing mattered. Jackson had everything he needed. He didn't miss her dad, nor did she, for that matter. She closed the door and stood there for a moment, sipping the dark coffee. The bitter taste and the cold, gloomy day fit her mood. She was probably in shock. She had cried, but was able to fall into a restful sleep. This morning, she was numb to the emotional pain. Saturday night had been wonderful. She had played well, made an impression, and likely gained a champion in her desire to go to Rice, but did it matter? The plan was for all of them to go. To live together, to experience college life, and that was gone. She'd be alone.

"Tanya, can you make me one of those?" Her mom pointed to her cup of coffee.

"Sure, Mom." She poured her a cup and brought it to the table.

"Mom, do you believe in good and evil?"

"I guess I do. People do bad things. But they also do good things, charity, helping the less fortunate."

"I believe."

"Honey, I can't imagine the pain you're in right now."

Tanya nodded, "I am, and I'm not. I just feel numb, like there's nothing I can do. I'm on a train speeding toward a bridge that collapsed over a large ravine, and everyone around me is panicking, running around, trying to save themselves or jump off the train. But I'm sitting calmly in my seat, watching the scenery pass. I know it's coming, and since I can't do anything about it, I'll just wait until it happens."

Her mom watched her, sadness in her eyes. "Honey, bad things happen. We don't always know why, but people recover."

"I want you to move with me when I leave for college. There's no reason to stay here."

"We can talk about it. I just got the new job."

"Mom, I don't want to be alone. I need you. Do you really want to stay in this house?"

Her mom looked around the kitchen. "Not really. You're right. A new beginning will help us both."

Ding!

> Yusef: Tanya, this is Imam Yusuf. Let me know when you are ready to talk.

> Tanya: I'm ready. Do you want to come here?

> Yusef: No, let's meet somewhere in the main library. Will one o'clock work?

> Tanya: Yes, I'll be there.

"Who was that?"

"Amara's imam. He was there yesterday when we found them. I said I wanted to talk to him. I don't have anyone else."

"Do you want me to go with you?"

"No. Rest. I'll take an Uber there and back."

"Ok. I know this is a lot. You can talk to me, too."

"I know, Mom. I love you."

"Love you, too."

Tanya ordered the car to pick her up and went to her room to get her things. She went upstairs, packed her laptop, and waited for the car.

As she walked into the library, she headed towards an area near the large windows, bypassing the main desk. She loved this library. The large windows extending from the floor to the ceiling brightened the building. At night, the library returned the favor by shining into the darkness.

She saw the imam sitting at a table along the windows, away from the main desk. Only a handful of guests were present. She suspected she was one of very few from her school with a library card.

When she caught his eye, he nodded as she headed to his table. He had several books open and laid out in front of him. She approached. He looked stern, focused. Unlike at Amara's house.

"Imam, Yusuf. I'm sorry, I don't know the proper level of respect."

"Imam Yusuf is fine. These are troubling times. I brought my notes from my discussions with Amara. May Allah have mercy on them. I am not sure how much Amara shared with you."

Tanya sat across the table, her eyes drawn to the books. "She said that you and her father discussed what was happening and agreed that there could be something and that someone was going to bring us wards against evil."

"Ok. Let's start with the symbol on the wall. I believe it represents the name Al'Hiyal. It was first found in ancient Persia. Researchers believe that several family lines from that time were ended suddenly. These symbols represented prominent families, but not leaders in the community. It is odd because the tendency is to move to positions of power to become community leaders. I made a few calls to scholars more familiar with this period. These stories have remained unknown and buried for a long time. They told me they do not wish them to become public knowledge as it could damage the perception of the culture. You can imagine our current culture of punishing the people of now for the sins of the past."

Tanya nodded, "Cancel culture."

"Yes. It is widely accepted that Allah created humans by breathing life into clay. Thus we are from the earth and given life through the divine breath of Allah."

Tanya nodded.

"Are you familiar with angels, demons, and devils?"

"Yes."

"Please take no offense. In our current age, not all of these things are taught." He paused. "There is a process believed to have occurred at the beginning of time. Before humans, there were angels formed from light and created by Allah. The West ignores other beings, but they appear in other Eastern cultures. The Jinn. Some believe that Allah created the Jinn by combining wind and fire and breathing life into them. Still, others believe they are different beings from another plane. It is unnecessary for our discussion, but I wanted you to have an understanding."

Tanya was unsure where this was going. "Are you saying a Jinn is doing this?"

"I do not know yet. The term Jinn is like the term human. If I told you a human did this, you could judge the comment but would understand that you cannot apply the actions of one to the whole, correct?"

"Yes."

"The same applies to Jinn. There are many different races of Jinn, some good and others evil. Some have accepted Allah and the Quran, and others have not."

"Like us."

"Yes, with an exception. They have known the Earth before us, have had dealings with angels and demons, and have their desires and goals."

"What type of Jinn could do everything that's happened, and why?"

"I am not sure yet. I still believe it to be a Ghūl."

"What can we do?"

"It would be dangerous to go down the wrong path. There are many types of Jinn, and any of them could do what we've seen."

Tanya sat back, exasperated. "I don't understand. This, whatever it is, is all around me. I feel like the walls of a prison are closing in on me." She leaned forward. "I didn't feel anything this morning, no emotions. The sadness, the desperation, all of it are right there, but," she paused, looking away ashamed, "I don't care anymore. I'm alone, and I've lost so much."

"Tanya, you must resist these feelings. What of your parents?"

"My mom was in an accident. Both of us are going through a tough time. She's at home, but I don't think she understands. I don't think I do either. I'm scared because every time I say something about evil or darkness being around, someone dies!"

He looked at her. His dark brown eyes showed compassion. "I know you are not Muslim, but Allah cares for you. We are never truly alone if we embrace Him."

Tanya sighed, "I feel helpless."

His smile was one of mercy. "Of the seven houses I spoke about, there are legends that they were each cursed. The nature of the curses is questionable. I will continue to look into them. My colleagues understand the severity of our situation. If it is one of these houses that has resurfaced, it could be catastrophic. Al'Hiyal is one of the seven."

"Could someone have found this out and been faking it?"

"Of course, but the knowledge is not widely known. You will not find it on the internet. They would have found someone that knew the old stories and passed them down."

"What am I supposed to do? I don't have anyone. My circle of friends is gone. I have one friend left and I'm worried something will happen to her."

"You have your mom. Believe in her, and you have me. I do not want to see this darkness spread."

"Doesn't this put you in danger now?"

"I have Allah with me. He will not forsake me."

The hair on the back of her neck stood up. Someone was watching. An image of her and the imam from outside the window flashed in her mind for a second. She spun, shoving her chair back from the table. Two burning embers looked at her from a shaded area much darker than it should have been in the afternoon.

"It's here, outside, in the shadows of the trees. Two burning red eyes."

The imam turned and looked. "I don't see anything."

When she looked back to where she had seen the eyes, they were gone. The feeling remained. She wanted to go home. She needed to get back to her mother.

"I think I need to go home."

"Of course. Would you like me to take you home?"

She thought about it, but didn't want him in danger. He believed her and may find something to help. "No, thank you. I'll call an Uber. What can I do now? If it is a Jinn, how will I know?"

"I don't know. Stories of the Jinn are old, and there isn't much written about them. The means of dealing with them are archaic. Be cautious of anyone new coming into your life. I'm hesitant even to say this as there is no evidence in the modern era, but they can affect your perception. It is a common belief that they can shape-shift."

Tanya stared at the imam. She shook her head. "I guess my feeling of numb acceptance is warranted." She stood up, getting an alert that her ride was close. "Thank you, Imam Yusuf. I hope I see you again." She lowered her eyes, worried that something bad would happen to him soon.

Chapter 45

Monday Afternoon

Her mom was fine. Tanya had gotten home to find her standing on a step-stool, putting dishes away on the top shelf.

"Mom! What are you doing? Let me."

"I'm fine," she said, standing on the third step, a plate in one hand, her other arm in a sling.

"If you slip, how are you going to grab something? Just let me do it, please."

She helped her mom down. "Will you just relax? I've got it." Tanya climbed on the step-stool and put the plate away.

Arr, Arr, Arr, Arr, Arr.

She looked out the window. Jackson was running back and forth, barking at the back fence.

"I'll get him."

"Let him go, Mom. He's fine, just running around. Probably looking for Coolio."

"Ok, I'm going to sit in the living room and catch up on my Netflix shows."

"Good. I'll make some popcorn and join you in a minute."

She took the rest of the dishes out of the dishwasher and stacked them under their cabinets. She put the step-stool away and returned to putting the dishes in the cupboard.

Arr, Arr, Arr, Arr, Arr.

"Ok, Jackson. I guess we're all lucky Dad's not here."

She closed the last cabinet and stepped to the sink to see what Jackson was doing. She froze. A shock ran through her body and fear gripped her. Jackson was sitting in the middle of the yard, looking up at a shadow. The form was faintly visible in the daylight, but it looked like a person. Jackson sat looking up at the form. His head tilted to the side as if listening to what the form was saying. The figure turned its head to look at her. It had two eyes, the color of burning coals. It darted just outside the window, looking at her. The face was a shadow.

She screamed, jumping back, expecting the ethereal form to appear in the kitchen.

"Tanya, what happened?" she heard from the living room.

Tanya ran from the kitchen through the swinging kitchen door and into the living room toward the front door.

"Mom! It's here. It's here." Terror gripped her heart. She needed to get away as fast as possible.

Her mom jumped up. "What's here?"

"Mom! We have to go!"

Her mom followed her. She opened the door, looked back toward the kitchen, ran out, hitting something solid, and screamed. She tumbled down the front steps, landing on something soft and rolling, trying to disentangle with whatever had her.

"Tanya! Ow, stop!"

The voice pulled her out of her fear. "Yasmin?"

"Are you trying to get us back to the hospital?"

Her ribs hurt, as did her right wrist. "Ow, something was in the backyard."

"What?"

"I don't know." She got up, helping Yasmin. "I'm so sorry. We have to get out of here."

"What was it?"

"I think it was a Jinn."

"A Jinn? I haven't heard that name since I left Iran."

"I don't know. It was almost invisible but had burning eyes. Jackson saw it, and it came at me. It had no face."

Yasmin looked askance at her, "Are you sure?"

Tanya felt more calm with Yasmin. Her mom came down the steps. "Are you two ok? You need to calm down, Tanya."

"Mom, I saw it. It had burning eyes. I couldn't make out any other features. It came at me."

"Ok, honey. What do you want to do? The car is in the shop."

Tanya looked around, realization hitting her. "What if it's still there?"

Yasmin started up the steps, "I can look."

"No, the imam said that we couldn't fight it without prayers."

"Ok, I'll pray then. I think I'll be fine."

Tanya's eyes darted between her mom and Yasmin. "Ok, let's all go. We need to stick together."

Her mom nodded. "Ok, let's stick together."

They went back into the house. Nothing was different. Everything in its place. Tanya held her mom's arm as they approached the stairs and the hallway to her dad's office and the laundry room. Yasmin pushed the door to the kitchen and they all piled in, not seeing anything. When she opened the door, Jackson trotted in, going to his water bowl for a drink.

"Jackson thinks everything is fine, and you know they say animals can tell."

Tanya let out the breath she had been holding. "I swear I saw it."

"I believe you, honey." Her mom looked at her, forcing a smile. "I'm going to get the pistol from my room." Her mom left the kitchen.

Tanya felt helpless. She knew that look. Her mom didn't believe her. Her mom was humoring her. She looked at Yasmin, who was smiling at her. "Where did you hear about Jinn?"

"Oh, my gosh, you don't know." She felt overwhelmed and moved to the kitchen table, pulling a chair out and sitting. "Amara and her family are dead."

"What?" She looked shocked. "How?"

"Something killed them. There was blood everywhere."

Yasmin was studying her. Her stoic expression was holding. It's another reminder of her past. *I can't tell her about the heads. It's too much like her mother.* "I went looking for Sheri." Emotion overwhelmed her, breaking through the numb feeling. She started crying. "They're gone. All of them."

"I'm sorry, Tanya. I wish I could have been here for you."

"It was like the center. So much blood. Her imam was there, the one she talked about. I spoke with him. He said that the symbol I dreamed about was from an ancient family, Al'Hiyal. Have you heard of it?"

"Does he have a way to help? Legends and stories are fine, but won't keep you alive."

"He's working on it. He's contacted other scholars." She pulled a napkin from the metal holder in the center of the table and wiped her eyes.

"I'm glad that you're alright."

Tanya reached over and put her hand on Yasmin's, tears rolling down her cheeks. "I'm glad you are as well. I'm scared."

"Of course, we all should be."

"It's all around me. I'm afraid something will happen to my mom and you. I've lost everything else," she sobbed.

Yasmin turned her hand over, taking Tanya's in hers and placing a second hand over it. "We'll get through this. Look at what we've been through together. We need to be strong."

Tanya continued to cry. "I know you're right. It just feels so hopeless." She looked up, scared. "What are they going to say at school?"

"Ignore them. None of them matter. Where have any of them been through this? Your friends are the only ones who stepped forward after what we witnessed at the church. Who came forward to show kindness or compassion? None. They are all selfish, self-absorbed sheep."

Tanya watched Yasmin. Her expression was one of disgust. But she was right. No one had come forward. They were cowards. "I'm glad I have you."

"I'm glad we have each other."

Chapter 46

Tuesday Early Morning

Ka-lack! Ka-lack! Ka-lack! Ka-lack!

Tanya walked into the heart of Dallas in the middle of the empty street. Her black heels reverberated with each step. She wore a dark gray, almost black, women's business suit. The jacket is buttoned with moderate-sized diamond-shaped brass buttons up the front. On her lapel was the blood-red metal symbol of Al-Hiyal. She was not afraid. Her eyes focused forward, ignoring the pleas of the people on either side.

A small boy rushed into the street toward her. He was familiar. She stopped, watching him approach. She examined his features, seeking to make the link. *Dad.*

"You'll never amount to anything. Do you believe this is real? You're nothing." He ran to her, striking her on the leg as if throwing a tantrum. She could feel his anger, jealousy, and contempt. She raised her hand and brushed his cheek, and he froze, fear entering his eyes. The color drained from his face as his blood seeped out of his body onto the surrounding street.

Leaning down to the boy, Tanya looked into his drying eyes and offered, "I give you this flesh for nourishment."

Flame consumed the boy's body, burning through his dry, bloodless form. The flames gradually engulfing him.

"Does your soul feel pain, Dad?"

Tanya sat up, her pajamas soaked in sweat. It felt so real. The sounds of her shoes and the wailing of people. The touch of the boy's skin and the smell of burning. She checked her phone. The time was three-forty in the morning. Tanya knew she would have to stay awake for the day and would suffer the consequences later when she felt exhausted in class. Her mom told her she didn't need to go to school, but she wanted to. It remained as her last source of stability, her solitary constant. There would be stares and comments and whispers. But she could clear her mind and focus on learning. She wanted to get lost in differential equations, history, and English literature. The dream should have bothered her, but it didn't.

She left her home, glancing once down the street where Sheri would have come from. She missed her friend and still held a glimmer of hope that she had escaped. Unlike the other cases, she was missing, with no indication of harm. Her heart was heavy as she crossed the street for the walk to school. This would be the most arduous walk to school—the first day after losing Sheri and Amara. Her heart felt empty. The trees were almost bare of leaves, having shed them to prepare for the approaching winter. Looking down the road, the colorful tunnel created by the trees reaching across with their fall-colored branches was gone, replaced by a mix of gray, white, and brown bare limbs stretching across and highlighted by an overcast sky.

The squirrels were missing. She thought about this as she walked, allowing her mind to disengage from guiding her. Only vultures roamed the area, devoid of any other animals. The dark birds that had invaded the neighborhood at the end of summer. At first, there had been only a few, and then more. Over a dozen perched on the roof, both the top and the lower eaves.

The second-floor window was always open. The white curtain moving with the slightest breeze. Shadows played across the door, casting an ominous darkness over the front porch. Unlike the other houses on the street, the door had a dark wood finish. It looked heavy. Leaves covered the front yard, hiding the boundary between grass and sidewalk. The dark, vibrant green of the bushes along the front of the house was the only sign of life. Someone owned the home, but no one came and went.

Krsssshhhk.

She heard the vulture's cry, and the rustle of anxious wings, but they didn't matter. She stared at the birds, challenging them to do something. What was hiding behind the door? Was the house open? She could knock on the door, maybe even check to see if it was locked. She would likely get away with it. No one was around. She only needed to climb a few steps.

The warble of a police siren broke her train of thought. Tanya stood at the steps in front of the Vulture House. She raised her gaze and witnessed a dozen pairs of black eyes, all fixed on her. The birds were still waiting to see what she would do. She looked around. Who would really care? She was walking on the opposite side of the street. She had crossed without knowing it. How did she get here? She turned to see Officer Hendercriss getting out of her patrol car.

"Tanya, are you ok?"

"I think so. I was walking and my mind was wandering. Because I wasn't paying attention, I didn't realize where I was going."

"Do you know the residents?"

"No, ma'am. I've never met them. The birds creep me out."

Krsssshhhk.

She jumped, looking up. They were all still watching. "See."

"I was just making a round through the neighborhood. Do you want a ride to school?"

Tanya shook her head, "No, thank you. It would just add to the gossip everyone will have, anyway."

"Alright. Remember, you can call me if you need anything, even if it's someone to talk to. It may not be obvious now, but you will recover. You won't forget your friends, but you can move forward."

Tanya adjusted her backpack on her shoulder. "Thank you, Haley."

She saw the concern in the officer's eyes. Maybe she could be trusted. Or she'd think she would lose it in a post-traumatic meltdown. Tanya waved and turned toward the school, shaking her head. She looked back at the house. She didn't remember crossing the street or approaching the home. It felt like a dream, but she had been thinking about it. The birds didn't react to her. Something told her they wanted her to go inside. But that couldn't be. She shook the thoughts from her head and picked up the pace as she neared Amara's home.

She didn't want to look up. Glancing at the sidewalk, she noticed the once immaculate lawn, now scattered with the last leaves from the neighboring trees in their yard. Mr. Qadir would never have stood for that. She thought of Amara, her body half on a couch, the head missing. How do you explain that to people who have never experienced it? She clenched her jaw, feeling her teeth grind together as she raced past the house.

The thought of what she would meet at school weighed on her. She should have been happy, celebrating with her friends. The recital was amazing. Unfortunately, people wouldn't remember her as the outstanding musician who helped bring down the house. People would know her as the poor girl whose friends had been murdered. Some people would be oblivious to anything that happened, at least at first. They would greet her and tell her how great her song was. Then, later, they would stare and whisper about her. She thought of turning back, taking her mom up on the pass to skip school, but pushed ahead. It would be the same every day until she faced it. Better to do it now.

The *Walk* light turned white, and the crossing guards rushed out to hold up their stop signs to let the students cross. She raised her chin and walked in deference to the looks she was getting.

Chapter 47

Tuesday Midday

The cafeteria was quieter than usual. The presence of two police officers contributed to that. Tanya sat by herself at a small round table along the windows. Her lunch comprised of fruits and a peach yogurt. She had hoped that the sweet and tangy flavor would cheer her up like sunshine breaking through the clouds, but she preferred the tart taste more than the sweet.

She saw Yasmin enter the cafeteria before heading for her table. When she sat down, a smile spread across her face. "You look different. I like it."

"Darker eye shadow. It's menacing and keeps people from asking questions. If you are scowling, people stay away."

"I should have done that."

"How was the morning?"

"Not as bad as it could have been. More looks than anything else. Amara was the most popular of our group. Some of her friends had to go home early when they found out."

Yasmin nodded.

"The tough questions are about Sheri, whether I know if she's ok and if she knows about her dad. I don't have anything except to tell the truth. I don't know. Everyone's on edge. Other students are missing. None that I know. I'm sure that's why the police are here."

Tanya rubbed her temples. "How about you?"

"I feel like you do, and I only knew them for a short time. Please don't take this wrong, but I feel more for you and what it is doing to you."

"I get it. We have things in common. Not good things."

Yasmin nodded, sat back, and looked around. She stopped and glared. Tanya felt the intensity of the stare and followed it to the table of freshmen boys, maybe sophomores, who were now looking away or down at the table. "It's something they haven't experienced yet."

Tanya looked at Yasmin. "What do you mean?"

"Some people go through life never experiencing death. Most, however, will face the death of someone they know or care about in their life. It has the potential to alter them. It's not something they expect. It just happens."

"Yeah."

"Others, like us, experience death and keep going, taking strength from the grief." Yasmin turned back to her, holding her gaze. Tanya felt warmth in her chest. Her look exuded strength. She had refused to accept helplessness from her mother's experience.

"I see that."

"Have you heard any more from the imam? Yusuf?"

"Not yet. He was looking into the Al'Hiyal symbol and whatever else he could find on Jinn. He talked about angels, demons, and lots of stuff, but I'm not sure I understand enough to believe. If Jinn exist, why isn't there more information on them?"

"Maybe they are good at staying hidden."

"From the internet? I know you don't have a phone, but you have to have seen social media on your computer."

"Of course."

"Then you know. Someone will make a video about it, even if it is a completely unjustified conspiracy theory."

Yasmin thought about it. "You're right."

"I know. There are already over a hundred videos about the Blood Pool Killer."

"I try to stay away from that. What do they say?"

"It could be me, Diane, my Dad, the police chief, a celebrity, or even the son of the Zodiac Killer trying to one-up his dad's record. Most of it is garbage pieced together from the news stories and whatever they make up."

Yasmin shook her head. "People will believe whatever fits their narrative of the world. They don't trust their eyes anymore."

"Well, I thought about what you said yesterday. I probably imagined what I saw in the backyard. I'm exhausted, and my mind has been playing tricks on me." She leaned in. "This morning, I was walking down the street, thinking about everything, and I almost walked into the Vulture House."

"Walked in?"

"Yeah, Officer Hendercriss saw me and stopped to talk to me. I didn't say anything to her. But between you and me, I don't know how I got there."

"Maybe you need some time away from all of this. You look tired."

Tanya slumped. "I've been sleeping ok, but I woke up early and couldn't go back to sleep."

"Did you fill out your applications?"

"I can't. I just can't concentrate."

Yasmin turned on her. "It might help get your mind off all of this. Focus on the future. We can't let this define us."

"You're right. If I keep putting them off, I'll miss the deadlines."

"Don't forget Bernard's card and offer."

Tanya looked at Yasmin with surprise. "Bernard, huh?"

"I liked his smile, and he was duly impressed with your playing. I told my grandmother about the recital. My description didn't do it justice. The majesty and magic of the song were beyond anything I expected."

"You're biased! It was your song and you're my friend."

"Maybe, but I asked if there were other songs and she said she would look."

Tanya perked up at the thought of playing similar music. She thought of the song and found that part of her was happy. The music helped to set aside the pain she felt. "That would be incredible. I don't think I'll ever be able to describe how I felt playing the song, and because you were there, it was so much better."

"I was there for you."

"I know."

Tanya felt herself grinning. A slight pang of guilt washed over her, yet the memory of playing brought happiness. She looked up at the clock on the wall.

"I've gotta go. Thanks for cheering me up." Tanya leaned over and hugged Yasmin. She felt her friend hug her back. Her joy was replaced by the reality of an unknown killer still on the loose. While clutching Yasmin tightly, she prayed the curse wouldn't ensnare her. She saw a glimmer of hope that there could be happiness, but the reality was that one or both of them would likely die. She let go and looked at her friend, aware that her eyes betrayed her fear and sadness.

Chapter 48

Tuesday Evening

Tanya reached over the stove and hit the fan. The smoke billowed up and around the filter, contributing to the already thick layer of smoke in the kitchen. The cast iron pan filled the kitchen with the loud sizzle of cooking meat. Abruptly, the fan kicked in with a loud whir. Jackson sat at the back door, looking up at her.

Arr, Arr, Arr!

Jackson danced around in the commotion, dodging her quick steps to move about the kitchen.

Using a fork, she flipped the steaks in the pan. Biting back the pain, she felt grease splatters hitting her arm. She hastened to the door and opened it. She secured it open, and the smoke was pushed out of the house.

"That was clo—"

Beep, Beep, Beep….

She took the small towel over her shoulder, stood at the living room's closed kitchen door, and vigorously fanned to push the smoke out.

Beeeeeeeep!

She ran to the microwave and hit *End*. Then, went to the stove, grabbed the steaming broccoli pot, and poured it into a waiting bowl.

The smoke was being replaced with cold air. She stood by the stove and fanned the smoke a little more before closing the back door. She looked at the clock, took the steaks out of the pan, and set them on a plate.

The kitchen door swung open.

Her mom came in, a questioning smile on her face. "Is everything ok in here?"

"Yeah, of course," her voice broke at the announcement.

"Are you sure? Because I peeked in a few minutes ago, you were running around the kitchen waving a towel."

"Mom! Why didn't you come in and help?"

"You had it under control, mostly."

"Well, nothing is burnt. I tried a new rub. So pull up a seat and tell me how work was."

Her mom sat at the table, examining the plate of food in front of her. "It looks good. Fluffy potatoes and the broccoli is a lovely bright green." She cut the steak and took a bite. Her face showed a hesitation before she finished chewing. "The steak is a little bitter, but looks good." She added A-1 sauce and took another bite. "It's good."

Tanya knew she didn't like the steak. She sat down and started eating. A hint of bitterness lingered, but it was tolerable. "How was work?"

"It was good. I got my desk. The accounts I started will be up tomorrow. I got a tour of the offices, met a few people, and filled out lots of paperwork. How was school?" Tanya saw the look of concern.

"I'm not gonna lie, it was hard. I kept looking around, expecting to see them, and didn't. Yasmin and I talked at lunch and after school. She's had it rough, too. She was friends with them."

"Is she coming over?"

"No, but that's ok. I think I want to play tonight, if I can find the motivation. Is that going to bother you?"

"Of course not, honey. I love hearing you play. I apologize for missing your recital. I still feel terrible."

"I'm not sure I'm up to playing it tonight, but I'll play the song through for you sometime." Tanya felt a pang of sadness.

"Take your time."

"You made it, so I'll clean up."

"Ok." Tanya planted a gentle kiss on her mom's cheek. Her mom was doing better. Going to work seemed to have helped relieve the stress her father caused.

With a small cup of chamomile tea in hand, she went upstairs to her room. Later on, she planned to go down for a second cup, aiming to calm her mind for a good night's sleep. She considered looking for a song to play, but in the end let her emotions choose. She turned her desk chair toward the window in the direction her music would normally be.

Tanya took her flute from the stand, took a deep breath, and played. She didn't know what she would play and let her fingers lead her into "Million Years Ago," by Adele. The three girls had listened to the entire album when it came out, sharing stories about the artist and enjoying the summer. This song made them cry when they read the lyrics and sang along. She had played it last year during the spring recital. Her mom had been there and cried at the song. She thought of Sheri and Amara and let the sadness take her as her fingers danced over the flute. She played with her eyes closed, letting memories of her friends bring brief glimpses of the happy times they had. The grief that filled her swiftly replaced the feelings. It felt like a cork had been removed and her emotions rushed in. Tears streamed down her cheeks. Despite the despair wrapping around her, she played through. In the room, she envisioned Amara and Sheri standing beside her, listening to her play just like they had since the first year. She released the grief she had for them, realizing that she had been suppressing her emotions. She let the notes drift off as she neared the song's end. As she sat, she gazed at the pictures over her desk and cried.

Chapter 49

Wednesday Morning

Tanya opened her locker and saw the notification flashing.

> Yusef: I have found the information and need to see you soon.

The text was from earlier in the day. She could try to leave at lunch but wasn't sure she would make it back before afternoon classes started, and she had a quiz right after lunch.

> Tanya: I can meet after school, is 4:00 ok?

> Yusef: Yes, that will work.

Her mind raced, trying to figure out what it could mean. She had one more class before lunch. Concentrating on calculus would prove challenging. If she tuned out Mr. Grays and started on her homework, it would probably go faster. She looked around for Yasmin but didn't see her. Maybe she could come along.

The bell rang, and the students shuffled toward their classes. Tanya walked down the hall to her next class.

Tanya couldn't wait to see Yasmin. She set her tray down at the table and opened the water. She picked at the salad. She had chosen the one with spinach, cranberries, and feta. Amara had warned her about eating salads at school, but Tanya was hungry and didn't feel like eating anything fried. The smell of the serving line turned her stomach. With the bite halfway to her mouth, she paused at the thought of her friend. Losing her appetite for the salad, she set her fork down, peeled a banana, and took a bite.

She looked around the lunchroom. She caught a few people looking at her and promptly turned away. The noise in the lunchroom was lower than the day before, almost a return to normal for the school. She watched the surrounding students. Most didn't seem to have a care in the world. Despite the murders, they were unaffected. People were laughing and joking around with their friends. How was she supposed to act? She shook her head and looked at the banana and salad.

The police were still at each entrance, watching students and faculty come and go. She wondered how long that would last. She looked at the closest officer. From one end to the other, he carefully surveyed the room. He smiled and greeted students but returned his focus when left alone. He took the threat seriously. Tragedy loves company, but everyone besides the police doesn't care. The intense feeling of yesterday was more measured today. Tomorrow would be even less, as everyone moved on to the next story of interest.

"Hey." Yasmin sat down at the table. "Salad?"

"I didn't want anything heavy, and I was thinking of Amara."

"Are you still getting looks? It's only been a day, but people seem to have moved on already."

"That's good. We can get back to our lives."

"I guess. Some of their friends are still out to grieve."

"And yet, not her closest friend."

"Are you busy after school?"

"I'm not sure yet. Why?"

"I got a text from Imam Yusuf. He said he's found some information and needs to see me immediately."

Yasmin didn't look happy. "What does he know about any of this?"

"He was looking at the symbol, Al'Hiyal."

"I talked to my grandmother last night. I told her what the imam told you. She said it was all nonsense. The teller always manipulates stories from that far back to make themselves shine in a better light."

"You think he's making it up or that the story's just a myth?"

Yasmin looked out the window. "Whatever happened was a long time ago. Don't you remember what Mrs. McCarthy told us at the beginning of World History?"

"The victor writes history and rarely tells the tale of the oppressed."

Yasmin smiled. "Good impression."

"Thank you. But, even if it is a skewed story, it's something. How can we explain a symbol on the wall from a family in ancient Persia?"

"They'll think you're crazy. Did you tell anyone else about the symbol after you dreamed about it?"

Tanya thought about it. "I only told you, Sheri, and Amara. I don't think they would have told anyone."

Yasmin pulled out a piece of paper and a pencil and drew a similar symbol on the paper. The flourish was not as pronounced, but it was near.

"That's it. Where did you see it?"

"I've been thinking about it. Where would you have seen the symbol? And I think I figured it out. Do you remember what Diane wore at our meetings?"

Tanya looked up to the left. "Jeans or blue slacks and a long-sleeved shirt, red or maroon usually."

"I think she wore a necklace outside her shirt. It was gold, but I don't remember what it was. Could it have been something like this? Maybe it was a friend or someone important, with the initial B."

Tanya thought about it. She remembered the outfits but not the necklace. She was also nervous and looked more into her eyes. "I guess. Do you believe in the Jinn?"

"Of course, people in my culture talk about them. Often, the stories are used to scare children into behaving. Like Western stories of monsters under the bed."

"Well, if you want to come along, I will head to the main library after school."

"I don't know. I don't have a good history with holy men."

Tanya remembered the story of Yasmin's mother. "Oh my gosh. I am so sorry! That was insensitive." She placed both hands over her mouth.

"It's ok. I think I'll head home. I've been finding peace in the garden, and my squash looks amazing." Yasmin's smile wavered.

"Ok, I'll let you know what he says."

Yasmin reached up and patted her hand. She felt the tingle of a shock. "Maybe I'll see you tonight?"

"Yeah. I could come to your place if you are tired of coming to mine."

"No. Your house is better. I never know when my grandmother's friend will be there."

"How has everything been?"

"Better. I confronted him. He tried to bully me, threatening to kick us out of the apartment."

"Oh, no."

Yasmin smiled. "I set him up. He yelled at me while my grandmother was cooking through the open window. She came out and put him in his place."

Tanya smiled. "Your grandmother seems like a feisty woman."

Yasmin looked out the window. "She can be."

Chapter 50

Wednesday Midday

Yusuf shuffled through the documents on his dark desk. The manuscript he had received this morning already had several sections tabbed, with small cloth ribbons to protect the pages. Using his tablet, he rapidly typed an email, attached a file, and sent it to his assistant. He wanted to be prepared for the meeting with the young woman, Tanya. He placed the manuscript, a few documents, and his Qur'an in his worn leather satchel.

"May Allah watch over us and protect us from malevolence. It is written that Allah only puts forth challenges that we can endure. Guide me in assisting this young woman and protect her with your divine grace."

He turned to leave the office and looked back once more to make sure he wasn't forgetting anything. Despite its cluttered appearance, his office wasn't disorganized. His dark wooden writing desk, with a single center drawer, was surrounded by shelves containing books, old and new. His prayer rug and collections from his years of study decorated the book shelves and most other horizontal surfaces. As he left his office, he remembered his teacher reciting a verse from the Qur'an that had stuck with him through all his studies: "He grants wisdom to whom He pleases, and whoever receives wisdom indeed receives a great good, and only men of understanding comprehend it."

The words had touched him the first time he read from Surah Al-Baqarah. He had devoted his life to the pursuit of knowledge and teaching what he learned to those he led. This pursuit of knowledge had opened the doorways to the scholars who had provided the manuscript he now carried. Allah is remarkable in his preparations. The initial dark foreboding he felt at the discovery of the Qadir home was supplanted by the blessing of the Lord. He found himself where he was meant to be. A link to knowledge that may save the girl, and more if the prophecy were to be believed.

Yusuf felt a slight bite in the air as the cold hit him in the face. The sky looked to be in turmoil, with the low clouds drifting across the sky. He drove through the township toward the Qadir home. He shook his head at the city, which was putting up its decorations for Christmas already. Silently musing, he considered that the reason was to help people embrace the festive season earlier, to escape the growing challenges of life, extend the holiday from mid-fall to mid-winter, and profit from the holiday-related spending.

He looked to the left at the high school, wondering how the young woman, Tanya, was doing after the traumatic events of the weekend. His mind wandered back to his time studying in Qom. Iran was more stable than other areas in the Persian Gulf region, leading to less exposure to violence before moving to America.

At the light, he turned right and drove at a leisurely pace toward their home. He searched his jacket pocket for the pass the police had given him as the family's spiritual leader to ensure he had it in case anyone asked why he was entering the home. He exited the car and rushed up the steps to the front door. The door stood cracked open, and he could hear voices emanating from inside. He knocked and stepped in. Both men turned to look at him.

"Sir, this is still an active crime scene."

Yusuf nodded. "I will stay out of your way. I have a pass. He pulled it out and showed them. I only need a picture of that." He pointed to the symbol.

The younger officer, with short cropped hair and a thick mustache, looked at the symbol and then back at him. "Do you know what it means?"

"I'm not sure. I am sending it to a few scholars I know."

The older officer, a short, stocky man, slipped off a blue glove and pulled a card out of his pocket and handed it to the imam. "If you don't mind. I'd appreciate it if you could let us know what you find out. We've had a few people from the lab on it, and the working theories are anything from a gang symbol to an occult ward."

Yusuf nodded and took the card. "I will." He used his phone to take pictures of the bloody symbol. "Thank you. That's all I needed."

He left the home, shutting the door, and stopped on the porch to look at the images. He swiped through each and then attached them to a message and sent it. His friends had requested the photos.

He went down the steps and headed to his car.

Krsssshhhk.

He turned toward the sound and saw Amara walking a few houses down toward a worn gray home that looked abandoned.

"Amara!"

The girl turned and looked at him before going up the steps into the house. Did he see correctly? His eyes weren't what they used to be, but it looked like her, and she turned when he called her name.

"Amara!"

The girl didn't come back out. He thought she was dead, but now he was unsure. The bodies they discovered didn't have heads. They were missing, except for the father. He locked his car and headed toward the home. As he neared it, he saw the vultures roosting on the roof. He bowed his head, "Allah, watch over me."

As he ascended the steps, the earthy smell became more prominent. He looked around, noting the surfaces' mold growth and other fungus. Leaves from the trees covered the porch, forming a layer of yellow and orange across the wooden planks. He extended his arm towards the door and hesitated. He knocked. There was no answer.

"Amara? It's Imam Yusuf."

He waited for a moment before calling out again. When he tried to open the door, he realized it was unlocked. He cautiously pushed the door, the earthy smell becoming stronger. "Hello?"

He stepped into the entryway. It was dark inside. He reached to turn on the lights, but they didn't work. The rooms on either side of the door were empty. Light wood panel flooring and white walls. The mold from outside hadn't made it inside, despite the smell.

"Is anyone home?" his voice echoed in the empty rooms. He listened but didn't hear any response. The staircase to his right went up and ended at a 'T.' He could see the door to the left was open, but the room was dark. He looked down the hall that led back to the kitchen and moved forward. To the right, under the stairs, there was a hall that carried on. The light wood flooring reflected light from the door behind him, casting his shadow ahead.

Creak!

The sound came from upstairs.

"Amara, are you here?" He waited for an answer, but the house was eerily quiet.

Creak!

Yusuf backed up to the main entrance and peered down the hall before ascending the stairs. Everything was meticulous. The walls were clean, the wood floors polished, and no dust was on any surface. The run-down look outside made for an odd mismatch.

Creak!

He crept up the steps. He slowed as he neared the top of the landing, listening. His shadow fell on the wall in front of him. He cautiously looked around the corner and saw an open door down the hall. He attempted to remain silent, taking careful steps as he got closer.

Leaning forward, he peered into the room. A woman stared at him. She pressed her foot to the floor.

Creak!

"I could smell you when you entered O' holy teacher, Yusuf Ahmed Al-Fortwani."

He hid his surprise, stepped into the room, and prayed to Allah to protect him. The woman was dark, her skin black as the starless night sky. Her hair rolled in long curls over her shoulders. Her eyes were burning embers. She wore a long midnight blue wrapped skirt, with the faintest orange gold lined slit up both sides, showing long slender legs. Her top, made of the same cloth as her skirt, wrapped around her neck and crossed over her chest, exposing her midriff. Her feet were bare but crossed strands of fiery orange metal twisted up her calves to the knees from gold anklets.

"Allah is with me; you have no power over me."

She took a step closer; a sly grin broke on her face. "If only that were true, holy teacher."

Yusuf stood in defiance. "You have no power over me."

"I could kill you where you stand, and your God would do nothing except welcome your faithful soul." Her voice was smooth, alluring.

"To be with Allah is the reward of a faithful life."

She walked up to him and lifted her hand toward his face. He tried to step back, but the door frame stopped him. He felt her fiery touch on the side of his face. It burned, then turned soft, as her finger traced down his jaw. *Allah is with me.*

She leaned in, lowering her face to his. The blazing coals of her eyes kept his focus. Her skin was smooth like obsidian. She smiled, revealing sharpened teeth. "You're lucky, holy man. This is the longest anyone has beheld my true form and lived longer than an instant."

"What do you want?"

"We have similar desires." She took one step back. Her body moved with seductive fluidity, resembling that of a serpent, with complete control. He swallowed.

"There is hope for you. Let me teach you of the Qur'an."

She flinched. "No, O' holy teacher. I will not let myself be lured like others of my kind were. We are not of heaven or hell; our place is here, not locked within the City of Brass," she sneered at him. "Soon enough, though, the time of our imprisonment will end."

"What do you want with the girl?"

"She is of no concern to you. You should be more concerned with why you're still alive. I would prefer to feast on your flesh, but I must resist."

"Ghūl!"

She sneered, the yellow-red of her eyes continuously shifting. "I think a slow death is more fitting. After all, you need time to praise Allah before you meet Him." Her hand flashed up, revealing long, thin nails extending from the ends of her fingers. They glistened with moisture.

He felt a scratch on his neck. "That's so you don't run away."

She flicked another finger, and he felt the prick of a needle. "And that is so you die like a dog."

He tried to move but paralysis overcame him. He tried to speak but couldn't. *Allah is with me. I am His servant. He does not present tests we are not capable of overcoming.* Despite the fear creeping into his chest, he continued to pray. He was determined not to lose faith.

She effortlessly lifted him and carried him downstairs. The scratch on his neck was burning. He felt it spreading. Sharp pain formed in his stomach. He couldn't see. It was as if he had swallowed razor blades. He could taste blood in his mouth.

She lay him down in the grass. He could see tall, thin, evergreen cypress trees along the back fence. She placed him in a position where he was looking up toward the roof. A dozen pairs of black eyes watched him. The vultures! With greater intensity, he prayed in his mind. He was to be eaten alive. Determined, he steeled himself and kept praying.

She stepped over him, straddling him and leaning over to lick the side of his face. He caught a quick flash of the forked tongue. "Holy man, Imam Yusuf Ahmed Al-Fortwani. I gift you a test of faith. One

278

last chance to prove to Allah the extent of your devotion." She smiled at him and moved out of his view. *Allah is with me. I am his faithful servant. Have mercy on my soul. Grant me strength, oh Lord.* The large black birds shifted, flexing their wings, and watched him.

Chapter 51

Wednesday Afternoon

Tanya arrived early for the meeting at the library. The last time she had been on time, it looked like he was already deep into his research. Imam Yusuf said it was urgent, so she assumed he would be here, ready to talk, but he wasn't. The librarian at the desk stated that there were only a few others in the library, none matching the imam's description. Tanya used the reference computers to find information on the Jinn. She found it surprising that the Qur'an contained several references to them. Taking a copy with English translations, she went to the table they had met at before. She opened the back and read the passages that focused on the Jinn.

They were beings created by God, like humans, given free will to choose good or evil. Some had converted to follow God and were benevolent, while others rejected the teachings, choosing evil. They were believed to have mystical powers or abilities that made them more powerful and deadly. They could fly, become invisible, and change their appearance to that of an animal or person. The thing she saw in the backyard, standing over Jackson, saw her and appeared in the kitchen window. She instantly noticed her proximity to the large glass windows. Fear weighed on her heart as she lifted her gaze and scanned outside the window.

"It could be watching me right now." She felt her skin prickle. She checked her phone, turning it to read the time. He was late. She checked her texts, not finding anything else from him. She was worried. Everyone who got close to understanding was dead. Her eyes darted around the library as she noticed the varying sounds. The smell of the books overwhelmed her. She had no one else to turn to. Who could help her? The imam had given her a spark of hope that there was something she could do to protect herself. What about her mother? Was there anyone else that knew about the Jinn? She had no way of finding out who Imam Yusuf was talking to. The Ghūl would get to her. Was this part of the torture? Did the others know they were being hunted before they died?

She wanted to run. The library felt too enclosed to her. There weren't enough people here. Leaving the books on the table, she gathered her things. She should have at least taken them to the desk, but she decided against it, wanting to get away, go home, and lock herself in her room. She went to the main desk and called for a ride. The lights didn't appear as bright as she thought.

"Are the lights dimmer?"

The man at the desk looked around. "No, they seem normal."

She went outside as soon as the red Nissan Sentra pulled up. She heard the driver turn down the hip-hop music. Wrapping her coat around her, she got into the car. The car was warm and smelled of evergreen car freshener. The driver glanced at her in the rearview mirror before pulling out. She watched the world pass by in silence. She wanted to see her mom. The car pulled up in front of her house and let her out. A silver Hyundai sat in the driveway.

"Thanks." She clicked five stars and headed into the house.

"Mom, I'm home! Are you here?"

Her mom came out of the kitchen. "Hey honey, how was your counseling?"

"He didn't show."

"That's odd, no texts?"

"No. I'm sure something important came up. I'll try again later."

"Do you want to talk about it while we drive around the neighborhood?" Her mom pulled her coat on.

"Why would we do that?"

"Jackson got out."

"When?" It should have hit her harder, but it was just another bad thing in her life.

"I thought I brought him in before work, but now I'm not sure."

Tanya's heart sank. The vultures. He was small enough that one of the birds could get him. "Yes! Let's go now."

"Ok, just a sec. I need the fob. The car won't start if it's not near."

"Is that a new car or rental?"

"Rental from the dealer while they fix my car."

"Should you be driving with your arm?"

"I'll be careful." When Tanya gave her mom a puzzled look. She shrugged. "I have to get to work."

"Mom, do you need me to drive?"

"No. If you need to jump out, he'd be gone before I could get out of the car."

They got in the Hyundai. It smelled new. Her mom started the car, and Tanya felt warmth on her legs and back.

"Seat warmers?"

"Yes, nice isn't it?"

"Uh-huh. Go up the road toward school. There are vultures."

"They won't go after live animals unless they're sick."

"These will. They're black vultures, not the turkey vultures. Something's different with them. A few flew at us when I took him on a walk. We ran home. Drive slow."

Her mom drove slowly up the road and around the surrounding streets for the next hour. They saw a dead opossum on the side of the road that the vultures hadn't found, but no sign of Jackson.

They pulled up to a stop sign before returning to their house. Her mom looked over at her. "He usually comes back. He'll be hungry soon."

Tanya nodded, looking out the window. She hoped he didn't get taken by the large birds. She looked up the street and saw a metallic blue car gradually nearing their house.

"Mom, slow down. That's Dad," she pointed to the car.

Her mom pulled over a few houses away. He stuck his arm out of the window. He was taking a picture.

"What's he doing?"

"Looks like he's taking a picture. He shouldn't be there. I'm going to call the police."

"No honey, look, he's going."

"Why are you protecting him? He broke the law. He should get called out for it."

Her mom nodded, "Yeah, ok, you're right. But technically, we're not there, so he is still outside the restraining order distance."

"Mom, don't let him push you around or manipulate you. You know he will. He's a monster and we're better off without him. He can't go in and out of the house whenever we're not there."

Her mom nodded, watching the car pull away. "Ok, I'll report it when we get back." Tanya thought something else was in the look, but it disappeared quickly.

When the car was out of sight, they pulled into the driveway.

Tanya looked around. The daylight was fading. "Jackson!" She waited a few moments before calling two more times. When he didn't come running, she went into the house, turning on the front light by the door.

Chapter 52

Wednesday Night

Tanya took a breath and stepped out the back door into the yard. It was dark, and with her dad gone, the motion sensor lights wouldn't get fixed anytime soon. Her breath formed a fine mist in the night air. She looked up, still clouds, though she thought she could see where the moon was trying to break through. All the leaves had fallen and spread over the lawn. The trees looked like bony tendrils spreading into each corner of the yard. She shined the flashlight around the back deck, just in case. The memory of Coolio flashed in her head. She dreaded the thought of Jackson being gone, but it was preferable to the certainty of his death. Hopefully they would find him soon.

In her mind's eye, she visualized Sheri being away at a relative's house, somewhere far off. It helped calm the fear that she was likely gone, too. She tried to push the thought of her best friend away. The more she tried to distract herself, the stronger the memories were. She felt the tears build in her eyes, the emptiness again in her chest. She went to the side of the house. The darkness outside the light caused her to pause.

She steeled herself and used the light to check every shadow. She walked the entire fence line, not seeing any holes where he could have dug.

"Jackson!"

She listened in case he had gotten into the neighbor's yards. Absolute stillness enveloped the surroundings, without even a hint of a breeze. She shined the light around the yard again and then onto the deck covering under her window. It was clear. She saw a shadow move and shifted the light higher and saw the glowing eyes of a vulture sitting atop her roof. The light reflected in its eyes, making them shine golden yellow.

Her cheeks were hurting from the chill. She went back inside and hung her coat on the hook in the living room closet. She made a cup of decaf coffee, a dark roast, nothing added, and took it up to her room. She saw the light under her mom's room and knocked on the door.

"Come in."

Tanya cracked the door open and said, "I'm going to bed."

"Ok, honey, sleep well."

Closing the door, she headed down the hall to her room. She closed the door, set her coffee on the desk, and changed. She went to the bathroom, washed up, and returned to the room, feeling refreshed.

"Hopefully, I can sleep tonight. No nightmares." She gestured towards the dreamcatcher hanging on the wall.

She opened her laptop to check her email. An email from Farid Amirzadeh caught her attention. She opened it.

Ms. Janessy,

My name is Farid Amirzadeh. I am an assistant to Imam Yusuf Ahmed Al-Fortwani. The imam asked me to send these files to you if I did not hear from him by 8 P.M. this evening. If you met with the imam, you should already have copies. If you did not, something may have happened to him. Please reply if you met. I am waiting in anticipation for your reply.

Farid Amirzadeh

Tanya clicked the link and opened the file. Pictures, notes, and documents were in Arabic, with notes in English on the side. She took time to read through.

The research focused on the Al'Hiyal family name. The family rose to prominence in northern Persia, pre-Qur'an, building a reputation for exceptional craftsmanship. She flipped through the images, finding a hand-drawn symbol she recognized as the one from her dream. The documents describe that the family was driven to exile, with many being killed for the most grave of crimes. She read through the files and found a note in another document about eating the dead. She recoiled, forcing herself to continue to read. Six other families were condemned at around the same time for similar crimes, but no specifics were listed.

An image of a scroll had the words "Zoroastrian" and "revelation" among notes in Arabic. She read through once more, absorbing the information.

"Eating the dead?"

She opened her search engine and typed in ancient Persia and "eating the dead."

The page contained examples of cultural relativism and emphasized the spiritual importance of consuming the flesh of the deceased. People have engaged in cannibalism throughout history and it continues to be practiced in certain regions of the world. The thought sickened her and brought an onslaught of images. The missing bodies. Were they being eaten? She closed the browser and opened her email.

Mr. Amirzadeh,

I waited at the library for almost an hour after our appointment. Imam Yusuf didn't show. I received the files. Thank you. Please let me know if he turns up.

Tanya

After hitting *Send*, she closed the laptop. Embracing an escaping yawn, she stretched her body. As she got up, she peeked out the window and saw nothing. She turned off the lights, keeping her nightstand light on, and pulled the cover up to her neck, turning to get comfortable. She didn't want to have nightmares. The information from the files and the events of the last few weeks would probably haunt her again, as they had most nights.

With a sudden burst of energy, she propelled herself upwards, snatched her calculus book from the desk, and flipped to the questions pages at the end of the chapters in a frenzy. She read and reread a few problems, hoping her mind would want to solve them instead of obsessing about the murders.

As she lay in bed in silence, her eyes felt heavier. From the window side of the bed, she rolled over and gazed at Smurfette, who returned her bright-eyed smile. *Gargamel always talked about getting rid of the Smurfs, but he never succeeded in killing all your friends.* Her eyes closed as her focus dropped from her shelf to her desk and then to her flute stand. *Where's my flute?* She drifted off to sleep. *A particle moves along a straight line, and its velocity function, v(t), is given by.* The thought drifted just out of reach.

Chapter 53

Thursday Morning

Tanya woke up, somewhat rested. The calculus trick had worked, though she felt she had worked on the same problem all night. She didn't remember exactly what she was working on, but the graph had been an oval extending to a point in space similar to a black hole. She remembered sitting at a computer, working out the math to elongate the event horizon from a circle to an oval with a ratio of 2:3. Thinking of the model with a fuzzy morning brain didn't help and made it even more confusing. As soon as she got out of bed, she remembered her flute was missing. She opened the case, and there was nothing inside. Unless it was on the stand, she never left it out. Had someone taken it?

Her mind was awake. This didn't sound like some torture of a supernatural being. This sounded like a mean and spiteful person. The same person who could get the dog to go with him willingly, without leaving a clue. That *bastard*! She went to the bathroom, hearing her mom moving around downstairs.

"Mom, are you up?"

"I'm in the kitchen," her voice sounded from downstairs.

Tanya walked into the kitchen, combing her hair. She had on jeans and a scoop neck long-sleeved blue sweater. She went toward the refrigerator, deviating when she smelled the cranberry-orange muffins on the counter.

"Oh, Mom." She picked it up, cut it in half, and spread butter. "Mmm, I love these."

"Tanya, thank you. I know you love them, and I wanted to start our day off well."

Tanya hugged her mom. "Thank you, this helps."

"Don't forget, Officer Hendercriss is supposed to stop by tonight, and I have mediation with your father this afternoon."

Tanya pivoted. "I think Dad was in the house. Jackson would have gone with him, and my flute is missing. Before you say anything, I never misplace my flute."

Her mom tilted her head. "You know. I'm missing a few things too. He might do something as petty as that to show he can get to us any time. Well, he's in for an awakening tonight. I'm putting my foot down. No more bullying, no more calls, and no more coming near the house."

"I can't wait to get out of here. We'll finally be free of all this. We'll start over, just the two of us."

Her mom smiled and picked up a muffin, placing it in a plastic bag before putting it in her lunch bag.

Tanya watched her go out of the office. Her mom looked happy, which was good. She deserved it. Tanya did not feel good. She wanted to get away as fast as possible. Her mom had done her best to help her and had set up the 'meeting' with Haley to help cope with the deaths of her friends, but no one understood what she was feeling. She wondered if today was the day she would die. She didn't have anything else to lose except…Mom. She ran out of the kitchen and jumped at her mom as she opened the front door.

"Mom, promise me you'll be safe. The killer is still out there."

"Tanya, I'll be fine. Straight to work, the mediation, and home. I'll see you tonight."

Tanya hugged her again. A sense of dread fell on her.

She watched her mom leave and ran upstairs, opening the files from Farid. She printed a copy. There were just over a dozen pages. She went to her dad's office and found an empty folder. She stopped to look at his things. Most of this would be gone soon. He had taken his computer and most of the stuff on top of his desk, but the shelves around the room held little reminders of his time in the Navy. On the wall was his athletic letter 'N' from playing lacrosse at the Naval Academy and a picture of his graduating class throwing their hats in the air. A photo of him standing on the pier in front of his destroyer, his navy officer's sword, a long-curved kukri, and a plaque from the ship were alone on a wall. She used to feel sorry for him and how depressed he had been, but now she knew who he was and felt nothing but contempt. There was some love there, linked to moments of happiness growing up, but there was also disgust at what he had done and continued to do to them and her, his daughter. She doubted if he still cared for her.

She took the pages off the printer, placed them in the folder, and left the room. All of this couldn't be gone fast enough.

Chapter 54

Thursday Midday

Tanya sat alone at a small round table near the window. Her lunch was on the left side. A cranberry-orange muffin was broken into pieces on her tray, which held a plate of tater tots and mustard. She wanted the bitter taste instead of ketchup's sweet, tangy flavor. It was still gloomy outside, overcast, and thick clouds. The cafeteria was louder than usual, the cold weather driving in most students who ate outside. The police presence was down to one officer at the main door.

Tanya sighed, turning back to her laptop. She had another email from the imam's assistant, Farid. The imam hadn't checked in. He told her he sent an email to an address in Iran. He didn't specify what the email contained, only that the group looked into odd occurrences. He didn't seem too worried yet, as the imam sometimes would research things he wished to discuss with the worshippers.

Before popping it in her mouth, she dipped a tot in the mustard. She hadn't seen Yasmin all morning. She kept looking up from her laptop, searching the room for her friend. What if something happened to her? Tanya felt panic rise. She sent a text to her mom.

> Tanya: Mom, I just wanted to say I love you!

> Mom: I love you, too.

Phew, she was ok. Why did they take one officer away? It wouldn't matter at all. She closed her eyes, trying to block off the negative thoughts. The noise swirled around her: darkness, screaming, and terror. She saw the dark shape in her mind flow across the officer at the door, his lifeless body dropping to the floor, and a shadow swept through the room. Anything that touched the dark cloud fell to the floor in a growing pool of blood.

Tanya opened her eyes, afraid of what she might see. Her heart raced, matched by her rapid breaths. The lunchroom was normal. Tables of friends carried on as if they didn't have a care in the world. There was no threat to them. Instead of envying them, she only felt pity. She finished her lunch and packed up her laptop. She hadn't had a chance to get to the music room. Band was still the highlight of her week.

Tanya entered the band room. She smelled the hint of oil used in the keys and levers of the instruments. She was alone. Mr. Bilby should be in soon. The others wouldn't show until right before class. She looked around the room and then went back to her prep area.

"Tanya, what are you doing?"

She looked up from her hands and knees. Her flute case was not under the instrument shelves.

"Hi, Mr. Bilby. I can't find my flute."

"That's not like you."

"I know. I think one of my parents moved it. I couldn't find it, and my mom had already left for work."

"We have the trial instruments. You can use one of them."

"Are you handing out music for the winter holidays?"

"You've got my pattern down. After you all performed so well last week, I think we have to step it up for our next performance."

Tanya nodded.

Other students started coming in, getting their instruments and tuning them. Tanya went to the shelf with the trial flutes and opened each case, looking for the cleanest one. They were all pretty good, but one looked almost new. She took it out, assembled it, and polished it with the cloth in the case.

When all the students were in place, Mr. Bilby went to the head of the class.

"Ok, let's start with our scales to warm up." He turned to his teaching assistant. "Pass out the winter music." The student nodded, went to a table next to Mr. Bilby's desk, grabbed the packages, sorted by instrument, and walked through the ensemble, placing the music on their stands.

Tanya played the scales up and down, changed the key with the group, and repeated their routine. She played with her eyes closed, hearing the soft sound of her flute. Slowly, she tuned out the other instruments and felt each note as she played them. She experienced something new when she transitioned to legato. An energy connected the notes. Each one had potential, depending on the following note and the transition. She saw the notes floating in the air, shifting shape from the symbology for the notes to something else, just out of touch. The notes stretched, flowing into lines along familiar but unrecognized patterns.

She heard a gasp and opened her eyes. The lights had gone out. Students were scrambling to move toward the front of the room to avoid sparks falling from the light fixtures.

"Careful, careful. Watch your instruments and be mindful of each other. Come on, students, out the front door."

Tanya's heart jumped at the power outage, fearful of another attack, and was relieved when the hallway was illuminated.

"Ok, well." Mr. Bilby looked back into the room through the propped open door. "Let's go back one or two at a time and grab your cases. I'll inform the office that you're released for independent study."

Tanya felt disappointed. She had felt something new with the music and wanted to play more. If she couldn't find her flute at home, she'd call her dad to see if he had *mistakenly* grabbed it. She knew it wouldn't be the truth, but it would give him an out.

She entered the room and stored the flute when it was her turn. The sparks had almost stopped, the burnt electrical smell filled the room, and the infrequent pops made her jump. She slid the flute case back on the shelf. As she left, she saw the text from her mom that she'd be home early. The mediation shouldn't last too long. She was going to order Chinese for dinner.

Tanya: Chicken Lo Mein, please. Good luck. Be strong.

Mom: You got it!

Chapter 55

Thursday Afternoon

Tanya closed her locker and checked her messages. The hall buzzed with her excited and loud classmates, ready to escape for the day. She looked across the hall to Sheri's locker. Since she was still listed as missing, the school hadn't cleaned out Sheri's locker like they had Amara's. Several sticky notes, offering words of encouragement and prayers, were taped in place. Tanya felt her throat tighten as she gave in to the belief that her best friend was gone. She checked her phone before exiting the school.

> Mom: After school, take an Uber to get Chinese food. Delivery is not available.

The message was an hour old.

> Tanya: Ok.

She waited for the car inside the building. When her rideshare arrived, she stepped outside. The wind hurt her cheeks. She zipped her coat up higher. At least it would be in the seventies this weekend.

Loneliness weighed on her. Other than the text from her mom, there was no activity. The silence reminded her that Sheri and Amara were gone. She leaned back in her seat, watching the other cars, until she pulled into the strip mall. She picked up the food and hopped back in the car to head home.

They turned down her street. She saw her house indicated on his map app. As they passed the run-down house, she saw someone standing on the porch. They were near the dark corner by the front door, but it looked like Yasmin. *I wish she would get a cell phone.* Someone was shuffling up the street, walking with a stagger. Their leg was hurt. It was her dad. His shirt and hands were stained with blood. He didn't look up. Her heart was overcome by fear. *Mom!*

She jumped out of the car.

"Mom!" Tanya dropped the food and her backpack and ran to the open front door. In the living room, she saw smoke coming from the kitchen, and she pulled her jacket up and across her mouth.

"Mom!"

Tanya froze. She heard popping from the kitchen and saw smoke above the door. She ran forward and put her hand to the door. It felt hot. She pushed against it, swinging it inward, and saw fire burning up the walls over the stove. All burners were on. The curtains over the sink were burning, and flames were coming out of the pantry to the left. She didn't see her mom.

"Mom!"

She ran upstairs to her mother's room. The door was open. Her heart stopped. She lay across the bed on her back, one hand on her chest, blood running between her fingers. Blood streaks spread across the bed. Tanya ran to her side.

"Mom!" Tears were in her eyes, and her hands were shaking. She tried to check her pulse. As she touched her neck, she felt for the carotid artery. It was faint. Her mom's chest rose slowly, and she coughed. Blood trickled down the side of her mouth. Smoke was coming from the doorway. She had to get her out. Tanya tried to put her arm around her mom, but she was too heavy. She couldn't lift her. Her mom's eyes looked at her, tears running down her temple.

"Oh God, Mom." She tried to grab her mom's arm to drag her out. Her hands slipped, now covered in blood. She coughed, the smoke getting thicker. She attempted to grab her mom's shirt and pull her, but her hands tore through it.

Tanya wiped her eyes. She couldn't move her mom.

"Mom, I'm so sorry."

Her mom's mouth moved. She leaned down to hear. "Go. Love… <cough>… you."

Tanya pulled a pillowcase from the bed and held it over her mouth. Her eyes were stinging. If she didn't go, smoke would overcome her. She tried one more time to pull her and slipped, falling on the floor. She lay there, smoke rolling overhead. Why bother? She could lay here and give up. She would be with her mom.

No! The voice in her heart rebelled. Get him! Adrenaline shot through her veins, as anger focused her on revenge.

Tanya crawled out of the room to the stairs, staying low. Smoke had filled the living room and the upstairs area. She took a deep breath, ran down the stairs, and out the front door. She fell on the front lawn. Smoke was billowing from her home, and she could see flames through the doorway. She reached for her phone. She needed to call 9-1-1. It wasn't in her pocket. She looked around. It must be inside. She heard a window break around the side of the house.

As she straightened up, watching everything she knew go up in flames, she glanced down the street. She took off running. He would not get away with this. She felt adrenaline course through her veins. She clenched her teeth in anticipation. She would do whatever it took to hurt him for this. Her legs ached as she neared the decrepit home.

Krsssshhhk.

"Fuck You!"

She bound up the steps and opened the door, bursting in. She looked around. The place was pristine inside. She looked to either side, not seeing anything. The banister railing up the stairs were twisted black metal. She ascended the stairs, attentive to any noise, and searching for anything she could use as a weapon. Darkness enveloped the area, and all the lights remained nonfunctional. She opened the first room. It was a small bedroom, the walls whiter than any she had seen. A small light hung from the ceiling, surrounded by crystal teardrops a few inches long. She left the door and turned toward the room at the front of the house with the open window.

She opened the door, and a chilly breeze hit her in the face, blowing in from the window. It wasn't open. It was not there. Although the frame was in place, the glass and the lower frame were nowhere to be found. The walls in the room were also white, but the wall opposite the window had the Al'Hiyal symbol scarred black into the wall. The symbol contained an intertwined script that someone had written in blood. She went to the last room. The door was locked. She tried to turn the handle hard and hit it with her shoulder, but the door didn't budge.

A scream from downstairs sent ice through her veins. "Yasmin!"

She bound down the stairs, looking in the kitchen before doubling back to the hall going toward the garage, and she guessed the laundry room. She heard a running faucet—the laundry room. She entered the room and saw the source of the sound. The taps for a washer were open and running into a shaped half-pipe of smooth gray-white material. The water flowed down the duct, leading to a large floor opening. She stepped forward, seeing steps made of the same material as the pipe lead down into the ground.

Chapter 56

Thursday Late Afternoon

Tanya looked at the dark passage into the earth. The passage extended further than she expected, bending and preventing her from seeing what was at the bottom of the stairs. This was the source of the earthy smell she had detected upon entering the house. The passage was dark, with the faintest light near what she suspected was a turn. She started down the steps, holding the wall to maintain balance on the steep steps.

The steps wound around almost ninety more degrees before opening into a basement as large as the home. She stepped off the bottom landing. The ground shifted slightly. A dim light shone from a crystal hanging in the center of the room. The air in the room was warm.

A figure lay on a stone slab. Plants created a chaotic scene of shadows. Plants—hyacinth, jasmine, and other scented flowers and spices—grew thick from the floor. She looked around the room. The plants were precisely positioned to create the illusion of a forest of fragrant flowers. She could feel someone watching her as she crept closer to the slab. A figure would appear, then fade when she tried to focus. She saw the man on the flat rock—her father.

Her face flushed as her anger returned, her hands clenching as she took the last steps to the edge of the stone slab. His shirt was open, exposing his chest to the light. Next to him on the slab was his kukri, the blade coated in blood. She closed the distance to her father and looked down at him. He lay on his back, looking up at the light above. His eyes moved about, catching hers. Tanya reached for the kukri, turning it over in her hand.

"Is this Mom's blood?" She clenched her teeth, glaring down at him as his eyes shifted to the blade she held over him.

"Kill him," a whisper floated out of the foliage. The scent of jasmine accompanies it. She looked toward the shadow, trying to find the source.

She looked down. "You deserve to die for what you did."

"You could kill him right now, and no one would ever know." She felt the allure of the whisper.

A shade drifted around her, its eyes burning embers. It faded from sight. Was she hallucinating?

She turned the blade, holding the point above her father's chest. She wanted to grab the blade with both hands and drive it down. Images of her father flashed in her head. Happy times at the beach in Corpus Christi. They were getting Jackson for Christmas eleven years ago. She lifted the blade a little. She thought of her mom, dead now in a burning house, their home destroyed by him. Tanya pressed down on the blade, feeling resistance, before seeing the blade cut his skin. Blood trickling from the cut. She saw movement and looked up to see Yasmin standing across from her. She hadn't seen her friend.

"How did you get here?"

"Who do you think caught and laid him out for you?"

"How?" She eyed Yasmin with additional concern. How could she have stopped her father?

"I have my ways." She started walking around the stone. "Do you like my garden?" She motioned to the myriad of plants that grew in the room. Tanya noticed the smell of hyacinth.

Tanya's focus remained on her father. "He killed my mother."

"He did."

"He should pay for his crime."

"He should."

Tanya adjusted the grip on the kukri and stepped away from Yasmin as realization hit her. "You're the Ghūl!" She backed away, bringing the blade up between her and her friend. "You're a monster!"

"Am I? What is the source of pain in your life?"

"You killed Amara!" She raised the blade, holding it.

"I defended myself. Who has been there for you the entire time?"

"You were using me."

"That is not true. Our friendship is genuine."

"What about Diane and the women? You took advantage of them."

"I removed their pain."

"By killing them."

"Yes." She smiled.

"You liked it."

"I won't lie to you. I did, very much," she replied in a menacing tone.

"Why are you here? What do you want?"

"I'm here for you." She smiled wider than a human should, her mouth filled with sharpened teeth.

Tanya felt paralyzing fear grip her. Was she going to die? She wanted to give in and accept her fate. Be with her mother. She lowered the blade in resignation, feeling the adrenaline rush leave her.

"Oh, no, don't do that. I want you to be angry. Remember all he has done to you and your mother. The pain, the abuse, her death. All at his hands. You lost the person who loved you the most. You couldn't save her. She loved you till the end."

Tanya looked down at the blade in her hand. She had lost everyone who mattered to her. What was left?

"Tanya, I chose you because you are special."

Tanya didn't look up. She thought of the night in the church building. The murderer had moved through the darkness, killing without compassion. Driving them out. Each time she had lost Yasmin in the dark chaos, someone died.

"The confirmation of your gift came when you played at the recital."

She saw the scene from Amara's house. The family murdered in their sitting room, their heads missing.

"I offer you a new life." She reached out, taking Tanya's hand.

Tanya looked at her hand, holding Yasmin's. She shouldn't. They were close. She could attack her. Tears filled her eyes, pain overwhelming her. What's the use? A glint of metal caught her eye. She let go of Yasmin's hand and kneeled to pick up the necklace. It was a sapphire heart surrounded by tiny diamonds.

Tanya looked up, holding the necklace in front of her. "You killed her! Sheri! You were friends!"

Yasmin stared at her.

Tanya jumped up, the kukri between them. "You were friends with them both! How could you?"

"I have only one friend."

"You think we'll be friends after this? You're a murderer!"

Anger flashed in Yasmin's eyes. She shifted, growing in size, her skin becoming black as coal, her eyes burning with the intensity of molten lava, her fingers extending into long, sharp black nails. She towered over Tanya.

"I chose you! I am Nafara Al'Hiyal! Don't presume to know me or my motives, human. I have walked the Earth longer than anyone in existence. I could raze this city and wreak havoc upon your world, bringing more pain and suffering than you can imagine." The heat from her gaze burning her skin. Nafara extended to her full height, towering more than a foot above her.

Tanya shrank back, the kukri shaking in her hand, her resolve faltering.

"All that I have shared with you is true. I find myself drawn to you. My offer of friendship is genuine, and I *will* kill those who get in my way." Nafara turned her back and took a step. "You are different." Her voice softened. "All I have done is protect myself and then you from the actual monsters. Who believed in you, supported you, and stood between you and him?" She pointed at her father. "I want to change this world, and I want you by my side. Monsters like him deserve to die. You must release your old life."

Tanya looked at her back. She could lunge forward, driving the blade deep. She didn't know if it would kill a Jinn, but she would die trying. Resignation hit her. She was powerless, Yasmin was her friend. She felt the bond connecting them, the soft melody of the song played through her mind. She couldn't do it. The kukri slipped from her grasp and clattered off the stone.

Nafara turned around, looking at Tanya.

Tanya couldn't look into the Jinn's eyes, her shoulder slumped. "Tell me what to do."

"You have one more link to your former life."

Tanya looked over at her father. There were no emotions. "Do want must be done."

Nafara glanced into her eyes before stepping around Tanya to her father on the slab. She placed her hand on his chest. "This is going to hurt." She smiled; the sharp teeth spread in a wide grin. She took her other hand and flicked a nail across his neck, leaving a wet cut.

She turned back to Tanya. "This is something you must go through."

"No. No. Let me go you—" He let out a blood-curdling scream as blood seeped from all of his pores. The scream continued for a while, his voice becoming more hoarse and finally ending as the last of the blood flowed from his body down the stone and into the grass. Nafara leaned down toward his face, locked in a mummified look of terror, and bit into it, tearing the dried flesh from his body. A glow like the embers at the base of a dying fire swept through his dried flesh and swirled up and into Nafara's mouth. Her forked tongue flicked out, cleaning any ash from her mouth.

Images from the crime scenes flashed in her head. Yasmin or Nafara had feasted on her victims. There was nothing she could do but serve.

Nafara produced a flute glimmering with an otherworldly aura and offered it to Tanya. "Your bonds are broken. You are free. Now we can begin your training, Magi. I have plans for us."

Chapter 57

Monday Morning, Early November

Tanya sat in a comfortable chair across from the school counselor. She was a young woman. Her blonde hair held up in a loose bun by a yellow number two pencil. It seemed strange since none of the high school students used them. Tanya looked around the office. The counselor was an Aggie. The Texas A&M diploma hung on a wall next to her master's in School Counseling. Her office was unexpectedly bare of decoration, accomplishments, or pictures.

"Tanya, your teachers have informed me you are doing well in all of your classes. I can't imagine going through all you have and bouncing back so quickly."

Tanya shrugged. "It helps to throw myself into my schoolwork."

She flipped through a few pages to one with a yellow tab. "It says here you moved."

"Yes, my aunt moved here and was able to buy the house just up the street from our old house."

Tanya smiled, maintaining eye contact.

"I reviewed your applications; they're impressive. If you keep it up through the end of the school year, you'll graduate as the valedictorian."

Tanya grimaced at the distinction. It should have been Sheri, but she bounced back. "Yes, ma'am."

"I have nothing else unless you do."

"No, ma'am, I just want to finish school and get on with my life. I've got big plans."

The counselor got up from the matching chair across from her and showed her to the door.

"Oh, I forgot to tell you. I loved your solo at the fall recital."

Tanya looked over her shoulder, a broad smile on her face. "Wait until you hear what I do in the spring."

She walked out of the office toward calculus. "Back to work."

End

Acknowledgments

I want to thank the people who helped make *Vulture House* a reality. As always, my wonderful wife, **Elaine**, for her amazing support and honest feedback.

My horror aficionado, and good friend, **George Engel,** who has continued to provide honest feedback on the characters, setting, and story. If you can get him to talk, he knows the full plot of the Jinn Prophecy series. **Addy Sheridan** for meaningful feedback, continuity recommendations, and vulture knowledge. I also want to thank **Tanya Jacquinet** for letting me know there is a house in Southlake ,Texas that vultures are attracted to and encouraging me to write a story about it. She planted the seed for the Jinn Prophecy series.

I also want to thank those involved in the creative process: **Suvajit Das** for the cover design, **Addy Sheridan** for the internal Art, **Maura Jacquinet** for media marketing, and my wife **Elaine** again, for her meticulous editing, proof reading, and continuity.

Thank You

Thank you, the reader, for entering the world I created, meeting the people inside, and hanging around for a while. My goal in writing is to tell an enjoyable story that was worth the time you took to experience it.

Reviews are an essential step in building credibility and extending an author's reach. If you have time, I'd greatly appreciate a review on Amazon, Goodreads, or any other site you use, which will help the story find more readers.

Again, *Thank You* for reading Vulture House, the first book in the Jinn Prophecy series. I hope to see you again in the worlds of my imagination.

Follow me on Amazon and get notified as soon as a new story is released:

About the Author

Don Wilburn Jr. is an international award-winning author, known for his captivating science fiction and global thrillers. His debut horror novel, Vulture House, plunges readers into a modern-day dark fantasy full of suspense. With twenty-eight years of government service as a Naval Officer and with the Transportation Security Administration, Don draws upon his experiences navigating the complexities of security and human nature. His travels around the world fuel his imagination, helping him craft stories that blend intrigue and terror. Don lives in Fort Worth, Texas, with his wife, two children, and two faithful dogs.